THUNDER

To Ginger,
Written with His grace
and for His glory!
Juanita Paslay

THUNDER

Passed on to you. May you
be blessed! Ginger

They heard God
and followed Jesus

JUANITA TURNER PASLAY

THUNDER

Cover Design by Melissa Caven
Cover Photo by Juanita Turner Paslay
Author's Photo by Bill E. Tinsman
Published by Juanita Turner Paslay

ISBN 978-0-9976971-0-0 (sc)
ISBN 978-0-9976971-1-7 (e)

Printed in the United States of America.

Dedication

To HIM

who planned every day of our lives
for His glory before we were born.

Endorsements

"Juanita has a great love and understanding of the Bible. She wields her pen in a way to make the Bible stories she writes come alive. For those not as familiar with God's Word, her writings will give them an incentive to read and learn more."

~ **Carol Kimsey**, Ridgefield WA

"Juanita Turner Paslay loves Jesus and His Word. It occurred to her there might be a story behind the Bible stories of Jesus' wonderful teaching and His power in needy people's lives. *The Ambassador* is a story of a desperate family who saw no way out of their problem. In a few words, Jesus transformed Ari. With the young man's obedience, the power of God and His Son Jesus spread to many people. God's grace is on Juanita as she writes."

~ **Sharon Ostrander**, Eugene OR

"Juanita's story *The Other Joseph* is fantastic. It really touched my heart. She is truly gifted by God, and I shall share her book THUNDER with others."

~ **JoAnn Miller**, Lowell OR

"Juanita Turner Paslay combines imagination with reality to bring to life classical stories from the Bible. Her book THUNDER shows what ancient people might have experienced in their daily activities and relationships with God."

~ **Geni J. I. White**, Eugene OR

"Dear Reader, you will not only enjoy Juanita Turner Paslay's stories and style, but you will also gain some insight into how that widow from Nain might have responded when Jesus, with a word, touched her life and healed her broken heart."

~ **Pastor Ellis Parker**, Biggs Assembly of God, Biggs CA

"Have you ever experienced a native American storyteller? Juanita Turner Paslay's stories are like that. They pull you in and transport you back in time and you are there watching living history. It is like a dream that you do not want to end. Keep them coming, Juanita."

~ **John Titman**, Philomath OR

"Juanita Turner Paslay has a heart for the Word of God and relaying its truths in her writings. She is faithful to research and study every topic she pursues. You will enjoy her debut book THUNDER and will be blessed by its content. Her style is unique and refreshing."

~ **Pastor Larry Gatlin**, Encounter Church, Canyonville OR

Contents

Thunder

But the Lord spoke with a mighty
voice of *thunder* from heaven that day . . .
1 Samuel 7:10 NLT (italics added)

Listen carefully to the *thunder* of God's voice
as it rolls from his mouth.
God's voice is glorious in the *thunder*.
We cannot even imagine the
greatness of his power.
Job 37:2, 5 NLT (italics added)

The Lord's voice will roar from Zion and
thunder from Jerusalem,
and the heavens and the earth will shake . . .
Joel 3:16 NLT (italics added)

When the crowd heard the voice, some thought it
was *thunder*, while others declared
an angel had spoken to him.
John 12:29 NLT (italics added)

Preface

THUNDER depicts twelve hundred years of possible conversations with Samson, the prophets Jonah and Samuel, King Saul, King David, Jesus, Peter, John, Andrew, Joseph of Arimathea and Nicodemus. These stories are based on characters and events recorded in the Bible. Other people and their experiences have been included that might have taken place during Bible times. While this is a work of fiction, scenes with direct quotes from Scripture are included to enhance the story line.

As I created the conversations, I implored the Holy Spirit to guide my thoughts and ideas while I imagined how the complete details of the story might have happened. I held to the truths of the story as it is told in Scripture.

I appreciate my many friends and critique groups that used their precious time to read and edit my stories. Their help was invaluable to me.

The Apostle John said if every event in Jesus' life was recorded, the world (or my library) might not hold all the books.

After reading this book, may you desire to read more of the wonderful stories in the Bible. Everyone will experience joy in reading the inspired Word of God and knowing the heart of Jesus, our Lord and Savior.

The Warrior Judge

Samson

A fearless man chosen by God and
deceived by a beautiful woman.

A story based on Judges 13-16

~ 1 ~

I am the Lord God Almighty, Creator of heaven and earth. When I brought My people out of Egypt, the land of their first bondage, I promised them victory over their enemies if they obeyed My commandments to serve and worship Me and none other. They failed to follow My instructions and they no longer had strong leaders like Moses and Joshua to lead them to victory. Their hearts bowed to serve false gods. Therefore, I allowed wicked kings and foreign people to harass and enslave them.

In the days before Israel served her kings, the Philistine people ruled the land that bordered the coastline. My people co-existed with their enemy in the land I promised to them alone.

Israel made decisions based on her sinful lusts. My people worshiped idols and intermarried with their enemies. When they repented and cried out for help, I appointed judges to guide them.

I chose Samson son of Manoah from the tribe of Dan as My twelfth judge. Samson instructed the people to burn their idols and worship only Me. My hand of blessing rested upon this judge and I gave him many opportunities to come against and defeat the Philistines.

~ 2 ~

"I am barren and not a young woman anymore, but I still desire to have a child if it be Your will."

God's Spirit imparted peace to Judith's spirit. She never complained she had no children, but in her humble way shared the longings of her heart with God.

"Almighty God of Israel, I know You love and care for me. You gave me Manoah, a kind and righteous man, as my husband. I am so grateful for my many blessings."

A strong breeze waved the oak branches one sunny afternoon as Judith prepared a small bag of dried fruit for a snack and left the house with a flower basket for her usual adventure in the meadow.

"I will pick the tallest white lilies I can find. Their strong sweet scent always lifts my spirit."

Judith enjoyed her frequent talks with God in the meadow. That day God sent her a special visitor.

She noticed a change in the wind. *The wind has calmed, but I think I hear thunder in the distance.* Her mind filled with questions. *Why is my heart racing? Is a storm coming?*

"Judith!" His voice sounded like none she had ever heard—bold but soft, mighty but compassionate.

Her basket slipped through her fingers as she turned toward the voice. A man unknown to her delivered a message that she had longed to hear for many years.

"Judith, I bring you good news today. You will become the mother of a son."

The woman dropped to her knees. "My lord, I have never met you. Is this astonishing announcement really for me?" *Am I dreaming?*

"I bring special instructions you must follow during the months you await his birth."

Judith held her breath as her eyes widened.

He continued. "You must eat a special diet."

"Special? Special in what way?" Still on the ground, she turned her face toward his.

"You must not consume wine nor any fermented drink. Abstain from all forbidden foods."

"Any other restrictions?" She shifted her position to get a full view of the giant of a man.

"One more commandment. His hair must never be cut."

Judith rose to her feet and smoothed her dress. "I vow to follow your instructions." She folded her hands across her heart as she whispered. "I shall obey your every word." On the verge of laughter, she grinned a huge smile.

"Your son will follow a special Nazirite vow of no wine nor forbidden foods. His hair shall never be cut. He shall be dedicated to God until the day he dies. As a young man, he will help lead the hearts of the people back to God. He will set in motion the rescue of Israel from the rule of the wicked Philistines."

Our son will be a mighty man of God! I must tell Manoah. In her enthusiasm, Judith made a quick bow at the waist to the stranger, forgot her basket of lilies, and ran home to share the incredible message with Manoah.

As she skipped through the meadow's tall grasses, she sang a song in loud volume for all the birds and angels to enjoy.

"I shall bear a child. I shall bear a son.
Me, a mother. A mother of a son!"

As Judith approached her home, she found Manoah pulling weeds from around the cornstalks. At the sound of her singing and running through the garden, he whirled around to focus on his adorable wife.

"Such a burst of energy. Why the hurry, my dear?"

"I . . . I heard . . . I heard wonderful news! . . . I must sit . . . and catch my breath."

"Come sit beside me in the shade. We both could use a rest. Did you find the lilies you wanted?" Manoah poured her a cup of water from the clay jug stored under the bench.

"Oh, I do not need lilies today. Wait until I tell you . . . what an awesome man told me . . . a few minutes ago." She paused to swallow a long drink of water.

Manoah gave her a squeeze. "An awesome man?"

"A beautiful man. Huge. Tall. Maybe an angel! I have never seen such muscles."

"Where did he come from?" His voice displayed a hint of teasing.

"He came out of nowhere. While I knelt and picked flowers, a magnificent voice called my name and there he stood—smiling. I jumped with surprise but not from fear. Do I make sense?"

"Not yet. Tell me more." Manoah hugged her close.

"He did not tell me his name and I did not ask. He gave me a message. He said that I shall become pregnant with a son dedicated to God as a special Nazirite. He spoke with such powerful authority that I knew God sent him to me."

"A son? A Nazirite? Oh, Judith, we must give thanks right now." Manoah's voice dropped to a whisper.

They knelt side by side at the old bench. Manoah

pleaded, "O God, we believe your messenger. Please send him again so I too may understand all his instructions about our promised son."

Three days later the Angel of the LORD appeared again to Judith while she meditated at her favorite place on the knoll behind their home.

"Please sir, do not leave. I will return with my husband."

She ran down the hill and spotted Manoah as he tended his sheep and goats in the back field. "Manoah, the messenger has returned. He waits for us. Hurry!"

Manoah dropped his staff and together the man and his wife raced hand in hand up the knoll.

Breathing hard with excitement, they both bowed prostrate before the stranger. "Are you the same man who spoke to my wife the other day?"

"I am." His awesome voice produced a musical echo.

Manoah rose to his knees. "When our child arrives, what rules shall we follow?"

"Your wife must obey all the instructions I gave her, partake of neither wine nor fermented drink. She and the child will eat no forbidden food according to Moses' laws. Remember, never cut his hair."

"We shall obey!"

Judith nodded her head in agreement with Manoah.

Manoah bowed before the angel again. "Will you stay while we prepare a young goat to eat?"

"I will stay, but I shall not eat. Instead, prepare a burnt offering as a sacrifice to the LORD."

Manoah still did not comprehend who talked with him. "Sir, your name please. We want to honor you after our son's birth."

"Do not ask me *that* question. I cannot reveal my secret name." The angel placed his hands on his hips as his face beamed in mystery.

The couple dashed down the hill to prepare their offerings.

"I shall kill a healthy, young male goat while you prepare a grain offering," said Manoah.

"I am so excited to make an offering to the LORD. I shall use my freshest flour and mix it with olive oil and a few drops of incense."

As he promised, the angel waited for them to return.

Manoah gathered tinder, twigs, and broken branches for a small fire. He laid the raw goat meat and the grain offering on a large flat rock and used his flint stone to start the fire. He stepped back to watch it burn.

"Judith, do not stand too close."

Suddenly, the blaze became intense with extreme heat and the sweet aroma of the thick smoke reached high in the air.

As the Angel of the LORD moved close to the fire, Judith whispered to Manoah, "What is he doing?"

Manoah warned, "Judith, move back!"

The fire roared twenty feet high in a matter of seconds. As the fire consumed their sacrifices, the angel stepped into the flames, raised his arms, and disappeared in the white smoke.

Judith gasped, then threw her hand over her mouth as she watched the incredible scene.

Manoah stammered and fell face down on the ground. "We shall die! We have seen God!"

Judith reassured him with a hug. "No, Manoah, God will not kill us. See, the LORD has accepted our burnt offerings."

"I believe we experienced a miracle today!"

Judith whispered, "I am confident we will see more miracles as God uses our son in His plan of deliverance."

~ 3 ~

Judith named the promised child Samson. She taught him to eat the required diet according to the Angel of the LORD's instructions. Samson learned what it meant to live in the ways of a Nazirite dedicated to God.

"Samson, you must sit still. I know it hurts when I comb your thick hair. The Lord has given you a lot of hair. He said it must never be cut."

The young boy squirmed and frowned as his mother handled his hair. "Do not comb so hard, you are hurting me."

"I am sorry, my son. Your hair has now become so long we must make it easy for both of us."

"I do not like hair in my eyes."

"Braids might solve the problem. Do you want it in one large or several small braids?

"I want lots of braids. Can I have seven?" The young boy was excited. "I do not know any kids with seven braids."

When the child grew into manhood, he moved to the town of Mahaneh-dan near his parent's town of Zorah. God's blessing rested on Israel's new judge and Samson encouraged his people to burn their idols and worship only God as he traveled from town to town dealing with their legal situations.

Early in the spring of the year, the young judge traveled

home to Zorah. “Father, I met a beautiful Philistine woman from Timnah. I must marry her. Make the wedding arrangements for me.”

“But Samson, is there no woman in Israel for you to marry? Why must you marry a pagan? I fear you are disobeying God’s will.”

“Father, I want this one.”

Neither he nor his parents understood that this marriage would provide Samson many opportunities to fight against and destroy Philistines warriors.

As the family traveled to Timnah to make wedding plans, their son used his strength to protect his parents.

“Father, I hear the roaring of a lion close by. Wait on the trail until I return.”

“My son, be careful!” his mother warned.

Samson found the lion crouched on a crumbling stone wall around a deserted vineyard. The animal roared and threatened to ambush his family. To agitate it on purpose, he roared back at the lion.

“Your days are numbered. Wait till I get my hands around your neck. With my God-given strength, you are no stronger than a young goat.”

He chased the lion into the vineyard, but the lion turned and leaped on Samson. He killed the beast with his bare hands and partially buried it among the dead plants. The young judge dusted off his hands and returned to his parents.

“That beast will not bother us again.” Samson chuckled.

Samson’s parents and the Philistine woman’s parents arranged the wedding as the young man requested. They completed all the marriage details in two weeks.

On their journey back to Timnah for the wedding day, Samson took a detour.

"Father, I am going to walk through that old vineyard, but I shall meet you at the next curve in the road."

Samson did not wait for his father's response and sprinted into the field. *I want to admire my recent kill.*

The wild birds enjoyed a feast of decaying flesh and a swarm of bees hovered above their nest in the exposed carcass.

"Hey, dead beast, thanks for the gift." Ignoring the bees, Samson helped himself to the sweet honeycomb under the ribs.

He dashed to join his parents. "Mother, I brought you a gift." He grinned and handed her a generous portion of the honeycomb.

"Father, I'll share my portion with you."

He did not confess finding the treasure in the dead lion's rotten belly.

~ ~ ~ ~ ~

While his father prepared the final arrangements for the wedding, Samson planned a party at the bride's home.

During the party, the bride's father addressed his guests. "May I introduce Samson, an Israelite judge, who will marry my daughter. Samson, I invited these thirty young men as our guests."

"Welcome to the party. I love a challenge. I bet none of you can solve my riddle." Samson showed a mischievous smile.

The men agreed in unison. "We bet we can."

"If you fail to answer my riddle during the party, you owe me thirty exquisite linen robes. If you give me the correct answer, I shall owe you the expensive clothes."

"What is your riddle?" The guests were eager for the game to begin.

"Out of one that eats, came food to eat; out of the strong came sweetness. What are the objects? Provide the correct answer within seven days to win your prize."

With that statement, Samson folded his arms across his chest and grinned like a boy who loved to tease his younger brother.

"We agree to your terms. This will be a simple problem to solve," the men bragged.

The young men had confidence the first few days of the celebration, but as the week progressed, they ran out of answers.

On the fourth day of their challenge, they took the bride aside in a secluded room and threatened her. "If you do not get the answer for us, we will burn your house while you and your family sleep. That despicable Israelite plans to make us poor with his ridiculous riddle."

The woman cried and ran to Samson for help. "If you love me, you must tell me the answer to your riddle."

Samson frowned, then mocked her. "Why tell you? I have not even told my parents."

"But Samson, I need to know," she nagged and cried for the next three days.

"Woman, I am weary of your emotional outbursts. The answer to my riddle is sweet honey and a strong lion. Now stop your ridiculous crying." Samson sighed.

She hugged her groom and left in haste to locate the men who threatened her.

As the sun dropped below the horizon, the men of the town returned to the party and gave Samson their stolen answer.

"What is sweeter than honey? What is stronger than a lion?" They howled with laughter. "Now give us our prize at once!"

Samson was furious with his wife and her father's guests for stealing the answer. He left the marriage celebration to gather the promised garments.

The groom mounted his donkey. "God, I need your power today. I travel to Ashkelon for robes."

In the Philistine town, he strangled thirty men, stole their best clothing, and returned to the party with the prizes.

"Pick out your robe." Samson glared at the guests and tossed the garments in a heap on the ground.

"Where is my wife?" Demanded Samson who was not in a pleasant mood.

She came around the corner out of hiding. "I am here, Samson."

"I am so outraged with your deception that I am going home to live with my parents. I shall return for you after the wheat harvest."

Two months later, Samson wanted to make amends. He brought his wife a young goat and a beautiful gown as a gift.

When Samson arrived in Timnah, he announced, "I go into my wife's room to sleep with her."

But her father stopped him. "No, you cannot. I believed you hated her, so I gave her in marriage to the best man at your wedding."

"You did what?" Samson loudly exclaimed.

"You may have her younger sister. She is even more beautiful."

Samson stormed out of the house and shouted over his shoulder, "I shall bring revenge on you ungodly Philistines!"

The agitated judge sprinted to a nearby hill. *I know just where I am going—to where the red fox lives. There are at least a thousand of those red dogs in their dens this time of the year.*

"I will burn all their crops to the ground. I'll tie two foxes together so their tails will make the perfect torch." Samson's plan succeeded as he chased three hundred fiery animals through the Philistines' dried grain fields.

"Now I shall destroy their vineyards and olive groves. They deserve all the damage I give them."

When the Philistines discovered who destroyed their crops, they retaliated and killed Samson's wife and his father-in-law. In revenge, Samson attacked and killed his enemies wherever he found them in a radius of fifty miles.

The judge's unmerciful actions created a fresh war situation between the people of Israel and their Philistine enemies.

"LORD, I am a wanted man, so I must travel at night to counsel and judge the cases among Your people. During daylight, help me find refuge in a cave somewhere. Stay with me, LORD."

~ ~ ~ ~ ~

A brigade of Philistine soldiers camped in Israel's territory and raided the Israeli town of Lehi. They threatened the men of Judah.

"We seek Samson. By our gods, we will take revenge and punish him," their captain shouted.

"Take us to Samson if you value your own lives!" The Philistine threats vibrated loud and fierce in the elders' ears.

The men of Judah huddled together to discuss the situation. "Samson is our judge, but he is always causing trouble with the Philistines.

"Remember, Samson was chosen by God to help deliver us from this enemy," one elder cautioned.

"We should think of our own safety first," retorted another.

Most of the elders agreed to comply with the brigade and

approached the Philistine captain.

"We will do what you request. We will find him and surrender him to you," the cowards of Judah agreed.

Within the week, elders from the tribe of Judah arrived at Manoah's home in Zorah.

Judith peeked out the window when she heard unexpected voices. "Manoah, a crowd approaches our property. I do not recognize any of them. Do you?"

"Stay in the house. I shall talk with them outside." Manoah grabbed his staff and stopped the men at his gate.

"We belong to the tribe of Judah. Where is Samson?" their leader demanded.

"I have not seen our son for several months." Manoah answered truthfully. "Why do you want him?"

"We have a personal matter to discuss with him."

"If you need a judge, you might find my son in the hill country of Etam."

The dishonorable men left the property in a hurry and Manoah returned to his house.

He opened the door and whispered to himself, "What trouble seeks my son this time?"

Judith rubbed her hands together with concern. "Remember, Manoah, God always has His hand on our son."

"Yes, we will fear neither our people nor the Philistines, but I believe those men intended to deceive us."

~ ~ ~ ~ ~

Three thousand tribesmen from Judah, intimidated by the Philistines, searched the area and eventually located and confronted Samson in his hideout.

"Samson, you must remember the Philistines rule over us. Why do you always seek to aggravate them?"

"You know God has appointed me to punish our enemies." Samson reminded them with a hint of anger in his voice.

The spokesman for those cowardly men of Judah stepped forward with an air of confidence, though his hands trembled. "We came to surrender you to the Philistines for *our* safety and the safety of our families."

"But I am your kin, your appointed judge. Why do you send me to my death? I am astounded at your weakness." Samson frowned as his fists rested on his hips.

The traitors responded, "They will kill *us* if we do not deliver you into their hands."

"Do what you must. But remember, God always protects me." *LORD God, I know You are watching over me right now.*

His brethren bound his hands with a rope and descended the mountain to the Philistine soldiers stationed in the valley of Lehi.

A few hundred yards from their rendezvous point, an elder said, "I hear the Philistines shouting victory chants already. We must leave Samson here and run for safety to the hill behind us."

Samson stared at the Philistine garrison and dropped to his knees as they marched toward him.

"God, as You gave Gideon and his army strength to defeat the Midianites, give me Your power now. I am one weak man against so many. My LORD, my Strength! I shall not be afraid."

The Spirit of God came upon Samson and gave him power to break the ropes off his arms as if they were rotten threads.

"God, I see that decayed donkey carcass on the side of the road. Just what I needed."

He grabbed the dried jawbone, then attacked and pounded each soldier as they advanced row by row toward him.

"Run! Run, you injured cowards. Run back to your command post." Once again, Samson put Israel's enemies to flight.

Samson looked over his shoulder toward the hill where his countrymen hid. He shouted, "Traitors!"

"LORD, with Your strength, I killed about a thousand soldiers and won this battle today. You saw me pile their dead bodies in a heap. But now, I am so weak."

Samson collapsed on the ground to catch his breath.

"I am about to die of thirst. Will I fall into their heathen hands now? LORD, help me before I die!"

"LORD, You create amazing wonders! You just split the ground and designed a creek for me."

When he drank the cool water, his thirst disappeared, and his strength returned.

"LORD, thank you for that refreshing water. I trust You to help me win the next battle with the Philistines."

~ 4 ~

Samson had a weakness for women, especially beautiful, willing Philistine women. One named Delilah held his attention and affections above all others.

One scorching hot, sticky day, the five lords of the major Philistine cities of Ashdod, Gaza, Ashkelon, Gath, and Ekron traveled to Sorek to persuade Delilah to assist them in a devious plan to capture their enemy Samson.

The lords entered through her gate and the elder Cain knocked on her door. She opened it without hesitation.

"Delilah, we need water from your well to quench our thirst." Sweat dripped from his brow and down his chin.

"Yes, my lord. My servant will draw fresh water for all of you."

After they drank the cool water, Cain presented his challenge.

"We know Samson the Israelite spends many evenings in your home. He has given our kingdom grief. We want him. We swear you will benefit if you help us." Cain gave her a tight grin that showed his crooked brown teeth.

"What benefit?" She displayed her best enticing smile, placed a hand on her slender hip, and tossed her long hair over her shoulder. "What do you have in mind?"

"If you discover the source of his unusual strength, we will give you eleven hundred pieces of silver."

"Only eleven hundred?" She faked her response with a frown.

"Eleven hundred from each of us." Cain promised.

"Yes, from all of us," they each agreed.

"That amount of silver will make me a wealthy woman. But you will not kill him, will you?" she pleaded.

"No, just badly hurt him." Cain's huge belly shook with devilish laughter.

In three days, Samson made his next visit to Delilah's home.

"Samson, I'm so happy to see you. May I serve you a glass of wine?"

"No, but I am in the mood for some of your delicious food."

"Rest on my couch while I prepare some dried dates, fresh pears, and smoked fish."

After the meal, Delilah served almonds and olives in shiny silver bowls. As they reclined together on her plush couch, she placed wet red kisses on the back of his hand.

"Samson, I have never known a man with long hair like yours. I love it, but why do you wear it in braids?"

"As a child, my mother braided it for me. It is easy to manage this way."

"My strong Samson, what makes your muscles so firm? It must be impossible to bind you." She caressed and massaged his triceps and shoulders.

He returned the kisses and teased, "I am strong, Delilah, but if your servant tied me with seven fresh bowstrings, I would be as weak as your elderly neighbor."

He kissed her neck, then advanced to her mouth. An hour later, he sprawled on her couch, exhausted and snoring.

Delilah ordered her servant, "Go and tell Cain that

Samson is here, and I have his secret. I need seven untreated bowstrings now."

Cain and his soldiers were quick to respond.

While Samson slept, Delilah bound his wrists together with her tightest knots while the armed, yet cautious, men remained hidden in the adjacent room.

Delilah yelled loud enough to wake him from his deep sleep. "Samson, the Philistines have come for you!"

In two seconds, he jumped off the couch and broke the cords. The armed men observed what happened and remained hidden for their own safety.

"Samson, why did you lie to me?" Delilah pouted and focused on the silver she did not earn.

"Delilah, my sweet, you enjoy playing games, but the sun has set. I shall leave the valley tonight. I might return to you, and I might not."

Samson disappeared through the sagging wooden gate and slipped out of sight without making a sound.

Several days later, he again knocked on her door. Thrilled at his presence, she anticipated her promised silver.

"Samson, my handsome man. I waited all week for you to return."

"Delilah, Delilah! The sound of your name plays music in my ears."

Again, she set the scene—velvet couch, all the rich and delicious food a hungry man craves, and a strong scent of perfume. Nibbling on fresh fruit, they talked of nothing important in between caresses and kisses. Delilah was generous with her affections and Samson enjoyed himself, as usual. He grew excited by her strong embrace.

Delilah could wait no longer with her question. "Samson, on your last visit you shocked me with your lies. Can anyone keep you tied?"

"Oh, Delilah, why bother yourself with tough questions? Love me tonight and we'll both be happy."

She raised her voice as she tried to sound stern. "Samson, I am serious! Tell me your secret." She ran her fingers around his long braids with a soft tug, not knowing therein hid his secret.

He considered his options for the moment. He whispered, "New ropes. Ropes never used by anyone."

The night passed as before—Samson asleep on the couch. Delilah searched for new ropes. She acquired the necessary cords, bound him while he slept, and Philistine soldiers once again hid in the next room.

"Samson, Samson! They are here. Get up!" Delilah spoke with faked panic in her voice.

Her lover sat up, yawned, and stretched his arms. The ropes snapped like thin cotton thread. The men stayed hidden for fear of Samson's anger.

"Delilah, you and your silly games again. Come, we will lie until morning. I must go home soon."

"I do not want to sleep with you again," she shouted, forcing the tears to flow. "You always deceive me. You lie. You do not love me."

"Come! The sunrise will soon chase away the darkness."

"I will, if you tell me the secret of your strength." She turned her back to him.

"Delilah, you wear me out. I need you. Come, I shall whisper in your ear."

As they reclined on the couch, Samson caressed her face and played with her long hair revealing her dainty ears pierced with golden wires wrapped around rubies.

Samson smiled as he gazed into her brown eyes. *I do not trust her, so I will tell her another lie.*

In a soft voice, he whispered his untruth once again. So,

while he slept to rest his body and armed men hid in their usual location, she weaved his seven long braids of hair into a web and fastened them to her heavy iron loom. She took extra care in this third attempt to subdue him.

All her weaving efforts and her warning of a Philistine attack produced the same results. Easy escape to freedom.

"Delilah, I am tired of your games tonight. I shall be back when you want to provide pleasant entertainment." He tied on his sandals and left through the rear gate.

Delilah tried not to act furious, though Samson had made her appear foolish three times. She called out to him as he trotted down the garden pathway.

"If you really loved me, you would quit this deception and tell me the truth." Her voice pleaded and whined.

He stopped and glanced over his shoulder. "Oh, you beautiful nagging woman. Do you honestly need my secret?"

"Yes, please." She smiled. *I trapped him now.*

She beckoned him back inside the house and onto her couch. After he finished another tray of excellent fruits and nuts, indulged in sensual pleasure, and before he dozed off to sleep, she asked the same question once again.

"Samson, my dear, why are you so strong?" She twirled a braid of Samson's beautiful long hair.

"Delilah, your food was delicious. I am afraid I over-indulged. What was your question again?"

"I want to know why you are so strong."

Too satisfied and too tired to resist that beautiful woman, he confessed with slow but honest words. "No one has cut my hair because I am a Nazirite. My strength lies in my hair."

He fell fast asleep on her infamous couch and dreamed of forbidden wine and kisses.

Delilah sensed Samson revealed the truth. She sent word

to notify the lords to bring their silver while her man servant used a blade to gently shave Samson's head.

The lords entered through the back door. Cain whispered to his accomplices. "Place the promised silver on her table. We will wait with our weapons behind her thick curtain. Do not say a word until Delilah wakes Samson."

For the final time, Delilah continued her game. Samson's head rested in her lap as he snored and received his first head shave. She woke him with her usual, "Samson, the Philistines have come for you!"

Samson roused himself, jumped up, and prepared for a quick fight. He was unaware God's strength had left him.

"Delilah, what have you done to me? You evil woman!"

His lover did not respond.

"Who shaved my head?"

The judge no longer possessed any strength to resist the Philistines as they bound his arms and legs with ropes. God allowed his capture according to His plan.

While Delilah enjoyed hugging her silver coins against her breasts, the lords held Samson flat on the floor and gouged out the eyes of her Israelite lover.

A beautiful young woman influenced and overpowered one of history's most powerful men. Eve was the first such woman to persuade a man and a wicked queen named Jezebel, wife of Israel's future king, would not be the last.

Samson's days were numbered as judge over Israel.

~ 5 ~

"Samson, you have a new job now," the prison captain laughed. "You will grind the grain for the inmates in this Gaza prison. And you do not need eyes to do it." The captain laughed louder.

When not tethered to the grinder area, bronze chains shackled his legs together to prevent the blind judge from trying to escape.

"Hoshea, I'm giving you a new assignment. You will be Samson's guide," the captain ordered.

"I know Samson. He is God's chosen judge for Israel. I will gladly serve him."

The next morning, Hoshea entered Samson's cold damp cell with his daily portion of cooked grains. He found Samson squatting in the corner with a lost expression on his face.

"Samson, I brought you some food." He placed a small clay bowl in Samson's hands.

"What is your name, boy?"

"I am Hoshea. My father named me after the great warrior Joshua." Hoshea dropped to the ground and placed his hands on Samson's knees.

"I am glad to talk with someone this morning. How long have you been a slave?"

"For three winters, I think." Hoshea whispered so no other inmate could hear their conversation. "These beasts killed my parents when they raided my village and took me prisoner."

"You are so kind to me. You would make your parents proud." Samson smiled for the first time since his capture.

"I am honored to serve you, even to wash your feet." He gave the judge a big smile that Samson could not see to appreciate.

"Never doubt what I say. Stay by my side and someday," Samson pulled Hoshea close to speak into the boy's ear, "someday I shall set you free from this horrible place."

Hoshea's brown eyes grew wide. "How soon?"

"I am not sure when, but I know God has a plan for us."

"When you say you speak for God, I believe you."

The next day when Hoshea brought Samson's bowl of mush, they engaged in a serious conversation.

"Commit your life to God and trust only Him. When I set you free, run to the town of Zorah. My mother will care for you. She is a kind and godly woman."

"Please tell me about her. I want to learn all I can about your mother."

He told young Hoshea how God chose Judith to bear a son destined to lead and judge the people of Israel. Hoshea sat cross-legged on the ground, spellbound by the story of the angel rising upward in the smoke.

"I can see the sparks in the sky now. Tell me the story again." Hoshea scooted closer to hear every word.

"I long for the old days when God's strength enabled me to chase and destroy our enemy." Samson's voice trailed off as he fell asleep.

The Spirit of God communicated with Samson in prison, and he treasured every moment of God's presence. Though still blind, he perceived hair falling across his eyes. The new growth gave him hope for the future.

O LORD, I am so weak. Will my strength return before I die? I know You planned my life before I was born. My faith is in You.

~ ~ ~ ~ ~

The five Philistine lords planned a great feast of celebration. The weather developed into a perfect day for the occasion—clear skies and a warm breeze.

"This festival will be the greatest ever. The entire kingdom has assembled in the arena to offer sacrifices of thanksgiving to our god, Dagon," a Philistine lord confided in Delilah as he placed his arm around her waist.

Their honored guest, Delilah, enjoyed the privileged chair next to Cain, a sinister leader of Philistia.

"Our god gave us Samson!" The arrogant people proclaimed their victory over Israel.

Drunken men and women crowded the arena and the rooftop to overflowing. Their loud celebration echoed around the nearby hills.

"Our god conquered our enemy!"

They celebrated all day in high spirits, fine wine, and loud voices. They stomped their feet in unison.

"Bring us Samson!"

"We want Samson!"

Just before sunset, a prison official instructed young Hoshea. "I want you to escort Samson center stage for all Philistia to gloat over him."

Samson struggled to walk with his chains as young Hoshea guided him to the center of the building. The stocky prison captain made him parade back and forth across the platform while dragging his heavy chains behind him.

"LORD God, I raise my tired arms to You. Victory for Israel!" Samson shouted.

The drunken festive crowd recognized his obvious weakness. They laughed and jeered as their helpless enemy stood chained before them.

The captain placed Israel's captured judge right where God wanted him—between two pillars. They continued to laugh and shout curses at their prisoner who stood by the massive posts that towered overhead. The ungodly Philistines ridiculed their hostage and defied the LORD God of Israel. Not one Philistine pitied Samson, least of all Delilah.

"Long live Dagon! Our god has destroyed all other gods. We will conquer the world." The loud chants echoed again.

Samson whispered to the boy beside him. "Hoshea, put my hands on the pillars so I can lean against them."

Those two pillars were close together, allowing Samson to wrap his weak arms around them while he rested. Sweat dripped off his forehead as he whispered to his young guide.

"Hoshea, you still here?"

"Yes, master, I am right beside you."

Samson tilted his face to the heavens and prayed, "LORD God, give me back my strength this one last time. I want revenge on these animals for the destruction of my eyes and the oppression of Your people!"

Puzzled by his friend's behavior, Hoshea paid careful attention to Samson's prayer.

A soft rolling thunder sounded in the distance.

Samson leaned toward him and breathed, "Run, Hoshea, run!"

Hoshea disappeared from Samson's side without delay and ran to the closest exit out of the arena. All eyes were on Samson. No one paid attention to the young lad.

"Yes, LORD. Let me die with these wicked Philistines!" Samson shouted his final words as thunder rolled again.

Samson's faith remained firm, and his weakness vanished for his last moment of glory. God restored Samson's strength to greater than ever before. As he pushed the two pillars apart, the entire roof, with three thousand people sitting on benches, collapsed and every wall and pillar crumbled beyond recognition. The horrific noise was deafening, and people found no safe place to hide. Mass confusion reigned as the entire arena crumbled as if destroyed by an earthquake. Dust from the crushed stones filled the air, blinding and choking the few survivors as they screamed curses at Israel's God.

~ ~ ~ ~ ~

Hoshea escaped unnoticed out the city's main gate and never once looked over his shoulder for Philistine guards. Within the week, the young lad, dirty and hungry, arrived in the town of Zorah.

Hoshea questioned an old man resting at the city gate. "Sir, please tell me where I can find the home of Manoah."

"It is the last house that way." The man stroked his beard and pointed to a grove of myrtle trees. "You will see an iron gate."

This has been a long trip, but I am almost home. Hoshea was excited to meet his new family.

The young lad walked through the broken gate, down the path, and knocked twice on the door.

Judith, now living alone since her husband died, slowly opened the door. "Who are you looking for?"

"My lady, I am Hoshea. I just escaped from the prison where Samson was confined. He was like an older brother to me. Samson told me to come and see you."

"Please, do come in. You look tired. I shall get you a drink."

Judith gave Hoshea a cup of water and a slice of fresh bread as he rested on the couch.

"Please tell me what you know about my son."

"Because the Philistines blinded him and kept him chained, I was chosen to feed and guide him around the prison compound. Last week, God answered his last prayer. Though he was very weak, God gave him super strength to destroy the arena and kill thousands of those cruel heathens. But I am sorry to tell you that Samson died with them that day."

She cried, "Oh, no, my son, my son! I heard about that terrible destruction, but I did not know Samson was with them."

When Judith stopped crying, she whispered, "We were so proud of him. He was a judge for twenty years. Many times, I heard him warn our people to turn from idols and serve God. His father and I did not always approve of what he did, but he was God's chosen judge."

"I was Samson's guide, and it was my privilege to serve him. I stood by him at the end until he told me to run."

"We must bury him with his father," Judith said.

She dried her cheeks and turned her attention to Hoshea. "Where does your family live?"

"All my relatives were killed by the Philistines when they invaded my town. I have been their slave ever since. Now I am free, thanks to your son."

"I am alone now, too." Judith paused, then asked, "Would you like to live with me?"

"I would be honored to live with Samson's mother. He told me all about your visit with the angel and the fire story."

"I still remember that amazing day when God promised

us a special son. Now, you can be my second special son."

Judith smiled and held out her arms to Hoshea.

"I would love to be your son and take care of you." He stood over her and gave her a long hug.

~ ~ ~ ~ ~

Samson's relatives retrieved his body and buried him with honors in the tomb of his father. Manoah died the year before his promised son perished in the arena.

Israel's twelfth judge died as he killed three thousand men and women, including the five lords and Delilah, a beautiful woman with a beautiful name and a deceitful spirit. God allowed Samson to kill more enemies in his death than during his entire lifetime as judge.

As predetermined by God and foretold by the Angel of the LORD, Samson judged and instructed Israel in the ways of God.

Epilogue

I am the LORD God Almighty, Creator of heaven and earth! I chose Samson as judge and deliverer. He fought against My people's enemies as did Gideon more than one hundred years prior. Seventy-six years after Samson died, I anointed a young shepherd boy named David son of Jesse, from the tribe of Judah, to lead My people to victory over their enemies. This humble shepherd became Israel's second king. The future heir to the throne of David is Jesus Christ, the King of all kings and Lord of all lords.

The King's Daughter

Michal

King Saul offers his daughter to
the warrior who kills his enemy.

Each princess desires to marry the hero.

A story based on 1 Samuel 1-19, 21, 22;
2 Samuel 3-6; 1 Chronicles 15

~ 1 ~

Hannah and Elkanah from the tribe of Ephraim sat near the charcoal fire in their kitchen, watching the dying embers slowly fade. The air had turned cold, and Hannah moved her cushion closer to Elkanah.

"Hannah, you are very precious to me. You know I love you with all my heart even though you have not given me a son."

Hannah responded to her husband's love. "I adore you too, my husband. Though we have been married several years, I do believe some day God will give us a son."

Elkanah cleared his throat. "Please be assured of my love for you when say that I plan to marry Peninnah. I hope she will give us children."

Tears quickly filled Hannah's eyes. She turned her head away from Elkanah's view—her heart broken. She abruptly left their house, climbed a nearby knoll, and sat and cried until dark. *O God of Israel, See my sorrow. I need Your comfort. Please do not let Elkanah make the same mistake as Abraham when he married a second wife.*

~ ~ ~ ~ ~

As Elkanah hoped, Peninnah gave him children, but with the children came family stress and tension. As they prepared the evening meals together, Peninnah enjoyed taunting Hannah because she was childless.

"The years have been favorable to me. Elkanah has given me children. Too bad he cannot give you children as well, but the LORD must have closed your womb."

Peninnah had no respect for Hannah and loved to display her scorn whenever she had the opportunity.

Hannah's daily prayers came from her heart. *O God of Israel, I know you see my sorrows. How can I bear Peninnah's hurtful words? I need Your wisdom and patience.*

When the family made their annual trip to sacrifice at the tabernacle in Shiloh, Peninnah would belittle Hannah to her face. Those were intolerable days for the childless woman.

One year when Elkanah presented his sacrifice, every member of the family received their portion of the meat as usual, but Hannah refused to partake. She walked off by herself to cry.

Her husband followed her. "Hannah, why won't you eat? See, I have given you a double portion because I love you so much. It does not matter to me if you give me no children. My love for you is more important than ten sons."

Elkanah could not understand her sadness nor why the two women were not kind to each other.

Hannah responded, "Husband, please leave me alone now. I go to the tabernacle to pray."

With tears and sobs Hannah poured out her heart before the LORD. She spoke no words aloud because of her anguish.

"God in heaven, hear my cry. I desire a son like other women. Please have mercy on me."

Her spirit calmed as she prayed in the tabernacle to her God. When the tears stopped flowing, she made a promise.

"O God, if You would see me worthy and give me a son, I promise to dedicate him to Your service forever as a Nazirite." In faith she said, "His hair will never be cut."

The priest Eli watched from a distance, then approached her.

"Woman, I see you have drunk too much wine. You should not come here in this condition. Go back to your husband."

"Oh no, sir! I have been praying from deep in my heart and I made a promise to God."

"In that case, I am sorry I misunderstood your actions. May God grant your desire. Go in peace."

Hannah left the tabernacle with energy in her steps and joy written all over her face. She went back to the camp to partake of the sacrificed meat. She spoke to her husband when they were alone.

"I made a vow to God. When he gives us a son, I promised he would live with the priest in the tabernacle forever."

"My dear Hannah, that is quite a heavy promise, but I accept your vow. May the LORD help you keep your promise."

According to the will of God, Hannah gave birth to a son and named him Samuel. They took him to Shiloh to serve Eli in the tabernacle when the child was old enough.

Eli the priest blessed Elkanah and Hannah. "May the LORD bless you with more children to take the place of the son you brought here to serve the LORD."

Hannah was full of joy that day as they all worshiped the LORD together. She quietly sang a song of praise.

My heart rejoices in the LORD!
Oh, how the Lord has blessed me!

No one is holy like the LORD!
There is no one besides You;
There is no Rock like our God.

The LORD blessed Hannah with three sons and two daughters. Her first son, Samuel, grew up in the presence of the LORD. Samuel heard His thundering voice many times.

~ 2 ~

A voice called Samuel's name in the middle of the night when he was about twelve years old. He assumed the voice belonged to Eli who was almost blind, so Samuel tied his garment around his waist and ran to Eli's bedside.

Samuel pulled back the tattered curtain to Eli's sleeping quarters. "My father, do you need something? I heard your voice."

"No, Samuel. Go back to bed." Half asleep, Eli turned over and covered his head.

After the third interruption to his sleep, Eli understood the situation. "Samuel, I am sure it is God who calls your name. Talk to Him."

Next time, the lad responded with caution to the mysterious voice. "I hear You, LORD." *I think.*

The words from God sounded loud and distinct like rumbling thunder in his ears.

"Because Eli's sons continue to disobey me, I shall keep my word concerning their punishment. Neither sacrifice nor offering will earn them forgiveness now."

The young boy trembled at those harsh words. *I just heard God speak! I am scared to tell Eli what He said.*

He stayed awake the rest of the night, afraid to go to sleep. *What else might God tell me?*

The next morning as Samuel opened the tabernacle

doors, Eli questioned him. "I know God talked to you last night. God might punish you if you do not tell me all He said. Tell me the truth," Eli said as he shifted from side to side. The old priest was in a bad mood due to lack of sleep the night before and in fear of God's message.

The lad tried to calm his shaking voice before he told Eli every word.

"God knows the right action to take. So be it," Eli whispered. "Follow me."

The priest motioned for Samuel to sit beside him on a bench outside the tabernacle.

"Samuel, I need to tell you a story."

"A true story?"

"Yes, a prophet visited me many years ago. It was late winter and black storm clouds had gathered in the hill country. A violent wind on a mission threatened to damage the structure of the weathered homes in Shiloh. Loud peals of thunder scared the children and startled livestock.

"On that stormy day, a stranger in a prophet's robe arrived at the tabernacle with a severe warning for me. That intruder brought a dreadful message from God—a promise of future judgment. As the man of God pounded on the door with both fists, I heard more thunder rolling in the distance."

"Loud thunder scares me," said Samuel, moving closer to Eli on the bench.

"The stranger woke me from my morning nap as he shouted for me to open the door, but I will not open doors to strangers. Now on my feet, I asked who knocks on my door. I opened the door a crack and asked him what he wanted.

"He said, 'I bring you a message from God. Because you have failed to restrain your sins and the sins of your sons, none of your family will live a long life. Your rebellious sons, who treat the LORD's offerings with contempt, will die on the same day.' The stranger pointed his crooked finger in my face a few inches from my nose."

"Then what happened?" Samuel's eyes widened.

"That unnamed prophet, with his outer robe wrapped tight around his rain-soaked body, left Shiloh riding his donkey as mysteriously as he appeared. His words put fear in my heart, and I hope I never see him again."

~ 3 ~

Late spring brought refreshing showers to encourage the growth of colorful wildflowers on the hillsides. Spring also brought war. The aggressive Philistines attacked Israel's troops near the town of Ebenezer, thirty miles west of Shiloh. Their anxious wives camped along the main road at the gate waiting for their men to return. As they prepared the evening meal for their children and the elders, one of the women stood up and alerted everyone.

"Look! A man comes down the road. But he is alone. That must be a bad sign. God help us!"

Beniah, one of the few surviving messengers, escaped the bloody battlefield and returned on foot to Shiloh.

At first, Beniah's wife did not recognize her wounded husband. She groaned, "Beniah, Beniah! Tell me what happened. Why have you torn your clothes and covered yourself with dust?"

Dragging his wounded leg, Beniah approached the town's broken gate. Weak from exhaustion and loss of blood, he said, "I must tell Eli that we have been defeated. Take me to him."

The aged and blind Eli listened to the pandemonium of the women and moved from under the shade of an oak tree.

As he approached the injured man, he asked, "My son, what has happened? Tell me everything."

Beniah paused to catch his breath before he told the dreadful details. "You need to sit down before I answer you."

A woman ran to bring a bench for Eli.

"We were defeated once again. Most of our thirty thousand soldiers lay slaughtered on the plains south of Gilgal. Wounded soldiers follow behind me now. Your two sons were killed, and our sacred ark has been captured by the Philistines."

Eli wailed, "The ark! The ark of God! I sinned when I allowed my sons to remove the ark from the tabernacle and take it into battle." He choked, gasped for more air, then his face turned blue.

Beniah was quick to reach out for him, but Eli slipped through Beniah's bloody hands and fell backward over the bench. "Eli, speak to me!"

But Eli did not respond; he died of a broken neck. Then Beniah collapsed at the priest's feet and breathed his last breath.

Eli had reigned as Israel's judge and priest for forty years and died at age ninety-eight. As God said and the unknown prophet prophesied, Eli two sons, Hophni and Phinehas died on the same day.

~ ~ ~ ~ ~

After seven months and a series of bad luck that included a deadly plague and the mysterious destruction of their god Dagon, the Philistines were frightened to keep the stolen ark any longer.

"We must get rid of this trunk that belongs to the God of Israel. It has brought us nothing but trouble!" All the Philistine leaders agreed and conceived a plan of action. They placed the ark on a cart drawn by two cows. As if an unseen hand guided the animals, they arrived at the closest Israeli town of Beth-shemesh.

A week after the ark arrived, the Israelites of that town met with the elders.

"We have disobeyed God and we are afraid to keep the chest in our possession. God was angry with us when the townsmen looked inside the sacred ark. We buried seventy men that day."

They moved the ark to the Israeli town of Kiriath-jearim without consulting Samuel, the new priest.

Because the ark did not reside at Shiloh with Samuel, the people of Israel were now concerned and told Samuel, "It appears God has deserted us."

The elders said, "We must repent of our disobedience. We want to return and follow the ways of God."

"If you are serious about your decision, destroy all your foreign gods and idols of Baal and Ashtoreth." Samuel instructed them, "Meet me at Mizpah and I shall pray for you."

All Israel assembled there for a day of ceremony and fasting.

Samuel assured them, "God will give you victory over the Philistines *if* you continue to worship the LORD and Him only."

As Samuel grew into young manhood, God continued to speak words of prophecy to him as His priest and judge. Every message Samuel proclaimed to the people came true. Israelites from Dan to Beersheba acknowledged that a true prophet of God and a judge lived in their land.

Israel had more lessons to learn.

~ 4 ~

When Samuel decided he was too old to travel as their judge throughout all the towns of Israel, he appointed his two older sons, Joel and Abijah, to hold court for him. Samuel did not seek the will of God in that decision. He experienced the same problem with his sons that Eli had encountered with his dishonest sons.

In late summer as the lower pasturelands turned brown, Ohad, an elder from Bethel, sat at the city gate with his neighbors. "Samuel's greedy sons make corrupt decisions and cheat us out of our rightful money."

"I agree! We cannot trust their judgments." Eldad pounded his fists on his knees.

Another elder suggested their leadership needed to change. "Samuel is almost too old to serve us now."

"I shall go to the elders at Gilgal and Mizpah to talk with them," Ohad stood up and mounted his donkey for the trip.

Eventually, all the elders of Israel agreed to meet with Samuel at Ramah and discuss Israel's deteriorating situation.

Samuel stroked his white beard with apprehension when he saw the delegation approach the gate at Ramah.

"What serious matter has brought you all together?" Samuel asked.

Ohad, chosen as the spokesman, addressed Samuel with

his strong voice of authority. "We know you are aging and someday you will be replaced. Your sons do not make honorable judgments. We all agree Israel needs a king to lead us."

Samuel frowned as his mouth fell open in shock. He responded after a long pause. "This request is absurd! I must talk with the LORD about this. I shall bring you His answer later."

"I shall wait right here until you return," Ohad said.

Everyone nodded their head in agreement with Ohad as they made themselves comfortable on the ground.

Samuel left them at the main gate and climbed the hill overlooking Ramah. He knelt before the altar and raised his voice to God.

"O LORD! Moses, our great deliverer, said a time would come when these people covet a king. Is this the time, LORD? You heard the demands of these elders. They do not want me or my family as their judge anymore."

Faint thunder rolled in the distance.

God spoke with clarity to his old prophet. "They do not reject you. They reject Me. They have continued to rebel since I delivered them from the Egyptians. Give them what they demand but warn them of the severe consequences."

With slow steps and a discouraged heart, Samuel returned to the elders with the LORD's somber message.

"The LORD has spoken. He will grant your request to be like other nations. But beware! Your king will demand your strongest sons for his army. He will take your daughters and force them to work for him. A king will take your best fields and vineyards for himself along with your favorite slaves. He will demand your finest cattle and donkeys. I would tell you more if your hearts were willing to listen."

Ohad expressed his determination shared by all the

elders. "We do not care about the cost. We want a king!" In defiance, the elder stood with arms folded across his chest.

"Very well, but I promise you, a time will come when you wish he was not your king."

Samuel returned to the LORD's presence at the altar and repeated the elders' decision.

God responded, "Give them what they want."

"O God! I fear for Your people, but I shall do what You say."

Samuel lingered in mediation at the altar, then returned to address the elders, "Go back to your homes until I call the nation together to choose your king."

The elders turned their backs to Samuel and with lighthearted steps, mounted their donkeys and returned to their towns to await Samuel's next instructions.

Several months later, God directed the prophet to call every family of Israel to meet at Mizpah.

"Today, you all stand here in the presence of the LORD. He reminds you that He was always your Deliverer, but now you reject Him. You want a king. The LORD grants your request. I remind you again that a king will demand the best of your fields and livestock for his own use. Your young men and daughters will be forced to obey his orders."

With all the tribes represented at the meeting, they cast lots for their king. The tribe of Benjamin was singled out, then the family of Matrites. Saul son of Kish was chosen just as God revealed earlier to Samuel. Saul was known as the most handsome and tallest man in Israel.

In a loud voice, Samuel addressed the people. "This is the man the LORD has chosen as your king. There is no one like him in all Israel."

The people shouted with exuberance, "Long live the king! Long live *our* king!"

Samuel quieted the people and demanded their attention.

"Listen to me! The king has many rights and duties as he leads God's chosen people to victory over their enemies. I have recorded them on this scroll to be stored in the tabernacle. In two months, everyone must gather at Gilgal to crown Saul as your king."

At the appointed time, the people gathered for the long-awaited ceremony with celebration of joyful dancing, the best of wines, and uncontrolled laughter. The people brought bulls, goats, and lambs for Samuel to present as peace offerings to the LORD.

Saul wore a linen robe of deep purple trimmed in gold thread. His wife Ahinoam in a shimmering white gown was by his side. Dressed in crude military attire, their sons Abinadab, Ishbosheth, Jonathan, and Malkishua stood with pride alongside their father. Saul's beautiful young daughters, Merab and Michal, positioned themselves beside their mother.

When the excitement subsided, Samuel demanded their attention.

"I served you from a boy and now I stand before you an old man. I did as you demanded and gave you a king. I warn both you and your king to always fear and worship the LORD. Do not worship false idols as your enemies do. If you continue to sin, you and your king will be punished. Do you remember the times in your past when you forgot God and served other gods? When you repented, God sent men like Gideon and Samson to rescue you. I am warning you now. If you and your king rebel against the LORD, you will suffer grave consequences again."

The crowd expressed to one another their agreement.

"We will support the king."

"The LORD God is our God."

"We will be faithful to Him."

Samuel pointed his finger at the king. "Saul, listen to me! You must follow the instructions of Moses to read the law every day to avoid becoming proud. You must learn to fear God so your descendants will reign for many years."

Samuel's warning left a somber impression on everyone.

"I promise to pray for you and teach everyone the ways of the LORD as long as I live." Samuel pledged to them and then sent everyone home.

A new era of victory and defeat, blessing and rejection dawned upon Israel.

~ 5 ~

King Saul and his commander Abner discussed their army's dire situation.

"The Lord instructed Israel to conquer Philistia when we entered the Promise Land," said King Saul.

"But we never claimed total victory over the Philistines. Their army is better equipped than ours; plus, we are outnumbered." Abner was not in a positive frame of mind.

"If we only had blacksmiths to make metal weapons. We are forced to hire a Philistine blacksmith to sharpen our farming equipment. That is humiliating!" Abner continued.

King Saul was determined. "Well, we will someday! For now, we will steal the weapons at every opportunity."

Only King Saul and his favorite son Jonathan possessed illegal swords.

Early one morning Jonathan, without telling his father, confided in Hirsh his shield bearer. "I want to sneak over to our enemy's outpost at Geba and attack them. I believe our God will help us. No one can stop God, right? He can win a battle with a large army or a few brave warriors."

Hirsh picked up his club. "I am ready for a good fight. I am with you all the way! What is your plan?"

"We will cross over the valley, hike up the ridge, and let them see us. If they say, 'Stay where you are or we will kill you', we will stop and not approach them. But if they say,

'Come and fight,' then we attack. I shall accept those words as God's sign that He will help us."

When the enemy saw them coming, they laughed and shouted at Jonathan, "Look! Our little moles have crawled out of their holes. Come up here, and we will teach you a lesson you will never forget."

Jonathan whispered to Hirsh, "Just the words I wanted to hear. Let us go get them. God is with us!" Jonathan drew his sword from its sheaf.

"Charge!" yelled his shield bearer. Hirsh carried Jonathan's shield and swung his own wooden club.

With God's help, they killed twenty Philistine warriors. Their bloody bodies fell scattered over half an acre of pastureland. Those who survived retreated like cowards. Jonathan and Hirsh claimed many metal weapons that day.

The report of their surprising defeat reached the enemy's main camp. Those in the field, including the outposts and raiding parties, were also aware of their slaughter. Panic set in and the enemy ran in all directions.

Then the unexpected happened. An earthquake struck! Thunder echoed in the distant hills. All the Philistines were filled with fright. Terror in the enemy camp grew louder. Confused, they attacked and killed each other. Bedlam ensued everywhere.

When Jonathan defeated that small garrison at Geba, their enemy became even more enraged. The Philistines came looking for Saul in full force with three thousand chariots, six thousand charioteers, and countless warriors.

"Abner, the Philistines are on the move again. What's your best action plan?" King Saul rubbed his hands together.

"Sire, most of your main army has already scattered to nearby hills to hide in the caves. I saw many troops escape across the Jordan River. At this hour, we are safe here in

Gilgal."

Saul's men lost their resolve and did not hear about the victory at Geba.

Saul complained to Abner. "Why hasn't Samuel the prophet arrived to pronounce his blessing? He is seven days late and many of the troops have deserted to the Philistine army."

Totally discouraged, Saul took matters into his own hands and offered an unapproved burnt offering to God. At that precise moment, Samuel arrived on his donkey.

"Saul, what have you done? I smell the smoke of a sacrifice."

"I needed the LORD's favor, and you were not here. The Philistines are about to destroy us. I need His blessing."

Samuel shook his finger at the king. "Why did you act so foolish? If you had obeyed the LORD, your kingdom would have been established forever."

"I had no choice. I had to act without hesitation." Saul tried to stand taller with his shoulders held back.

"No, Saul! You made the wrong decision. Now God will seek a man after His own heart, a leader who loves to obey His law. In fact, He has already chosen a new ruler for His people!"

After Samuel declared God's stern edict, he spun around, mounted his donkey, and left Saul standing next to the dying embers of his makeshift altar.

~ 6 ~

God spoke to Samuel as he worshiped at the altar in Ramah.

"You must deliver an urgent message to King Saul."

Without delay, Samuel mounted his donkey and rode twenty miles east over rough terrain to the king's residence in Gibeah.

"I must see King Saul at once."

Itamar, the gatekeeper, recognized the man wearing the usual robe of a prophet and opened the gate without delay.

"Sir, follow me." Asher, the king's servant ushered Samuel into a secluded room where King Saul reclined.

"King Saul! The LORD says, 'Now is the time to punish the nation of Amalek.' These people brought death and destruction upon Israel. They have been our enemy since the LORD liberated us from Egypt. The whole nation must now be destroyed—all the people and every animal. Show no pity on the people, covet no animal, take no spoils. Do you understand the LORD's instructions?"

"Yes, Samuel. I shall do as the LORD commands."

Saul gathered his troops. His son Jonathan called together his garrison. They prepared for the three-day journey with wagons filled with flat breads, raisin cakes, and wine. For their supply of fresh meat, shepherds drove flocks of sheep and herds of cattle behind the warriors. The king and his army headed south to Amalek.

Before sunrise, more than two hundred thousand Israeli foot soldiers hid stationed in the tall grass of the fertile valley near the capital city. From his vantage point overlooking the heathen kingdom, Saul shouted foolish instructions contrary to Samuel's distinct orders from God.

"Men, I order you to save the best herds and flocks for us but destroy all undesirable animals. Kill all the people, young and old alike, but save King Agag for my royal trophy."

As Saul's army pushed through town after town, the attacks caught the enemy by surprise. With God's help, Israel's military won a great battle that day. Every citizen of Amalek died. Abner captured King Agag as instructed. Saul's army now possessed more swords and spears.

Saul's heart swelled with pride at his victory over the Amalekites. After the battle, King Saul dismissed his army and returned to his home in Gibeah.

"Ahinoam, God blessed us today! Merab and Michal, once again I won a great victory. My troops destroyed our enemy Amalek. Bring our best wine from the vineyards of Gath-hepher."

His younger daughter Michal ran to their wine cellar for her father's favorite drink and returned laughing with excitement.

"Father, you have saved this skin of wine for a special occasion. Today must be that day. May I pour a glass for each of us?"

"Michal, my darling daughter, you have chosen the best. We shall celebrate!"

Ahinoam beamed with pride in her husband. "Israel has the greatest king of all the nations. No one can defeat you."

Saul raised his glass for a refill.

~ ~ ~ ~ ~

Again, the Lord woke Samuel in the middle of the night with a strong message that devastated His prophet. He always recognized the majestic voice of God.

"I regret making Saul the king of Israel. He pretends to honor Me but refuses to obey My commands. Saul is not following your instructions to read the law every day to avoid becoming proud. I have watched Saul develop into a prideful, disobedient king."

Samuel, grieved with this proclamation, cried out in prayer all night on Saul's behalf. His much-needed sleep escaped him.

"O God, I beg You to change the heart of Saul, at least for the sake of Israel."

Before the sun rose above the mountain, Samuel set out on his donkey to find Saul as the Lord instructed him. At the town of Carmel, the people said Saul left there yesterday after he made a monument.

"Saul built a monument to himself? O God! Forgive him. Who is this man becoming?" Samuel raised his moist eyes toward heaven. "O God, show mercy!"

Elam, a town elder, whispered, "You'll find him in Gilgal with his troops now."

The next day, Samuel located Saul in the garden as he strolled among his favorite flowers. The king was eager to report his victory to Samuel.

The king boasted, "I achieved what the Lord revealed to you. We won complete victory over the Amalekites."

"What do I hear in the green pastures behind us? The noise sounds identical to hundreds of sheep and goats. Do I also hear the mooing of cattle? Saul, meet me inside your tent to explain yourself!"

Leaving the garden, King Saul followed behind Samuel's hurried stride. They entered the room and King Saul, unconcerned, reclined on his couch.

At that moment, Abner entered the tent and stood at attention near his king.

Saul glanced at Abner for support, then tried to convince Samuel that his disobedience was justified.

"My army saved the best of the herds and flocks, but they belong to the LORD. We plan to sacrifice them to the LORD your God, but we destroyed everything else."

Astonished, Samuel's mouth fell open. *The LORD my God? He is your LORD too, and now your Judge!* The prophet raised his voice another octave. "Stop your excuses! Why did you disobey the LORD?"

With no regret Saul insisted, "I did what your LORD commanded. My troops wanted the best animals to sacrifice to the LORD your God."

The LORD my God? He said that again. LORD, why doesn't he understand that You are our God? "Listen to me!" Samuel stomped his sandal on Saul's dusty rug. "Obedience always proves better than sacrifice. Obeying the LORD's commandments rates higher than all your selfish offerings."

Saul whined, "My people influenced me. They celebrated as I paraded the tied and beaten King Agag down the streets of Gilgal." Saul's shoulders now drooped as he sat on his couch.

"Your rebellion and stubbornness are as evil as idol worship." Appalled, Samuel shook his head in disbelief of Saul's stupidity. "God has rejected you as king!"

Saul remained quiet for a moment, then tried to appear remorseful. "Forgive me. I have sinned."

"Where is your fear of God? Last night, *your* LORD told

me word for word what you did on the battlefield." Samuel turned his back to the king.

As the prophet moved forward to leave, Saul jumped up to detain him. He grabbed Samuel by his robe, tearing his old fragile garment from the shoulder down to the hem.

Samuel spun around and glared with fire in his eyes. "The LORD has torn the kingdom of Israel from you today! He has given your throne to a man with a heart to worship and obey the LORD. God will not change His mind!"

The prophet paused as if inspired, then roared, "Where is King Agag? Bring him to me!"

Abner vacated the room to retrieve King Agag from the dungeon. He unbolted two heavy prison doors and shouted to the captive huddled in the dark corner.

"You, disgusting swine, get on your feet! The prophet of God wants to see you."

The prisoner's knees shook, but he tried to appear brave.

"The king has spared my life. I am sure the prophet will do the same."

Abner roared, "Do not plan on it!"

The defeated monarch hung his head to shield his eyes from the bright sun as he exited the dungeon. Abner forced him, bound hand and foot, down the path to Saul's tent.

As Abner and King Agag approached, Samuel shouted to Agag, "Kneel!"

"O Prophet of God! I beg for your mercy!"

Samuel turned and scowled again at Saul for his weakness to obey God's orders, then glared at trembling King Agag.

"Your swords have killed many sons in Israel. Now your mother will grieve for *you*!"

With those prophetic words, Samuel grabbed Saul's sword from its sheath. Saul's hands shook not knowing what to expect. As King Agag knelt, Samuel brought the blade down across the foreign king's neck. Then with righteous anger, he cut Agag into pieces.

Samuel shouted, "Drag this vulture out of my sight!"

The commander barked orders to the soldiers standing at attention along the rear wall of the tent.

"Remove this dead heathen from our presence!"

Abner left the bloody scene and followed his men out of the tent to a nearby graveyard for foreigners.

Exhausted in mind and body, the prophet marched out of the room holding his torn robe together and returned home to Ramah.

"LORD, I shall never again request an audience with Saul. My spirit mourns for him as if the king has already died."

~ 7 ~

Due to his great affection for his king, Samuel despaired day and night over Saul's disobedience. After the severe judgment on King Agag, Samuel returned to Ramah to weep and pray for Saul.

Samuel grieved, *O king, my heart weighs heavy for you! Why have you become so rebellious? The LORD was with you in your victories. Why did you not obey His instructions? You are too proud.*

Months passed as Samuel resolved to remain out of public view. He preferred to make himself available to the school of the prophets at Naioth. Saul had grown evil and paranoid after God's rejection; therefore, the prophet no longer desired to meet with the king for any reason.

Again, God spoke to Samuel, "How long will you mourn for Saul? You know I rejected him, but My hand still rests on you. You have agonized long enough for Israel's disgraceful king. Get up off your bed and prepare for a trip to Bethlehem."

"Why must I go there? You know I prefer not to travel anymore." *Can I talk God out of this trip?*

"You shall anoint a son of Jesse as the future king of Israel."

"Now LORD? When Saul hears of my journey, he will have my head. You know he has become even more wicked, and he would not hesitate to send Abner to kill me."

"Take a young heifer with you to offer as a sacrifice."

"Clever idea. A sacrifice will conceal my ultimate purpose for this trip." Samuel smiled at the LORD's perfect plan.

Before daybreak, Samuel prepared for his journey. One of the young prophets helped him pack his supplies.

"I shall carry my horn of perfumed olive oil and select a perfect young heifer from the field for the sacrifice. It is a three-day journey, so I need to fill my leather pouch with dried lamb, raisin cakes, and fresh bread for this trip south. Thankfully, there are several creeks along the way to provide fresh water for me and my donkey."

As Samuel approached the town of Bethlehem, he wore his usual attire—the mended robe. The elders sat assembled at the main gate for their usual meeting to settle any disputes and legal transactions.

"Look, a prophet is coming down the road. Should we be concerned?"

Another elder questioned, "Did one of you invite him?"

The town leaders halted their business dealings, stood and bowed low in respect, then addressed Samuel.

"O man of God, why do you visit our unworthy town? Have we disobeyed God?"

"Do you come in peace?" Another man questioned with raised eyebrows.

"Do not be afraid. I come to offer a sacrifice. I ask all of you to sanctify your bodies and your hearts. Meet me on the knoll above the town for a feast within the hour. Bring dried fruit and your best wine."

Samuel continued down the lane to Jesse's home. Jesse also showed concern when he saw the prophet at his doorstep. His forehead dripped with nervous sweat as he bowed and kissed the visitor's wrinkled hand.

"Why this pleasure of your visit, O man of God?"

"I come to sanctify you and your sons. You will join me as I offer this heifer as a sacrifice." Samuel nodded to the calf standing behind him.

Jesse summoned his sons. "Come quickly! Samuel the prophet has arrived to bless us."

They gathered and knelt before Samuel as he prayed to God for them. Jesse's family joined the town elders for the long walk to the hill east of town.

Samuel took Jesse aside and whispered the real reason for his unexpected visit. "The LORD has instructed me to anoint one of your sons as Israel's next king."

"Oh, Samuel, your words are most unexpected. God honors our family beyond my imagination."

"Which one is your eldest son? Point him out to me."

"Eliab wears a brown garment. He roasts the heifer."

"A fine-looking man." *LORD, he must be Your chosen one. He is mature and has the presence of a man with authority.*

God spoke to Samuel's heart as soft thunder rolled in the distance. "Do not be deceived by his good looks. I read the heart of every man and I shall choose a leader who will honor and obey Me."

While the heifer roasted on the coals, Samuel walked a slow pace among the sons, pausing at each one to wait for God's leading. No loud announcement, no soft voice, no faint thunder spoke to Samuel.

LORD, am I not hearing You? I believe I followed all Your instructions. Samuel rubbed his forehead.

The prophet guided Jesse away from the crowd and spoke to him. "None of your sons appear chosen. God would not send me here by mistake. Are you sure all your sons attend this feast?"

"I have another son, but he is too young. He tends my goats and sheep in the upper pasture."

A large grin covered Samuel's face. "Send for him at once. We shall not sit down to the feast until he arrives." *God, he is the final son. I know You will make Your will clear to me.*

Soon a shepherd boy tanned from long days in the sun arrived at the feast with a lamb following close at his heels. Samuel observed this half-grown handsome lad and his soft brown eyes caught Samuel's attention. They expressed a spirit of joy and confidence the prophet had not witnessed in a long time.

"Samuel, I present my youngest son, David."

Yes, LORD! I hear Your voice of approval on this young shepherd boy. Samuel's eyes filled with tears as his heart responded to the LORD's message.

As David bowed and kissed the prophet's extended hand, Samuel directed him and Jesse to join him away from the other men.

Samuel did not raise his voice for all to hear.

"Young man, the LORD instructed me to anoint you as the next king of Israel. Now, we will join the others."

The guests, unaware of the significance, watched as Samuel picked up his ram's horn and poured scented olive oil over David's head.

Jesse watched with amazement as oil flowed down to his son's shoulders and onto his garment. *God, what does this mean for my young son?*

Questions also filled David's mind. *My LORD, I feel Your Spirit heavy upon me. This reminds me of the day You gave me strength to defeat a lion that attacked my sheep. Will I face another battle?*

With the sacrifice completed, all the men enjoyed a feast of dried fruit, fresh roasted beef, and wine. Only David and Jesse learned the real reason for the prophet's visit that day.

Samuel returned home to Ramah with great satisfaction and a sense of anticipation in his heart. After Samuel anointed the young shepherd, Samuel sensed the Spirit of God now completely abandoned King Saul. In Samuel's mind, he would no longer refer to Saul as the LORD's anointed.

"God, will I live to see David sit on the throne of Israel?" The elderly Samuel received no answer.

~ 8 ~

Five years passed. Spring rains arrived. Barren fields turned green once again and colorful wildflowers bloomed on the rolling hillsides of Gibeah.

"My dear Saul, it is springtime. Is it time for war with our enemies?" asked Ahinoam.

"I find it difficult to concentrate on my duties of leading the troops into combat. It is easier to avoid visitors and stay indoors." Saul was not honest with his wife.

Saul could not erase Samuel's threatening words from his mind. *When will a king take my kingdom from me? Dare I go to battle ever again?*

Often, he became enraged for no apparent reason. His wife Ahinoam stayed close by his side and tried to comfort him.

"Saul, why are you so fearful? What caused you to change?"

The king turned his head away from her and would not respond. She was unaware of the message Samuel spoke to her husband when he killed King Agag.

The king tried without success to fight off his periods of despondency. All who communicated with Saul noticed he exhibited strange behavior. Asher, one of his servants, stood in his place at the rear of the great hall ready to meet the king's every need. Asher was much aware of Saul's change in personality.

Saul hollered at his wife. "Ahinoam, bring Abner to me at once! I know the Philistines plan to destroy us." *These thoughts torment me day and night. I must be going mad!*

Saul's shouting unnerved Ahinoam. She gave Asher instructions to bring his army commander to the hall.

"The king suffers from extreme depression. He needs help. Tell Abner the situation looks urgent!" Trembling, she returned to the family's living quarters and left Saul alone to await the arrival of Abner.

The king's wife gathered their two daughters, Merab and Michal, around her and they cried together.

"Mother, I am sure Father will be in a better mood after Abner talks with him." Michal sat curled up at Ahinoam's feet and forced a smile for her mother's benefit.

"My lady?" Asher, the king's servant appeared at the open door. "Itamar and I believe a tormenting spirit attacks the king. Ask his majesty if he will see us right away. We have encouraging words for him."

"Oh, thank you! Wait here until I return." Ahinoam entered the great hall and bowed before her husband.

"Has Abner arrived yet?"

"Not yet. Two of your servants want a word with you. Will you listen to them now?"

"Yes, yes. But let me know as soon as Abner makes his appearance."

Ahinoam embraced her husband and left the room. She returned with the attendants following behind her. The men bowed low and tried to conceal their nervousness by speaking slowly.

Itamar spoke first. "O king! We know a tormenting spirit attacks you, but we bring hope. Give us permission to call an excellent musician to play the harp to comfort you. His melody will work miracles and you will be your usual self once again."

Asher, the older servant, presented his suggestion. "There is a young man from Bethlehem by the name of David son of Jesse who plays excellent music on his harp. People say the LORD speaks to him in songs."

At that moment, Abner arrived and entered the room. He approached and kissed the king's extended hand. "Sire, are you not well? Tell me what you need."

"I am always fearful and distressed over nothing important. Asher has suggested music might be a cure. Do you know David son of Jesse?"

"No, but I'll send for this man without delay if Asher recommends him."

"I want the best musician in all Israel. Find him!" Saul pleaded. Asher's idea brought hope to the king's heart.

~ ~ ~ ~ ~

David, covered with dust, arrived at Gibeah on a donkey loaded with fresh bread and a wine skin full of Jesse's best fruit of the vine. A young goat followed close behind the donkey. Jesse, a common sheepherder, was proud that Saul called for his youngest son and sent along humble gifts for the king.

Merab and Michal watched from their window as David approached the king's residence. Michal was impressed with what she saw and questioned her sister.

"Merab, do you recognize that good-looking young man?"

"I understand he goes by the name of David and comes to comfort Father with his music."

"I want to listen to his music, too. I think my heart needs

comforting."

"Oh, Michal, you are acting silly!"

The servant met the young traveler at the gate. "You must be David. My name is Asher, our king's trusted servant. Please follow me to the music room."

He escorted David to a small private room off the great hall where Saul reclined with a silver cup full of red wine. A thick blue curtain separated David from the king's vision.

"This is where you will sit and play twice a day for the king, in the morning and again in the afternoon before his evening meal. You are not to speak to the king, just play your harp and sing with a quiet voice. Wait here for me."

David seated himself in a far corner of the room and ran his fingers gently over the strings of his small wooden harp, humming as he played a melody.

After five minutes, Asher smiled to himself with satisfaction and slipped out of the room. *David was a fine choice.*

Within the hour, King Saul relaxed and fell asleep. Asher left his position at the rear of the great hall and returned to escort David to a sitting room.

"Your music worked wonders on King Saul. This will be your room while you are here. I shall bring your meals to your room and shall call for you when the king needs you." Asher then returned to his post in the great hall.

When the king awoke, he called Asher forward. "I could listen to that music all day. Send a messenger to his father. Say that I am pleased with his son and shall need his service on a permanent basis."

"I shall send someone to Bethlehem right away."

Often, each princess lounged in the hallway and listened to David as he sang and played his harp for their father.

"David's music puts a spell on me. I do not want to do

anything all day except listen to him play," said Michal.

"I love his soft voice. I wish he would sing to me," Merab whispered.

David's musical performance was helpful to encourage the king to relax. King Saul looked forward to David's regular visits. When Saul's spirit remained calm for an extended period, the shepherd returned to his sheep in Bethlehem.

A new chapter began in the life of David.

~ 9 ~

Again in early spring, the Philistines challenged Israel for possession of the land God promised to Abraham. Saul's army camped on a hill overlooking the valley of Elah. Across the valley darkened by gray storm clouds, the Philistines positioned themselves on another hill. Neither army advanced nor retreated. Days turned into weeks with no action from either side except threats that echoed from both sides of the valley.

Two of King Saul's sons, Jonathan and Abinadab, discussed the seriousness of the situation.

Jonathan said, "That Philistine giant must be at last nine feet tall. Watch how he and his armor bearer strut back and forth across the valley."

"I see their bulging muscles from here. I refuse to fight either one of them," whined Abinadab.

The giant's deep voice rode the wind, and no one misunderstood his message.

"I am Goliath of Gath, the invincible Philistine. I captured your ark and killed your priests Hophni and Phinehas when I was only a lad. I shall do the same to your king! If he is brave enough, send your son of Kish to meet me face to face with his sword raised. If he is afraid, send your strongest warrior." His arrogant laugh vibrated in the chests of Saul's fearful men. "The gods will decide the winner. If you defeat me, we shall be your slaves forever."

Abner rushed into King Saul's tent. "Did you hear that beast? He insists we engage in champion warfare—their god versus our God."

Saul rose off his chair and paced back and forth. "They know we outnumber them, and this challenge is the only way they can beat us—one on one. That is their stall tactic for more recruits."

Abner did not project confidence that day. "When the sun breaks through the clouds, his full body armor shines like solid brass. He carries a long javelin strapped on his back between his shoulder blades. His spear is the largest I have ever seen. If it is solid iron, it must weigh six hundred shekels."

"Abner, bring me our strongest and bravest volunteer!"

Abner showed no confidence in winning that battle. *I wish the old prophet Samuel were here right now. God, we need a miracle. If our king, the tallest man in Israel, will not fight Goliath, neither shall I!*

He left the cowardly Saul in his tent and walked the lines of the troops and stared into the eyes of the officers and captains.

"I want to see our bravest leader step forward to accept the challenge of Goliath," Abner shouted.

He paused in front of King Saul's son Jonathan who recently won a victory over a full garrison of Philistines with only the support of his armor bearer.

"This battle is not for *me* to win." Jonathan said. "But I am confident Goliath will be overcome!"

Saul's commander returned to the king's tent with the verdict. "No one wants to fight the giant."

"There must be one brave man. If he succeeds, I shall give my daughter as his wife and his family will be free from all taxes."

Abner muttered to himself as he left Saul's presence. "I do not think that reward is large enough for this challenge. No reward is!"

All, including the king, were afraid and not one soldier agreed to the demands of Goliath that day or any other day. The nights continued to drag on and neither army left their campsites, and none raised a spear or club against the other side.

Every morning and every evening for forty days, the giant invaded the once peaceful valley and roared his threats to God's chosen people.

~ 10 ~

With the daily chores completed, Jesse in Bethlehem of Judea presented the usual prayer of thanksgiving to God for His provisions. The head of the household reclined at the table after the evening meal with his wife and family.

"Nitzevet, your roasted lamb and root vegetables tasted delicious once again. You are an excellent cook."

"I am glad you are pleased, my husband."

Jesse expressed concern for his three oldest sons who fought in Saul's army.

"We have not received news from Eliab, Abinadab or Shammah for several months. I am worried about them as they fight their latest battle with the Philistines.

David showed concern for them also. "Father, do you want me to go to the war zone and talk with my brothers? I could report back to you the next day."

"Yes, I shall send you to the battle line. Your brothers should be low on food by this time. Nitzevet, my dear, please prepare a bushel of dried corn and loaves of sweet bread for David to take with him. Do we have extra cheese for their captain?"

Nitzevet nodded to David. "I made cheese yesterday, so the cellar is well-stocked. I shall have all the food ready for your trip in the morning."

"Leave before dawn because the trip will be a long one. The valley of Elah is more than sixteen miles southwest of here. Son, I am proud you want to help your brothers. God will be with you." He embraced his youngest son.

Jesse always remembered the day and the message when Samuel the prophet visited their home.

The next morning, excited to begin his trip, David left his father's flock with a hired shepherd and loaded a mule with bags of food supplies. He mounted his trusted donkey that transported him back and forth from the king's residence. Months had passed since he last played his harp for Saul, always behind a heavy curtain.

Maybe this time I shall have the privilege to meet King Saul face to face. David anticipated an unforgettable experience but was unaware to what extent God would use him that day.

The trip lasted five hours due to the rough terrain, but time passed unnoticed as David prayed with passion.

"I trust in Your protection even though wicked men string their bows and shoot from the shadows. I know You will cause the godless nations to vanish from our land. You are King forever! I give praise to God alone!"

As David headed for the battlefield, he found the journey a convenient time to commune with his Lord. The shepherd looked toward the sky and sang in his rich baritone voice.

"O Lord. Your name is most excellent!
Your glory reaches far beyond the heavens!"

David arrived at his destination in late afternoon. He saw the king's troops in formation and listened to their excited chatter as they fell in line to attack the Philistines. The young man left his brothers' provisions and his animals with the supply keeper and hurried to the battle line to see his older brothers. He searched for an hour among thousands of warriors before he located Shammah.

"Brother, how goes the battle? I brought grain and fresh bread for you."

Before Shammah could respond, Goliath made his entrance into the valley once again and raised his loud voice with the usual threat. Saul's troops retreated up the hill in fear.

David followed the men to higher ground and demanded, "Who is this uncircumcised Philistine that threatens God and His chosen people?"

The soldier nearest David answered his question. "His name is Goliath. He has badgered us for forty days, but no one is brave enough to meet his challenge."

Outraged, David continued. "How dare he blaspheme the living God! That disgraceful pig will be slaughtered!"

"The king looks for a brave challenger. Saul offers a large reward—valuable riches and the king's daughter—but no one will claim the honor."

When Eliab saw his young brother in deep conversation with a soldier, Eliab approached him and shouted, "Why are you here? You belong at home taking care of your little flock of sheep. Does Father know where you are?"

Why is Eliab so angry? I only asked a simple question. David sighed. *I am sure the stress of the battle must weigh heavy on all the warriors.*

David turned his back on his brother and walked over to another soldier. That warrior repeated the same promise of the reward.

"His family will pay no taxes in support of the king."

A captain named Simon overheard their conversation and reported their discussion to the king. "Saul, a young lad asks questions about the reward to kill the giant."

"Bring him to me at once!"

Simon approached David and announced, "The king asks for you!"

David's mind whirled with energy. *Now I shall meet our king in person.*

He entered the king's tent and bowed low before him. He sensed a cloud of fear in Saul's tent and wanted to encourage the king. David spoke first.

"Let no Israelite lose sleep over this profane infidel. I, your servant, shall kill him where he stands!"

Saul raised an eyebrow in surprise, then sneered at David. "You are out of your mind, young man. You are too young and inexperienced. Goliath has been a warrior all his life."

"I, too, am a brave warrior. I killed a bear and a lion with my bare hands on several occasions. This giant is no stronger than one of those wild beasts. The Lord God of Israel helped me then and He will help me now."

"Since you are determined to fight our enemy, I suggest you wear my armor to protect yourself." Saul smirked.

Reluctant, he accepted the full armor—metal tunic, coat of brass, and bronze helmet. He draped the king's sword over his shoulder. Saul followed young David outside as the lad practiced walking back and forth outside the tent.

David laughed aloud. "I cannot walk in this over-sized armor, let alone fight wearing all this protection. My king, keep your battle gear. I brought all I need."

As David left for the valley below, King Saul questioned Abner. "Whose son is this crazy young man?"

Abner shook his head. "I have no idea."

"Well, find out!" Saul shouted.

Using his shepherd's staff, David walked down the steep

rocky bank through the tall brush to the stream on the valley floor. *My staff always comes in handy on rough terrain. I will choose smooth river rock from the creek for my ammunition.*

David planned his battle strategy. *This giant might have four brothers. Five large pebbles should be sufficient today. They will fit nicely in my leather pouch.*

With his pouch hanging from his muscular shoulder, he crossed the shallow river, reached for his slingshot, loaded one rock in the rawhide cup, and approached Goliath without hesitation.

Eager for their long-awaited challenge to begin, the giant Philistine and his shield bearer moved forward from their relaxed positions. As he drew closer to David, he saw not a warrior but a lad.

Seeing David's staff, Goliath cursed him and shouted, "You bring a stick to scare me away like a dog?"

David raised his voice in response. "You are more like a despised pig breathing its last!" He spoke with authority and enjoyed the exchange of threats.

"Come here little creature, and I shall offer your flesh to the wild beasts and the vultures."

David did not disguise his smile. "You might own a heavy sword, a sharp spear, and a long javelin, but I come against you in the name of the LORD God Almighty, God of the armies of Israel whom you foolishly dare to blaspheme!"

A wicked laugh came from deep in Goliath's throat. "There is no god who can conquer me!" He swore again.

"Oh, yes! Today the LORD and I shall strike you dead and cut off your head. *Your* body will feed the beasts and wild birds. Everyone knows this is the LORD's battle, and you lose! My God has trained my hands and He is my mighty shield!"

Hearing David's last proclamation, Goliath moved in close for the kill.

Without the slightest hint of fear or hesitation, David rushed forward to attack him. With his trusty sling loaded and ready, the shepherd wound up and delivered the stone where he aimed. The small rock embedded deep in Goliath's exposed forehead. The warriors on both sides of the valley were aware of heavy thunder rumbling in the distance.

Unconscious, Goliath collapsed on the ground, face down. A tremor vibrated under David's feet. The armor bearer dropped Goliath's heavy shield and bolted backward across the battle line. David ran forward to grab Goliath's sword still in its sheath. He raised the blade high with both hands and hacked off the giant's repulsive huge head before he regained consciousness. The blade now glistened with fresh blood. He held up the ugly trophy for all the enemy to identify. A slimy red stream ran down David's raised arm.

David shouted, "Victory for the God of Israel!"

He stuck Goliath's sword in the ground, dropped to one knee and bowed his head in a quick reverent prayer of thanks.

"O LORD my God, You performed wonders for us once again. Trusting You brings me such joy!"

He stripped Goliath of all his armor and weapons. *This coat of mail must weigh at least five thousand shekels. These souvenirs belong to me. I shall take Goliath's sword to my friend, the prophet Samuel.*

A deafening victory shout went up from Saul's army and their enemy screamed as they retreated as fast as they could. Abner called for the trumpet to sound the charge and led his excited troops down the hill and across the creek into the enemy's camp. The Israelites chased and attacked the Philistines, leaving dead and wounded bodies prostrate everywhere along the Shaaraim Road as far south as the town of Gath. The vultures and wild animals enjoyed a delicious feast that day but not on Israeli bodies as Goliath threatened.

When Saul's army returned from the chase, Abner announced to his men, "All the Philistines' supplies and swords belong to us now. Go back to their camp and claim all you can carry."

When they returned with their wagons full of spoils, the troops boasted to each other of their victories. To add to the celebration, the captains passed around wine skins full of refreshment for everyone.

After the merriment died down, Abner approached David. "King Saul is asking for you."

The young hero still displayed his blood-stained prize atop Goliath's spear. David collected his personal booty and followed Abner into the king's tent. As they entered, Saul stopped pacing. The king's heart raced from the excitement of the battle.

Saul demanded, "Whose son are you?"

"I am the eighth son of your servant Jesse of Bethlehem in Judea. I am the one who plays music to comfort you. What an honor to talk with you, my king!"

"Abner, call all your captains together. It is time for an official ceremony. We have a hero among us!" Saul beamed with extreme satisfaction. He opened his tent door and stepped outside.

As Saul made his appearance, all the troops cheered. "Long live our king! Long live King Saul!"

With a loud voice, Saul boasted to everyone. "We have a champion in our midst!"

Humbled by his conquest, David spoke his true feelings. "If we trust in God, there is no enemy we cannot conquer.

God gave us a great victory today!" He still held the atrocious head of Goliath as he stood beside King Saul.

Saul agreed. "Yes, God did. But *you* deserve my congratulations."

Saul quieted the men, then continued, "This is David son of Jesse. Today, we are proud to have this brave man in the army of Israel. David, you proved yourself strong and fearless despite the odds. You earned the position as captain of a brigade with your amazing feat of killing our enemy, the giant Goliath. You will now fight by my side."

All the officers showed their agreement with shouts of praise for David.

At that moment, one of Saul's sons stepped forward and raised his hand for silence. He embraced the young man. "I am Jonathan son of King Saul. I, too, trust in God for my victories. Today I saw the power of God at work to preserve the land He gave us—our land with streams of olive oil and rivers of sweet honey."

Jonathan embraced David again, then removed his outer garment. "I present you with my robe. Take my belt and tunic also. You are my brother. May our bond with each other always be strong."

Overwhelmed, David bowed to one knee, but Jonathan reached down and raised him to his feet. They grasped their arms together as family.

David's voice diminished to a whisper. "I accept your friendship. You are my brother, also."

"I present my bow and sword to you. We shall fight together, side by side."

"I know there are no swords for Israel's army, and you give me yours?"

"I have connections," Jonathan said as he nodded to his father. "Besides, we acquired many swords today, thanks to you."

"I am humbled, my brother. I heard how you alone with your shield bearer destroyed a full garrison of Philistines. Everything God does reveals His glory and majesty. Jonathan, you honor me with your friendship."

The troops, including David's brothers, cheered. King Saul was proud of their accomplishments, and the spirit of celebration hung in the air for many hours around the campfires.

More battles awaited young David.

~ 11 ~

After celebrating Israel's victory over the Philistines, Abner dispatched a report to Saul's home in Gibeah.

The messenger boy hammered on the iron gate and shouted, "I bring a message. I have a message for the king's family!"

Itamar opened the gate and called for Asher.

Asher smiled at the boy. "You must bring good news because you are jumping with excitement."

As he rested on a stone bench, the young boy said. "I ran all the way from the valley. Goliath is dead! David cut off his head. His reward includes the king's daughter."

"You brought the best announcement ever! Itamar, provide this young lad with fresh bread and water before he returns to the troops while I deliver this exciting message to the family.

Asher found Ahinoam and her girls as they reclined in their garden enjoying cheese and fresh grapes.

"My lady! I bring an important message. Our king comes home in victory! Goliath will no longer be a threat to us because David beheaded him!"

"Do you mean our David who plays the harp?" they asked in unison.

"Yes, that one." Asher smiled, knowing a secret he planned to share with the girls.

"He joined the army?" Ahinoam asked, showing a light frown.

"He has now. He proved almost as brave as King Saul, my lady." Asher sat down beside Ahinoam.

"Guess what David's reward will be."

Michal spoke first. "I bet father will give him a beautiful white horse from Egypt."

"Michal, his reward will be more valuable than a horse. Silly!" Merab considered herself more logical than her younger sister. "Father will give him a large house with a vineyard.

"Girls, I am sure your father will make him a captain."

"All your suggestions sound appropriate to me, but there is a much greater honor. Since the army knows the answer, I guess this reward is no secret. Are you ready for this?" Asher adored the family and enjoyed the mystery he created.

"Tell us! Tell us!" Both girls giggled with excitement.

"Asher, you have kept us in suspense long enough." Ahinoam nodded at Asher to continue.

"Yes, my lady. The messenger said David's reward includes the king's daughter in marriage." Asher turned his head toward Michal, then to Merab.

"The king's daughter, the king's daughter! I hope it is me, the reward must be me." Enthusiasm overtook Michal as she bounced up and down on her cushion.

Merab countered, "I must be his wife because I am the oldest. And more beautiful."

"No, you are not. Besides, I loved him the first day I saw him."

"Girls, no more arguing. Your father and I shall discuss this matter later, probably much later."

~ ~ ~ ~ ~

News of the conquest over the Philistines, including all the unbelievable details, reached every town and village in Israel long before Saul's army returned to their barracks in Gilgal.

"King Saul, you are a proud champion once again. Are you ready for our victory march down Gilgal's main street? The four of us will lead the parade," said Abner.

With their horses four abreast, King Saul, Abner, Jonathan, and David rode down the street with the army following. The young warrior still carried an ugly oversized head pierced atop Goliath's sword like a banner on a flagpole. Blood, now dark and dried, coated the ghastly souvenir of their conquest.

Old men and children from the surrounding villages lined both sides of the road. Women played their timbrels and sang joyful songs of celebration. "King Saul has killed thousands! David has killed tens of thousands! Praise the God of Israel!"

Saul frowned and turned his head toward his commander beside him, "What are those women singing?"

"It appears they are singing greater praises to David."

"I hear the same. Next, they will give David my kingdom!" Sarcasm dripped from Saul's voice. *It will be in my best interest to keep a watchful eye on this young man!*

The hero did not return to his father's home but sent a messenger to Bethlehem to report that all Jesse's sons remained safe, and that David had joined the army.

"I am proud to store Goliath's armor and sword in my tent. Soon I shall visit the prophet Samuel and present my gift," David said to himself as he moved into his new home.

The day after Israel's victory, Saul developed a troubling spirit which agitated him to the extent that his wife became afraid of him. She called for their servant Asher, one of her few friends. He came as soon as he received the order.

"Asher, King Saul needs comfort again. Is young David in his tent now?"

"Yes, my lady. I shall bring him right away."

Asher located David and ushered him into the music room. Saul reclined in the great hall, but he proved too disturbed to sit still. During those times of discontent, he paced back and forth across the room. Always insecure, Saul kept a javelin nearby for protection.

David's melodies usually created a relaxing atmosphere but not to Saul's ears that day. As music filled the air, Saul hollered, "Open my curtain. Now!"

Asher jumped from his sitting position in the hallway and ran to pull back the heavy curtain and secured it.

The moment Saul recognized who played the harp, he shouted, "I shall pin you to the wall!"

He picked up his javelin and threw it. Out of control, Saul's aim lacked definite direction. David easily dodged the weapon. Saul cursed and grabbed a long spear. He threw again but watched his lance fall short without penetrating David or the wall.

"Asher," David whispered. "I think I am through for the day!"

"I agree with you. May God go with you, my son."

~ 12 ~

"Father, when will you let me marry David? You promised your daughter to the one who killed Goliath, but a year has passed since that battle. Father, can I marry him now?" Merab was determined to make her wishes known to the king.

"But Father, I am the one who loves David. Please let me be his bride." Michal complained.

"Oh, you are too young to marry," Merab chided Michal.

Michal persisted. "I must marry him. I know he loves me. I can tell by the way he looks at me with his soft brown eyes. I think we were born for each other."

"Michal and Merab, this decision requires more discussion with your mother. I shall not be rushed to give my answer now." *I had hoped my girls would never bring up this subject. David is the last person I want them to marry. I do not trust that young man!*

"Father, please do not delay any longer. Talk with Mother and make your decision soon." Michal's tears flooded her eyes.

In haste, King Saul rose from his favorite bench in the garden and left his daughters to their own selfish thoughts. *Something must be done about this man as soon as possible. I need to talk to Abner!*

As Saul returned to the house, he shouted to his servant,

"Itamar! Send for Abner at once!"

The day began sunny, but by midday, storm clouds gathered, and rain fell by the bucketsful. A greater storm raged in Saul's mind as he formulated a devious plan.

Itamar entered the great hall where King Saul waited. "Sire, Abner arrives."

"Good, good! Now leave us alone."

Itamar bowed and returned to his post at the gate.

"Sire, why have you called for me?" Abner gave the king a quick bow at the waist.

"We need to make plans for David. Since he acts the part of a mighty warrior, I want you to send him alone with his brigade on the next battle. Instruct him to attack the closest Philistine stronghold. I want to see how brave he performs under intense pressure." *Maybe he will not come back alive! Perhaps God will desert him too!*

Abner located the newest captain resting in his tent. "David, you have orders to take your men and attack the Philistine garrison north of Gath. King Saul has instructed you to leave at sunrise tomorrow."

"I shall leave for the barracks in Gilgal this afternoon to gather my men, then travel west. I will report to you when I return."

He sounds eager for his assignment. "God be with you, David."

"He always is, sir. I have proved Him many times." David spoke with confidence.

David won that battle with the LORD's favor. He returned in victory as usual and the people in Gilgal lined the streets to celebrate him. When he entered Gibeah, more cheers awaited him. King Saul's daughters stood along the roadside as their excited shouts resonated above the crowd.

"Hooray for David! Look, Merab, there is not a scratch

on him. What a strong warrior! Handsome, too."

"He does look handsome. I love his auburn curls," Merab giggled. "Remember, I am older, so I am sure Father will give him to me."

"Do not count on that gift!" Michal loved to challenge her sister.

King Saul watched the celebration parade from the upper window of his residence. He had no desire to join his citizens on the street, nor did he demonstrate any joy in David's victories. The battle did not end as he hoped.

I shall continue to send him out until his threat to my kingdom is eliminated. Why am I so afraid of him? Maybe God helps him. If so, I have a bigger challenge than I imagined.

~ ~ ~ ~ ~

When the chilly days of winter arrived, battle plans were delayed until warmer weather, but King Saul wanted to make an offer he hoped David would not refuse. Saul escorted himself to the young captain's tent to present the challenge. Saul paused outside David's quarters and listened as he strummed his harp and sang with a quiet voice.

"LORD, show me what path to follow.
I want to follow only You.
Light the road for me to travel.
I always put my trust in You."

Hum . . . those are comforting words. Saul considered reversing his steps but gathered his courage and called out. "David! I must have a word with you."

Based on past experiences playing his harp for the king, the young warrior hesitated to invite Saul into his tent, away from the view of the other captains. With caution, David stepped outside. He had learned to stay on guard for his personal safety.

"How can I assist my king? Do you have another assignment for me?"

"I am aware that you have not demanded your reward, but now is the time for me to fulfill my promise to the man who killed Goliath. I offer my first-born daughter, Merab, as your wife. But you must prove yourself worthy and destroy a full garrison of Philistines." *I will let them kill David instead of me getting blood on my hands.*

"King Saul, I am not worthy to be called the king's son-in-law. My family serves your kingdom as shepherds. Please forgive me for not accepting your gracious offer."

David's unexpected refusal irritated King Saul. Without another word, he whirled around and marched back to his residence.

"Well, that did not go as I planned. He proved a better man than I imagined," Saul mumbled to himself. "But I shall not be deterred from my mission to preserve *my* kingdom!"

~ 13 ~

"Ahinoam, there has been a change in marriage plans for Merab. David refused to accept his reward for killing Goliath."

"Oh, poor Merab. Did he give a reason?"

"He considers himself not worthy of the king's daughter because his family are shepherds." Saul spoke with contempt in his voice. *Is this man arrogant or humble?*

"Does Merab know about this yet?" A deep frown crossed Ahinoam's usual smooth forehead. "I wish happiness for my daughters, not misery."

Saul sighed, "No, I did not want to tell her. Her heart definitely wants David." *And I want him out of my sight—forever!*

"Do you want me to give her David's decision?"

"Not yet. We need a substitute to take her mind off David. Marzillai has a strong and able son named Adriel. He serves in my army as an officer. I am considering him as a husband for Merab. I know this family in Meholah can well afford our bride price."

Ahinoam said, "Oh, Saul, I know that name. I visit with his mother Sarah at the festivals. She is a fine woman. I am sure Merab will love Adriel's family."

"Then we agree. I shall send word to Marzillai. When I

receive a positive response, you can tell Merab the news. We can plan the betrothal as soon as possible. Since he is a young widower, there is no need for the one-year waiting period."

King Saul arose from his couch and left their private room to locate his trusted servant. He found Asher talking with Itamar near the front gate.

"Asher, I am giving you an important assignment. My father's brother, Ner, visits his relatives in Ramah. Locate him and announce I want to discuss an urgent matter with him."

"Yes, Sire, I shall leave without delay."

Saul's uncle arrived late the next day as the sunrays disappeared behind the Judean hills. Ner brought his nephew Joseph to meet the king.

"Saul, this is my sister's son, Joseph."

"I am glad to meet you, young man." The king teased him. "Are you ready to join my army?"

"I think I am too young, but I shall join when I grow up."

Saul and Ner both laughed at the boy's wide-eyed expression.

"Saul, today marks my first official visit to your royal estate. I am impressed with your fine home."

Ner enjoyed glancing from room to room as they walked through the house to the garden. The glow of the oil lanterns cast playful shadows on the path.

"We live here in comfort. Please join me in the garden. I have a private family matter to discuss with you. I trust you stopped at the captains' quarters first. Did you see your son Abner? He is an excellent commander of my army."

"Yes, Abner makes me very proud."

Saul led the way through the blooming acacia trees to a cedar bench. While Joseph chased the gray squirrels, the elder man and the king reclined at opposite ends of the bench.

"Ner, what do you hear from my father?" Saul shifted to face his uncle.

"Kish looks well. Prospers as usual. When did you see him last?"

"You know I lead a busy life as king." Saul frowned as he showed his impatience with where the conversation was headed.

Ner recognized the hint. "Saul, what is your important assignment for me?"

"I ask you to visit the home of Marzillai who lives in Meholah."

"Why?" Ner tilted his head, anticipating a story.

"Their son Adriel became a young widower six months ago and I chose him as the husband for my oldest daughter, Merab. No doubt his family will approve of marrying into the king's family. If Marzillai accepts your offer, arrange for Adriel to attend the betrothal ceremony here in Gibeah as soon as possible."

"I am sure none would dare to refuse the king." Ner's eyes twinkled with humor.

"Well, some might. But that is another story." *I make no confession to my father's brother.* "When can you leave?"

"If you serve pheasant tomorrow, we shall leave right after the morning meal." Again, Ner smiled with amusement.

"Thank you, Uncle. It is a pleasure to kill my enemies but not to deal with my daughters' love affairs."

~ ~ ~ ~ ~

The town of Meholah was fifty miles northeast of Gilgal. Ner and Joseph journeyed by camel, crossed the Jordan River, and camped near Cherith Brook.

"Uncle Ner, I am happy you asked me to come with you on this trip. I seldom have a chance to ride a camel. Plus, it is fun to join you on the king's business."

"I enjoy your company, too. Tell me, what do you know about this shallow brook by our campsite?"

"It flows near Meholah, and the water tastes good." Joseph laughed.

Ner loved to share his knowledge of the terrain. "Ravens make their nests in this area. They are a large black bird about two feet long. If you keep your eyes open, you might see one. I hear they can live a long time – about 20 years."

"That is a long life for a bird."

Ner grinned at his nephew. *He is a fine boy. I am glad I brought him with me.* "Tomorrow we will ride into town and find the home of Marzillai. I am sure they will be surprised by our visit but quite pleased with the message I bring."

~ ~ ~ ~ ~

Ner returned to the king's residence to announce his successful mission. Saul exhaled a sigh of relief and Ahinoam jumped to her feet with excitement.

"I shall tell Merab our good news."

Ahinoam made a quick search and found her daughter relaxing in the shady garden, the family's favorite place of retreat.

"Merab, Merab! Come sit beside me. We must make betrothal and wedding plans!"

"For me? I am so excited! Did David change his mind?"

"No, I am so sorry, Merab. I know he was your first choice, but your father chose a wonderful young officer in his army named Adriel. I know his mother. A marvelous lady!"

"Oh, Mother, is he handsome?"

"Yes, I am sure he is."

"Mother, you brought me such a wonderful surprise. Can I be the first to tell Michal?"

"Of course, my dear."

"One question. Can we plan a small quiet wedding? I shall be too nervous with hundreds of people watching me."

"Merab, the king's daughter can plan any size of celebration she desires." Ahinoam smiled and gave her daughter a big hug. "You will be a beautiful bride, my dear."

Merab's smile drooped for a moment. "I was sad that David refused Father's offer, but now I am excited to prepare for my betrothal and wedding to Adriel. My broken heart heals fast." She giggled and ran off to tell Michal.

Two weeks later, the king's daughter Merab celebrated her traditional betrothal ceremony with her parents and Adriel. Following Israel's custom, Merab met Adriel that day for the first time.

The heat of the day warmed the garden, and all were thankful for the cool breeze as they sat in padded chairs placed around a bronze table. Their servant, grinning with the excitement of the occasion, entered the garden with a bottle of red wine and four silver cups on a shiny brass tray.

"You may place them here on the table."

"Yes, Sire." Asher bowed low to the king, then retreated to the garden entrance to await further instructions.

Knowing the procedure, Merab rose to her feet and poured wine in three cups, leaving one empty.

She whispered to her mother, "I am so nervous, but I did not spill a drop."

Adriel was the first to speak. "King Saul, it is my

intention to propose to your daughter Merab. My large home is well-suited for a king's daughter. I have many acres of pastureland and large herds of livestock. I am a faithful son of Israel and a proud soldier in your majesty's army. I ask your permission to marry your daughter."

"I shall give my permission if you agree to my bride price." Saul said.

"King Saul, what is your price?"

"One hundred sheep and five hundred head of cattle."

"I accept your price." Adriel smiled, his voice a little shaky. Everyone expected him to agree to the price.

Now it was time for Merab to decide. If she turned her cup upside down, she refused the proposal. All eyes rested on Merab.

The young princess smiled, revealing both dimples. "I accept your proposal in marriage."

Adriel beamed with pleasure and rose to fill her empty cup with wine. Everyone drank together in celebration.

"Merab, I am proud to be your husband and I promise to care for you according to the laws of Moses."

He presented her with a delicate gold ring as a symbol of his intentions.

"Oh, Adriel, the ring is elegant and the brilliant ruby sparkles so. I love it!"

He slipped it on her finger. "It is a perfect fit for a beautiful woman." He turned his attention to the king.

"I shall have the herds delivered to your shepherds within the week. Merab, we are now engaged, and I shall call for you before the next full moon. I shall come when you least expect me according to our tradition."

He stood, bowed to Merab, and escorted himself out of the garden, leaving an excited Merab and her mother to arrange the perfect wedding plans.

~ 14 ~

"Father, I beg you to arrange my betrothal to David. I would be so proud to marry our famous warrior."

Michal and her parents relaxed in their secluded garden. The early afternoon weather was sunny and warm, a perfect day for sipping wine. The king, considering his pending battles, watched two ground squirrels chase each other around and up an olive tree like warriors pursuing their life-long enemy.

Saul's wife supported Michal's request. "I think David makes a fine choice for Michal. He continues to grow popular with our people and he conducts himself like a successful leader."

The king continued in his agony. *I need a better plan of eliminating my rival. I will send him out on another dangerous mission. I hope those despicable Philistines will kill him this time.*

"All right, I shall consent to Michal's marriage. I shall speak with him tomorrow and then contact his parents in Bethlehem because I insist they live here in Gibeah." *I must keep an eye on him.*

"Father, I am so happy! I believe David will agree this time."

"Now, do not make any wedding plans yet," Saul warned.

Michal and Ahinoam left the garden in haste, deep in conversation. Excitement and girlish laughter filled the air and entertained the birds.

Saul remained in the yard to formulate the details of his deceitful plan. After an hour passed, Saul went to David's tent.

Soft music drifted from David's open window as Saul approached. *Does he play his instrument every hour?*

"David! A word with you."

He laid aside his harp and stepped outside with caution. "Greetings, my king." He bowed with respect.

"I offer you another opportunity to become my son-in-law and take my daughter Michal as your wife. I shall expect your answer when I dine with my captains in the great hall tonight." Saul turned and left abruptly.

"Do I detect an attitude change in my king? It appears he approves of me at last—I think," he said to himself.

David walked the short distance and joined the others at Simon's tent where five captains along with Abner reclined in the afternoon shade. He shared the king's announcement.

"But I am not able to accept our king's offer."

"I would not pass up this opportunity." Abner encouraged him.

"I am sure the king approves of you. If I were you, I would not refuse him." Simon concurred with Abner.

"I have no means to pay the bride price, whatever it is, for a king's daughter. I am merely from a family of shepherds."

After a moment, David excused himself and with slow steps returned to his tent.

Abner also dismissed himself and jogged up the hill to report to King Saul. He pounded on the metal gate, attracting the gatekeeper's attention.

"Itamar, I am here to see King Saul."

He quickly opened the gate for the commander.

"Announce me to the king." He nodded to Asher.

Asher left his post to approach the king who reclined, as usual, in the great hall.

"Sire, Abner waits to speak with you."

"Send him in." Asher bowed low in respect and left the room to escort Abner into the king's reception hall.

"Abner, what do you learn from my captains this week?"

"No new battles, my king. Those ugly Philistines retreated to their camps in the distant hills. But on a different topic, I heard talk of another son-in-law for the king." Abner displayed a mischievous grin.

"Tell me more. What did you hear?" Saul prompted.

"David says he cannot afford the normal price and looks discouraged."

The king showed his crooked smile. "Well, you tell him I demand a price of one hundred Philistine foreskins delivered to me before the new moon. My project might keep him busy for two weeks. I am after vengeance on those foreign pigs." *I hope this will be the end of David, as well!*

"My lord, I will give him your message without delay." Abner bowed and quickened his steps as he left the king's presence.

Abner returned to David's tent within the hour.

"David, King Saul has named his price. One hundred Philistine foreskins. Do you accept his challenge?"

"Tell my king I will not join him for dinner tonight. I leave now to gather my garrison in Gilgal."

"God go with you."

"He always does!" David grinned with confidence.

~ ~ ~ ~ ~

Michal and her mother discussed plans for an elaborate royal betrothal and wedding.

"Mother, I know it is our custom for the bride to live near the groom's family, but since Father is king, I want to live here in Gibeah near you."

"I am sure that can be arranged with David's father," her mother nodded.

"There is a perfect place to live with David. I discovered a grassy knoll with tall pine trees a short distance from here. Come with me and I will show you where Father must build my home as my dowry to David."

Ahinoam hugged her. "Show me this afternoon, then I will speak to your father after dinner tonight."

"Remember, my home must be larger than Merab's." Michal's brown eyes were wide with anticipation. "I want everyone to talk about my wedding for many years. The celebration must be more glamorous, more expensive than anyone's in all Israel."

Michal would learn that not everything happens as the king's princess plans.

~ 15 ~

The report of David's latest military success reached Gibeah before he arrived at his quarters. Michal waited at the city gate with the other women who cheered and waved to celebrate his current victory over Israel's worst enemy.

Merab had been married several months and was in town visiting her parents. She arrived just in time to enjoy another victory parade.

Riding through the city gate, David paused in front of Michal, dismounted, bowed low in respect, and gave her a nod and a smile. Michal blushed. Her heart raced with excitement. She turned to her sister standing beside her.

"He is the most handsome man ever. Just imagine, this famous warrior will be my husband!"

"Well, I agree he is handsome. But my Adriel is the kindest man ever, and he will make the perfect father."

"A father? Merab, how exciting! Did you tell Mother?"

"No, I have not told anyone except you. Consider this our secret, okay? Promise me. Adriel and I plan to wait a few more months before we tell our parents."

"I promise. Oh, Merab, you told me the best news ever. Except, of course, David's return in victory."

Again, King Saul watched from his private window on the second floor of his royal residence that overlooked Gibeah's main street.

He groaned to himself, "Why is David always so successful? He is never defeated in battle. Must I kill the man myself?"

~ ~ ~ ~ ~

"David, come outside and tell us everything. How many Philistines did you kill?"

Rumors of his return from battle spread throughout the captains' quarters. Simon, the first to reach David's tent, was eager to enjoy all the bloody details.

Abner and his captains gathered around the young warrior as he bragged about the results of their surprise attack.

"Three days passed before we found the garrison. After dark, we hid our horses in the forest, then I sent my men into every Philistine tent in their camp, our knives drawn. Those drunken pigs were unable to defend themselves, making our attack quick and easy. One stab in the heart and then one slice below! We disappeared in thirty minutes."

Abner demanded a report. "How many men did you lose?"

"Sir, all my men came home unscathed. Our enemy did not hear us coming. Once again, God helped us. I give my Lord all the praise for this victory!"

"Did you bring back Saul's full bride price?" Abner asked, though he had already received the answer from the rumors.

"We stopped killing after two hundred. I obtained more skins than I needed," the young warrior boasted with a soft chuckle.

With raised eyebrows and a broad grin, David held up two bulging leather bags. "Abner, give Saul these sacks and the following message: I accept his terms of betrothal to the king's daughter."

The captains cheered with gusto and David returned to his tent. He spent the rest of the afternoon in worship as he wrote songs and praised the LORD while strumming his harp.

"My heart is confident in You, O God;
I will sing Your praises with all my heart.
May Your glory shine over all the earth.
I sing Your praises among my people."

~ 16 ~

The seasons changed and time passed quickly for Michal. Her father built her dream home for her dowry to David.

"Mother, I love my beautiful dress. You created a gown beyond my dreams! I love the rows of pale blue lace gathered along the bottom hem. The long train will make me look like a queen."

"You will be the most magnificent bride in all Israel! Your dark hair will shine with these threads of gold and strands of pearls woven together in your curls. Daughter, you are welcome to wear any of my jewels for your wedding."

"I am too excited to breathe! I love your long pearl necklace. Father said he completed my home and David's parents and brothers have arrived in town."

"Yes, and your sister and Adriel will arrive tomorrow, bringing our first grandson with them."

"Mother, did we forget anything important?"

"Now, Michal, do not be tense. I planned every detail of your big day. Now you must wait for David to call for you."

"When will he come? At sunset? Sunrise? I hope he does not decide to come at midnight." Michal could not sit still. She went to her window and gazed down at the captains' quarters in the distance. "I believe one hour before sunset would make a beautiful scene as David escorts me up the hill to our new home."

"Remember, the timing remains in David's hands."

"We shall be so happy together. I want five children, just like you and Father."

~ ~ ~ ~ ~

David reflected, *There will be a full moon tonight—perfect for a wedding!*

David remained inside his tent for most of the afternoon and reminisced as he performed a melody on his instrument and sang in a soft tone.

"I shall always sing to the LORD with joy.
Michal is a beautiful young woman!
I sing praises to the LORD with my harp.
Michal is a beautiful young woman!"

As the sun moved across the sky, David recalled his blessings of a loving family, wise parents, and fertile pastureland for his sheep. God brought him through many battles. He remembered the words of the prophet that day long ago and understood he faced more battles yet to come.

His mother brought him a silk robe of vibrant blues from Bethlehem. Jesse purchased perfumes of frankincense and myrrh for his son's garments. David declined to wear the customary gold crown in deference to King Saul's strained feelings toward him.

A garland of fresh flowers instead of a crown will be perfect for me. Time to pick flowers.

David laid aside his harp, stretched, and stepped outside his tent. He picked up a woven basket stored under a tree and headed for a nearby meadow that bloomed with lavender and white daisies.

"Hey, men!" Simon called to the other captains. "David

leaves his tent. He has an aura about him." Simon chuckled. "I bet he chose today for his wedding day!"

Soon a dozen men, laughing and running, followed close behind David.

"Hey, giant killer! Is this your big day?"

"Maybe!" He hollered over his shoulder.

David ran ahead of the other captains, leaving them gasping to catch up. "Who wants to help me pick daisies? Anyone man enough?"

David could not restrain his laughter.

~ ~ ~ ~ ~

The sunrays created a breathtaking sight as the sun, reflecting through the clouds, dropped below the horizon. Michal sat in the window seat of her bedroom with her eyes glued to the sky.

"The western sky glows with vibrant shades I have never seen. The golds and reds are amazing. This must be the day. Oh, David, please come. I am ready, I am ready!"

At that same moment, she heard her name, "Michal, my love, my princess! Come with me tonight!"

There in the shade of the garden, she saw her lover dressed in kingly apparel with a crown of tiny flowers playing his harp under her window.

Michal said to herself, "Oh, I love his music. David is so romantic!" She leaned out the window and called back, "I am coming!"

Michal turned and called out over her shoulder. "Mother, Mother! David is here. What shall I do now?"

Ahinoam ran to Michal's room at the sound of her daughter's voice.

"I am bringing your wedding clothes. It is time to

prepare yourself. David will wait, so do not get too excited. We will stay calm."

Word spread throughout the town of Gibeah. "The king's daughter marries tonight."

~ 17 ~

"You lost the LORD's blessing. Your kingdom belongs to another!"

King Saul remembered the words of his old friend Samuel that were ingrained in his mind. Saul continued to nurse his jealousy and fears toward his son-in-law.

David won every battle he fought against the Philistines and the Israelites celebrated his name after every victory while Saul harbored suspicions of David's motives.

"Ahinoam, my throne is in jeopardy! I know my kingdom will be taken from me. I do not dare trust anyone," King Saul raged.

Concerned for his welfare, Ahinoam tried to calm him. "Harp music has a relaxing effect on you. Do you want me to summon David again? He will put your mind and spirit at ease."

I like that suggestion. "Yes and leave the two of us alone. I need him this evening. Now!"

The king relished the idea of another opportunity to kill David. But as usual, his shaking fits of anger affected his aim and David dodged the spear once again as the weapon stuck in the wall beside him. The young groom escaped on foot into the night and feared the king's guards might follow him.

"If I return home alive, I shall never play music for him again, even if he is my king." David whispered to himself.

"LORD, please do not let his evil schemes succeed against me. I place this matter in Your hands. I must remember that You are the stronghold of my life. I will be afraid of no one."

When David arrived home, Michal greeted him at the door with a kiss. "My husband, you sound out of breath. What happened at Father's house?"

"He tried to kill me again."

"Oh, no!" Her hand went to her mouth as she gasped. "This situation between you and Father is hopeless. I believe Father will send his troops here tomorrow to capture you. They will kill you before dawn! Please escape tonight for my sake. I could not live if you died. Hurry!"

"I wish you were wrong about my danger, but I agree with you. I shall leave right now for Ramah to consult with Samuel. I always receive encouragement and advice from that godly man. I shall sing praises to God with Samuel and the other prophets. They will strengthen my soul and my resolve. I know the LORD will direct my steps, but I am not sure when I will see you again. Come with me now."

"If I left, my father would kill me, too."

They embraced for the last time and Michal helped him leave through a back window.

As David escaped into the darkness, he prayed, "O God, rescue me from my enemies. Protect me from those who want to destroy me. You, only You, are my refuge and my strength. Please protect my wife while I am gone."

As Michal predicted, soldiers pounded on her door before daylight the next morning.

"David! Open this door in the name of the king."

Michal opened the door a crack and whispered, "Go away! David lies sick in bed."

Her response surprised them, so they retreated.

When they reported back to the king, Saul spoke with

fury in his eyes. “Bring him to me at once, in his bed or on his feet. I can kill him in either position.”

King Saul’s guards returned to David’s house to discover Michal lied to them. They forced her to go with them to confirm their story.

Enraged, Saul shouted at his daughter, “Why did you let my enemy escape?”

“Father, David is not your enemy. He is captain of your bodyguards and my husband.”

“His days are numbered! How dare you trick your father.” Saul’s body trembled with anger.

“But Father, I had to. He planned to kill me if I did not tell you he was ill.”

Lying was easy for Michal.

“You will never see David alive again. He is no longer your husband. I shall see to that!”

“No, Father, no! I love him! I did not mean what I said. He did not swear to kill me. Honest!”

Within the year, King Saul gave his daughter Michal in marriage to Palti, a man from Gallim.

~ ~ ~ ~ ~

David’s escape route from Gibeah guided the brave warrior twenty miles west to Ramah. He arrived the next morning before dawn and enjoyed a pleasant visit with the aging prophet.

“Samuel, I wish we were meeting under different circumstances. Let us worship the Lord together. I need His strength for whatever He has planned for me.”

David borrowed a harp from one of the priests. Samuel praised the LORD with all his strength as David sang and played a recent song he composed.

Later, David traveled south to the town of Nob to see Ahimelech the priest who served in the tabernacle. Rubbing the sides of his robe, the priest was uncomfortable when he noticed David journeyed alone without other warriors.

David created a false story to put the priest's mind at ease. "King Saul sent me on a private assignment, but I left Gibeah without a weapon. Do you own a spear?"

"The only weapon here is the sword of Goliath the Philistine which Samuel stores behind the ephod."

I shall be proud to possess that weapon once again. "None compares to that sword. I am honored to take it. I remember the exact day I first used it!"

David left Nob and traveled to a wilderness area to avoid any contact with King Saul. Three weeks later, an early morning visitor brought him heartbreaking news.

"David! David! I need to talk to you."

David did not recognize the voice, so he stepped out of his hideout with caution holding Goliath's sword.

"Who are you? How did you find me?"

"I am Abiathar, the only remaining son of Ahimelech the priest. I begged the LORD to direct my steps today."

"Come. Sit and tell me what happened."

"King Saul ordered the killing of the priests at Nob. All eighty-five of them! God helped me escape before Doeg the Edomite killed me. I have come to you for protection."

Now aware of all the details, David fell on his knees before the LORD. "My heart breaks to hear what the king did. And why did he kill their families, too? O God, am I responsible for their murders? I was wrong to trick Ahimelech. I should not have said that Saul sent me on a mission. I lied!" David confessed, "O LORD, please forgive me!

David asked the LORD, "Why does Saul hate me so? I

would never harm the LORD's anointed. His jealousy over me increases by the month. O God, I need Your protection every moment!"

Abiathar trembled at the reality of his own situation. "I know Doeg will come looking for me."

"Abiathar, we must kneel and pray together."

David prayed in desperation, "Do not abandon us, LORD! Do not stand at a distance, O my God."

"We will need Your strength every day if we are to survive this trial," declared Abiathar.

Now, they were both wanted by the king—dead or alive.

~ 18 ~

"I am in a terrible storm, Lord. How long will it last? I looked for someone to help me, but You are all I need. Give me a new song of praise to sing as I wait in Your presence, Lord."

Thus, began many years with David on the run from Saul. One by one, a small army of six hundred dissatisfied warriors, including David's older brothers, left Saul's army and joined with David in his wilderness hideout.

David instructed his commander Joab, "My army will never pursue Saul, but we will fight battles against the Philistines and all other enemies of Israel."

He experienced opportunities to kill Saul but refused to allow his men to do so. David endeavored to stay as far away from Saul as possible.

David and his men had camped outside the town of Ziklag in southern Judah. After a recent victory, he rested in his private quarters when his commander entered the room with a message.

"David, a stranger arrived with a message concerning King Saul."

"The hour is late. Send him in but stand guard." David frowned. *Why does the man want an audience now?*

Thick dust covered his head. His clothes were torn to shreds. He knelt on the floor in front of David.

David cross-examined him. "Who are you? Where are

you from? What message do you bring?"

"I escaped from Saul's camp on Mount Gilboa. The Philistines attacked us. Now many brave warriors lay dead, including Saul and his sons. The army who survived fled in all directions."

David jumped to his feet and demanded, "Who told you Saul died?" His loud voice echoed outside the tent.

"The king fell wounded and told me to put him out of his misery. I brought you his crown, Sire," the man bragged.

He laid the royal diadem at David's feet.

David collapsed back in his chair and whispered, "Why? Why did you so boldly kill the LORD's anointed? You have just condemned yourself!"

David shouted to his commander. "Kill him!"

Joab ran his sword through the man and shouted an order to a guard. "Get his body out of here!"

"Joab, my heart breaks. Leave me alone now."

David left his tent and wandered off in the dark. He moaned, not caring who heard. "O Israel! Our pride and joy fell dead. Our mighty heroes will never rise again.

How I cry for you Jonathan, my dearest friend. I miss you so. I promise to honor your family as we agreed.

David and his men mourned the death of Saul and their beloved Jonathan. No one ate food the following day as they wept for the LORD's army and their cherished nation.

~ ~ ~ ~ ~

After Saul's death and with David no longer on the run, he and his followers camped thirty miles south of Jerusalem in Hebron, located in the Judean hills.

In the spring of that year, all the elders of Judah approached David.

"Will you be our king?" asked their spokesman.

"My heart shall be glad to serve you as king. God has been gracious to us all. I wish Samuel were alive to bless this day for us."

Everyone celebrated when David was crowned king of the tribe of Judah. The young girls danced in the street with their musical instruments. The women baked hundreds of loaves of sweet bread, and the men passed around skins full of their best wine. At the end of the day, David stood on the platform erected for the occasion and spoke to the people of Judah.

"I waited many years for the LORD to fulfill His promise to me. He heard my cry and set my feet on solid ground today. He has given me a new song, a hymn of praise to our God." David picked up his harp and moved his fingers gently over the strings.

"I will praise the LORD at all times.
I will always sing His praises.
I will boast only in the Lord;
Let us tell of the LORD's greatness;
Let us exalt His name together."

The people responded, "Long live King David! Praise the God of Judah and all Israel!"

~ 19 ~

Abner, commander of Saul's forces, remained loyal to Israel. He crowned Saul's only remaining son Ishbosheth as king of Israel after his father's death. As years passed, one hundred twenty thousand warriors who represented every tribe of Israel defected and joined David's army. The armies of Israel and Judah continued to fight battles against the Philistines. David and his army became stronger while Saul's dynasty grew weaker.

A violent rainstorm developed in early winter. The canvas flaps on the tents shook with the strong wind. Benaiah, commander of David's bodyguards, entered the king's quarters.

"Sire, Abner's messenger arrived moments ago. He requests an audience with you."

"Send him in but keep your sword drawn and stay alert." The young king frowned with suspicion.

A young man, drenched from the rain, rushed in and bowed low. "King David, I bring a message from Abner. He regrets making Ishbosheth king of Israel and no longer trusts him. Abner desires to defect to your army. He says he will support your efforts to bring the entire nation of Israel under your rule."

David showed no emotion and did not respond for a few minutes.

LORD, will You now complete Samuel's anointing? David wondered.

The young king answered him with a proposition. "Tell Abner that I will discuss his proposal on one condition. My wife Michal must return to me when Abner joins us." *She is Saul's daughter and my first wife. She owns the right to reign with me, though I now have other wives.*

The messenger rushed back out into the storm to deliver David's proposal to Abner.

~ ~ ~ ~ ~

A sad day dawned for Palti when Michal mounted a white steed and returned to David in Hebron. Abner accompanied Michal while Palti followed behind on foot.

"Michal, please do not leave me. Come back!" He wailed repeatedly. He covered himself with dust as mourning a great loss.

After three miles on the trail, Abner lost his patience with Palti. "You are disgusting. I order you to go home!"

Palti shouted to Michal. "I understood you did not belong to me. I will miss you so! Michal, you meant everything to me." He forced his feet to turn around, understanding he would never again hold her in his arms.

The day Michal returned to David, the sun shone bright, and David's happy heart anticipated their reunion. His private quarters held Michal's favorite scent of fresh lavender. He laid aside his robe and wore a plain garment.

He instructed Joab to escort Michal to his headquarters as soon as she arrived in town. "Abner must wait. I long to see my wife first."

Michal entered David's presence with her head held high like a queen.

He extended his arms to her. "Michal, I have been too long without you. Come and sit beside me. May I pour you a glass of wine?"

Their reunion did not go as David planned. No embrace. No kiss. Not even a smile.

"I shall neither sit with you nor drink your wine." Tears flowed down her cheeks. "If you had not left Father's army, he would still be alive today. It is your fault he died! Mother and I shall never forgive you!" Michal shouted her accusations for the benefit of everyone outside David's tent.

I never knew this side of Michal's personality. "You agreed I must leave you that night. Why did you refuse to come with me?"

Michal ignored the king's question. "I smell your scent of lavender, but it will not change my feelings. I shall not speak of this matter again!" She spun around and left without saying another word.

Abner slipped into David's tent and stood at attention.

In complete control of his emotions, David nodded to Abner. "Have a seat. Want a glass of wine?"

"Give her time. I am sure she will adjust to her life as the king's wife."

"Abner, what is your proposition?" David refrained from discussing his personal business with Abner.

"Forgive me for not supporting you from the beginning. King Saul had no reason to distrust or hate you."

David relaxed and breathed deep. "I always trusted God to protect me. Even when I doubted, He did not abandon me. Abner, praise God with me. He is eternal, I am just His servant."

Abner continued, "I consulted with the leaders of the tribes of Israel and Benjamin. They desire to make you king over all Israel, and they agreed to support you. I promise to stand behind you as well."

David stood to embrace Abner. "We have fought many battles together. I shall be honored to reign as your king. The LORD be with you."

"May He be with you also."

Tragedy struck before Abner completed the trip back to Israel with David's acceptance to rule as their king. Joab attacked and killed Abner because Joab distrusted him. He acted out of revenge because Abner killed Joab's brother in battle. David grieved when he became aware of the dreadful news.

Lord, I could not trust King Saul. Can I now trust Joab? I was honored to serve under Abner. I can only trust You, my Shepherd, who always protects me.

David served under Abner in Saul's army for many years and mourned over his former commander's murder. He sang during the funeral and refused to eat that day. From his actions, all Israel understood David did not participate in Abner's death.

Events continued to worsen as two of King Ishbosheth's captains killed the king of Israel while he slept. They brought the severed head to David as a trophy.

"You two are disgraceful officers! This head is no trophy for me. Leave my presence at once!"

The two men made a quick exit.

David ordered his bodyguard, "Kill those wicked captains when they leave town!"

King Saul's last son is now dead. My heart weeps again for Saul's sons. Oh, Jonathan, my friend, I need you by my side as we always planned!

~ 20 ~

The leaders of Israel and Benjamin traveled south to Hebron and joined with the elders of Judah to crown David as king of Israel. All twelve tribes now stood united behind their king. After the ceremony, the king assembled Joab and his captains together.

"The Jebusites have ruled the land around Jerusalem long enough. Jerusalem is the city of Melchizedek. Now I swear that I shall rule from that same city. I have committed everything I do to the LORD. I trust Him and I am confident He will help us."

Joab suggested, "First, we must capture their fortress at Zion. Those pigs have harassed us for weeks with a humiliating challenge of bragging their blind men can defend their fort against us."

"I agree. We take control of the whole area and move my headquarters nineteen miles north to Jerusalem. I predict the town will be called the City of God after I build a golden temple for the LORD. We will trust in the LORD and possess the land, the *entire* land, just as God promised."

"We shall attack tomorrow!" Joab rose to his feet and left the room with his captains to prepare for battle.

After David's army captured Fort Zion, they rerouted the water and moved in through the tunnel to capture the city of Jerusalem.

The LORD continued to protect King David and made him increasingly powerful over his enemies. David was quick to recognize God's blessing on His people Israel.

"O LORD, I believe You listen when we call for help. You promised to rescue us from our enemies."

When David and his troops resided in Jerusalem as planned, a foreign messenger arrived from the north.

"King David, a messenger from Tyre wishes to speak with you," Benaiah announced. "I removed his sword, Sire."

"Send him in."

A young man entered David's tent and knelt before the king. "I bring a message from King Hiram of Tyre."

"Tell me, soldier, what does he say?"

"The God of Israel has given you amazing victories over your enemies. My king offers his congratulations and his services. He says he will supply all the lumber plus carpenters and stonemasons needed to build your magnificent palace here in Jerusalem. He extends his kindness to you."

David appreciated the gesture of friendship and goodwill. *I understand this king's motives. Better an ally than my enemy.* "Tell your king I appreciate and accept his offer."

He envisioned his elaborate home of cedar, one far greater than the residence King Saul built for him and his wife Michal. "Tell your king that construction will commence at once with King Hiram's support."

~ ~ ~ ~ ~

"Joab, the ark of the LORD signifies the presence of God. I want it under my care and protection because I long to worship God in His presence. I designed and landscaped a peaceful garden of flowering trees and shrubs of every variety. I constructed a large canvas tent in the center of the oasis. I even lined the structure with white linen embroidered in blue, purple, and red pomegranates. It is time we bring the ark home."

Joab nodded. "It shall be moved right away."

Disaster struck the first time David tried to move the ark from the home of Abinadab. The king enlisted the aid of thirty thousand troops from his army for that journey. Uzzah, Abinadab's son, paid the ultimate price when he touched the ark to prevent the chest from falling off the unauthorized cart.

David raised his fist and shouted, "O God, why did You kill Uzzah?"

The LORD spoke loud and clear to David's heart. "You did not seek My will in this matter! Instead, you consulted with your captains and generals."

The sound of loud thunder shook David's nerves. That incident caused anger in David's heart toward God for not allowing his plans to move forward.

Three months passed, then David found courage to kneel and pray, "O God, my heart has heard You say, 'Come and talk with me.' I am coming, LORD. Forgive me for disobeying. Now I realize that You had designated only the tribe of Levi to attend to the ark which holds Your written law."

~ ~ ~ ~ ~

David spent limited personal time with Michal after they moved to Jerusalem because the king had other wives and their children. She kept to herself in her misery and David seldom conversed with her.

One evening in late summer with the strong scent of

white lilies in the air, he invited Michal to dine alone with him.

"Michal, I am pleased you agreed to share dinner with me."

"Well, I am available to join you anytime."

David detected jealousy in Michal's tone, but he ignored her insinuation of neglect.

"I wanted to share with you the longings of my heart. The LORD has blessed Israel more than I ever expected. He allowed me to build this palace for my family. This is the LORD's doing, not mine."

"I did not notice that your LORD provided the cedar. But I did hear about King Hiram's support."

David sensed bitterness in her voice. He changed the subject and continued. "Michal, tomorrow marks a special day for Israel and me—a wonderful day of worship and celebration. I want you to join me as we walk to the home of Obed-edom in Gath. The Levites will bring the ark home to the sacred garden. My people have missed its presence far too long. I shall bring the ark to this City of God. Will you walk with me?"

"I do not believe I shall. I share no interest in your affairs."

"Michal, I request your company as a king's daughter and your king's wife." His voice sounded strained.

"No! You show me no respect as either one."

David leaned toward her across the table, trying to relax his spirit. "I wrote a special song of praise for Asaph to sing tomorrow. Since you will not be there, will you listen while I play it now? I remember you always loved my music."

"No, I shall wait at my window for your return."

Michal stood and left the banquet room without tasting the dinner of roasted lamb and fresh figs.

With a sad but determined heart, David picked up his lyre and sang a few lines to himself.

> "Everyone give thanks to the LORD.
> The LORD's great love never ceases.
> Forever I will bless our LORD!"

The next day dawned warm without a cloud in the sky. The priests Zadok and Abiathar together with eight hundred Levites purified themselves according to the law of Moses by washing their clothes, washing and shaving their bodies, then sprinkled themselves with purifying water. Excitement filled the early morning air. All able-bodied citizens joined the parade headed southwest from the city of Jerusalem to Gath, one of the Philistine towns that David's army conquered.

Since David loved to sing and play music before the LORD, he ordered a large choir of Levite singers to harmonize joyful songs along the route. They sang with the musicians as they played their harps and lyres. Heman, Asaph, and Ethan followed behind and climaxed each song with the crash of bronze cymbals in assorted sizes.

The following afternoon, the parade of citizens entered Jerusalem with the golden ark in their possession. The walkers were tired and dusty but excited. Residents who could not make the long twenty-six-mile journey lined both sides of the main road. Their cheers and shouts of joy echoed for miles. Everyone demonstrated their excitement.

"Do you hear the trumpets and cymbals?"

"I recognize the priests in the distance."

"Here comes the golden ark, shining in the sun!"

"What a massive choir! There must be hundreds of singers."

"I want to sing with them!"

Seven priests clothed in white linen blew brass trumpets as they marched in front of the ark of God. Resting the ark on their shoulders, the Levites carried it with gold-covered poles placed through the golden rings as the LORD instructed Moses centuries ago.

"The king approaches! We will follow and dance with him." The boys and girls were excited to participate in the celebration.

David left his golden crown and elegant robe stored in his palace wardrobe. Instead, he wore a robe of pure linen topped with a tunic. He dressed as the Levites who carried the ark. Dozens of rams' horns sounded long and loud. The king lost himself in dance, song, and worship to his LORD.

When the brilliant cherubim-covered ark rested in its new home, King David with assistance from the priests sacrificed burnt offerings and peace offerings.

Everyone became quiet as the king addressed the crowd. "Today marks a momentous day of celebration for Israel. God has delivered us from our enemies. If we continue to honor the LORD our God and serve only God, He will never forsake us. Stand up and I shall pray a blessing over us in the name of the LORD."

David raised his arms and face toward heaven. "O LORD, we ask You to bless us, Your humble people. May Your holy name be praised for Your faithfulness! LORD, You alone live from everlasting to everlasting! Praise the LORD forever!"

Everyone shouted together in unison. "We praise our God!"

He continued to encourage the people. "Let us worship and kneel before the LORD. He is our God, and we are like sheep in His pasture. He cares for us, and we must always depend on Him."

He inspired the people to worship God for His unfailing love.

On their knees, everyone responded with “Praise our God!”

King David announced, “I offer you gifts of bread and sweet cakes for your journey home. God bless everyone!”

The celebration ceased and the people returned to their homes by late afternoon. All Israel celebrated that day, everyone except Michal.

~ ~ ~ ~ ~

As Michal promised, she watched from her window as the crowd led by David returned to Jerusalem. She complained to herself, “This king mortifies me. My father never acted so disgraceful!”

She could not comprehend the joy of the day’s event, but only experienced embarrassment from the king’s actions.

The golden red sun dropped behind the hills of Judea as David went home to pray a blessing over his own family. Michal met him in the front garden of the palace, one hand on her hip, and pointed her jeweled finger at David.

“How dignified my king acted today! Have you no shame dressed like a servant and dancing in front of all Jerusalem? Is this proper demeanor for a mighty warrior?”

Ready to defend himself, he explained. “I was not dancing for Israel. I danced before my LORD. As you well remember, God through Samuel chose me to replace your father. He called me to lead Israel, so I celebrated my LORD today. Do I care if you or anyone else calls me foolish? No! I intend to please my God, and Him alone.”

“You must show respect for me as King Saul’s daughter.” Michal held her head high with the palm of her hand.

"I am sure you understand that I want to share my throne with you, my first wife. Why are you so quick to rob my joy today?"

"You deserted me and married other women when Father gave me to another man. Then you ripped me away from Palti."

"Please come inside while I ask God's blessing on our household and family members."

Michal dropped her head and stared at the ground. *I refuse to admire this man.* "I have no respect for you."

"Michal, if you remain childless, there is no one to blame but yourself and maybe my God."

The princess turned on her heels and left her husband's presence once again, forever.

Epilogue

A king's daughter has no guarantees in life, neither does a king's wife. Michal developed into a bitter woman against her father for forcing her to marry another man. She resented David when he became a king instead of her famous warrior-husband. Michal refused to respect and praise God when life did not treat her as she expected.

Born a humble shepherd boy, David finished his life as an honored and respected king. He desired to follow God's laws. Though guilty of murder, adultery, and disobedience, he repented, then obeyed and praised his LORD. David's body and soul always longed to kneel in worship and sing a new song of adoration to his Eternal King. Psalm 5 is an example of David's spiritual commitment.

"O LORD, hear me as I pray; pay attention to my groaning. Listen to my cry for help, my King and my God, for I pray to only You. Listen to my voice in the morning, LORD. Each morning I bring my requests to You and wait with expectation. But let all who take refuge in You rejoice; let them sing joyful praises forever. Spread Your protection over them, that all who love Your name may be filled with joy. For You bless the godly, O LORD; You surround them with Your shield of love."

Juanita Turner Paslay

A Man on the Run

Jonah

He perceives himself a prophet to his Jewish people.

God designs different plans for him.

Learn the price Jonah pays when
his prejudices rule his decisions.

A story based on Jonah 1-4

~ 1 ~

"Jonah, you will be My prophet and speak all the words I give you!" The voice projected loud and distinct in Jonah's ears. Once again, he recognized the voice of God like the sound of gentle thunder.

"God, You know the tribe of Zebulun has lost their love for You. They no longer obey Your laws. They follow the ways of those heathen Gentiles who worship idols."

Jonah prayed, "LORD, how long will You allow Your chosen people to sin to this terrible degree? Surely, You will use me to warn Your people to repent of their sinful ways before punishment comes. I remember Your severe judgment on Israel in the days of Moses. O LORD, spare us and cause us to repent!"

Jonah meditated. *I envision myself a prophet to declare the words of Jehovah to my countrymen.*

As a young man, Jonah attended the school of the prophets on Mount Tabor. Located on the eastern end of the fertile Jezreel Valley, the mountain rose nineteen hundred feet in elevation.

"God, I recall the story of Samson, a not-so-perfect judge of Israel who yielded to his selfish desires causing the loss of his strength and his eyesight. You returned strength to blind Samson that enabled him to destroy thousands of Israel's enemies on the last day of his life."

The young prophets spent hours swimming in the large pristine lake at the base of Mount Tabor.

When the weather turned warm, a fellow student asked, "Hey, Jonah, are you going to compete in the swimming contest this year?"

"You know I am the best. I lovc thc challenge and I shall prove it again this year." Jonah laughed.

"I accept your challenge," the student laughed with Jonah.

"I told the LORD that I wanted the strength of Samson. I shall use every opportunity to improve my endurance in running and swimming," Jonah said.

When he finished his second year of training, a messenger brought tragic news from home.

"Your father sent me to tell you about your mother. I am sorry to say she became ill and died two weeks ago. The whole family mourned her sudden death. They understood why you could not be there."

After the man left, Jonah sat in the shade and reminisced about her kind and gentle spirit. *I loved my mother and I grieve not telling her goodbye. I know Father will miss her very much. I am glad he has the vineyard to occupy his time.*

Excited to return home after three years of intensive training at the school of the prophets, Jonah planned his four-day journey on foot to await God's specific instructions.

"LORD, I appreciate this time alone with You on my return trip home. I did not really mind the company of the other students, but I did get weary of eating, sleeping, and studying with them every day. Now, I can focus on Your plans for my life."

~ 2 ~

The young prophet traveled the road lined with colorful autumn wildflowers. He wore his prophet's robe, a gift from the master teacher. Each student received the garment upon completion of their spiritual training.

As Jonah walked through the towns and villages, he wore his cherished garment with pride, though he pretended to appear humble. People honored him with respect and offered food for his trip.

"Look! Here comes a prophet. I see his robe shining in the sun."

"Please, sir, share our evening meal with us."

"Man of God, you are welcome to stay with us tonight."

With gratitude, Jonah accepted what anyone provided, whatever their motive. As he approached the town of Jezreel, two young boys ran to greet him.

"O Prophet, may we walk with you for a while?"

"Of course. What are your names?" Jonah placed a hand on their heads.

"My name is Micah, and he is my brother Aaron." Micah playfully shoved his little brother.

Micah, the taller of the two, questioned the young prophet. "Where are you from?"

"My family owns a vineyard in Gath-hepher located in Lower Galilee. Our wine is sold in markets from Sidon in the north to Joppa in the south.

"Do you think your wine is sold here in Jezreel?" Aaron asked.

"Probably. More than two hundred years ago, my tribe of Zebulun brought their superb wine and excellent olive oil to King David for his crowning celebration."

"Sounds like your wine is famous," Aaron said.

"Yes, people as far away as the southern land of Tarshish coveted the red wine of Gath-hepher." Jonah was proud of his knowledge and loved to share it.

"Where have you been, and where are you going?"

"I studied at the school of the prophets on Mount Tabor. Now, I am going home."

"I know where Mount Tabor is. It is in Jezreel Valley."

"The judge Deborah and the armies of the tribes of Zebulun and Naphtali defeated the heathen Canaanites on Mount Tabor. That victory made it an ideal place to build a school for God's prophets."

At the school of the prophets, Jonah learned the experiences of victory and the persecution of the faithful men of God. The exploits of Elijah and Elisha ran through his mind as the boys escorted him away from Jezreel.

"Please tell us what you learned." Micah begged.

"There is too much to repeat, but I will tell you about the prophet Elijah. Once, Elijah brought a dead boy back to life—a true miracle! Another time, he challenged the prophets of Baal. Of course, our God won, and Elijah killed all the evil prophets."

"How many bad prophets were killed?" Aaron stopped walking and his brown eyes stared at Jonah.

"Eight hundred and fifty in one day. And that is no exaggeration."

Micah raised his eyebrows in amazement.

"Did you hear Elijah never died?" the young man wanted to impress both the boys with his knowledge.

"Never?" Aaron grabbed at the prophet's robe.

Jonah had their full attention now.

"Elijah rode a fiery chariot straight into heaven, the grandest entry I dare to imagine. What a thrill for the young prophets to watch from the hillside. I wish I experienced what they witnessed that day." Jonah's voice trailed off as he visualized the scene.

"We better go back before our father comes looking for us." Aaron said.

"Thanks for telling us about Elijah." Micah called out over his shoulder as both boys headed back to town.

Jonah waved goodbye.

As Jonah talked about the prophets, a question crossed his mind. "LORD, you allowed Elisha to heal a Gentile man of leprosy. Why heal a despised Gentile army commander from Syria? Why choose Naaman?"

He regarded Naaman often and considered that miracle a total misunderstanding of God's will on Elisha's part.

As the prophet walked down the path with a strong wind in his face, he contemplated how God might use him. "LORD, will I be a famous prophet? Will I perform miracles, preach judgment, or both? When, LORD?"

The young man believed himself ready for his prophetic ministry. "LORD, I hope You reveal my first assignment without delay."

Jonah did not understand that God's calling also held an enormous responsibility, but his future experiences became his greatest teacher.

~ 3 ~

Late autumn arrived, and with autumn came harvest time. Experienced vineyard owners know a cold spell with a light frost sets the sugar and creates the sweetest-tasting grapes and superior wine.

Amittai arose early one cool morning to evaluate the grapes for sweetness when he noticed a robe glowing in the sun and wrapped around a man who hurried toward his vineyard.

"Jonah is home! I would recognize him anywhere. Time for a race."

When their eyes caught sight of each other, they both hiked up their garments and dashed along the path between long rows of grapevines. They collided with a tight embrace.

"Jonah! Jonah, my son, I am so glad you are home. I have missed you beyond words.

"I am happy to see you, too, Father. You still like a good race. You always challenged me to run when I was young." He kissed his father's hand in respect.

"Come, we shall sit awhile. You must be thirsty and weary from your long journey." Amittai retrieved a bucket of cool water from the well for his favorite son. "It has been three long years. I am so proud of your desire to be a prophet of God."

Jonah drank a full cup before he spoke of his mother. "Father, I miss Mother's smile already. How do you manage without her?"

"It has been difficult, but I still feel her presence with me every day." Amittai sighed and wiped a tear from his cheek.

Father and son rested in the shade of an apple tree drooping with ripe fruit.

"I see news of your return has spread throughout the vineyard. No one will work today. Here comes your brothers and sisters to welcome you home."

The family members from every corner of the estate gathered around Jonah and Amittai as they bombarded their brother with questions about his years at the school of the prophets.

Amittai said, "I declare this evening a grand day for celebration. Jemuel, you are the oldest. I want you to plan the entire event."

"Jachin and I will leave for the pasture to select and butcher the finest calf for tonight," said Jamin.

Their sisters hitched the mules to a wooden wagon and traveled down the road to invite all the elders and neighbors to an evening of festivities. The brothers' wives prepared root vegetables and baked dozens of small loaves of wheat bread and sweet raisin cakes.

Excitement hung in the air as everyone gathered around the long banquet tables. After enjoying the sumptuous meal and merry dancing, the children went outside to play. The adults, eager to listen to Jonah, assembled in the great hall.

For the next several hours, Jonah recited parts of the law from memory and shared his years with the master teacher and the other young prophets.

Jonah said, "Many citizens in Israel have turned away from worshiping Jehovah God. It is my ambition to warn my fellow countrymen to repent and obey the words of God."

Long after the neighbors left, Amittai and his sons reclined around the indoor rock fireplace packed with dying embers and talked about old times.

"I remember the tricks I played on my brothers. I would hide from you in my secret place in the vineyard." Jonah said.

"You made us search hours for you." Jachin complained.

Jemuel said, "But you always managed to be found in time for the next meal."

Everyone laughed at Jemuel's comment.

They described childhood adventures their father was never aware of and other mischievous escapades he wished he had not heard.

"We miss our mother. Her sudden illness and death was so devastating to all of us," said Jemuel.

Their father was quiet while he listened to his grown children reminisce about events so dear to them.

Jonah stood and addressed his family. "I was eager to run through childhood and become an adult. I tried to be diligent to apply myself to my studies. Father, thank you for teaching us, your children, the law of Moses."

Amittai smiled to himself as he spoke quietly to God. "Jehovah, I am proud of my sons and daughters and their devotion to family and God. Thank you for their blessings to me."

After everyone departed for their homes, Amittai prayed concerning his son's faithfulness to God's calling. "Lord, will Jonah achieve the status of a mighty prophet like Elijah or Elisha, or continue his life in the vineyard and distinguish himself as a messenger to his own community? I pray Your will be done in his life."

~ ~ ~ ~ ~

Early the following morning, Jonah awoke eager to help with the harvest. After breakfast, Amittai escorted Jonah around the vineyard on an inspection tour.

"I love the smell of the sweet grapes. I still possess the ability to recognize ripe fruit. I remember helping make the pressed grape juice into finc winc," Jonah said.

"You learned quickly as a boy, but I'm sure God has other plans for you now."

"Father, do you still purchase your clay jars from Moshe?"

"Oh, yes, he is the best potter in Lower Galilee. He engraves each wine jar with a bold "A". Everyone recognizes my trademark and believes the jars hold the finest product." Amittai could not restrain his grin.

"Father, our God has blessed your vineyard." Jonah placed his arm around his father's thin shoulders and squeezed him tight.

"My family has blessed me, too. Everyone does their part. During winter when chores in the vineyard come to a halt, the women design next year's wine skins with the large "A" branded on each leather bag. They are busy all year tending flocks of sheep and goats for our needs. We are blessed with an abundance of dried meat, skins, and wool."

"I remember all those responsibilities—both in the rain *and* the hot sun." Jonah chuckled. In his heart, he believed those days for him were over; at least he hoped so.

~ ~ ~ ~ ~

With the harvest completed on schedule, Amittai's storehouses contained hundreds of wineskins and jars prepared for a long trip to local markets and the nearest seaports.

With faithful guards on duty at the vineyard, Amittai and his family traveled to Jerusalem for the Festival of Shelters as did every able Israelite. During that week, God's chosen people assembled to proclaim His blessings. They worshiped and praised God with the temple singers and musicians. The priests stood and blessed the people. For seven days, all Israel celebrated their bountiful harvest as they lived outside in crude shelters made of tree boughs and branches.

"Father, as a child, I enjoyed the adventures of camping outdoors. Now as an adult, I understand its meaning and appreciate the celebration of this annual event," Jonah said.

"Yes, I am proud that all my sons and daughters respect God and give Him praise for all the blessings we receive."

During the festival, Amittai, as head of the family, retold how God rescued their nation from the land of Egypt.

"Jonah, please honor us by offering our annual prayer of thanksgiving." Amittai smiled at his youngest son.

Jonah raised his arms heavenward. "Jehovah, we praise Your name, O Most High! We humbly give thanks for this bountiful harvest. You blessed the land You gave us. Thank you for our miraculous inheritance."

The family agreed together with an enthusiastic, "Amen, amen!"

The young prophet's spiritual journey had begun to accelerate.

~ 4 ~

Home from the festival at Jerusalem, Jonah welcomed his free time to wander the hills of the family vineyard.

Early one morning after his usual hearty breakfast of eggs, cream, and fresh bread, Jonah left the house alone and headed for his secret place of prayer that he discovered as a child. He wanted to avoid any interruptions by the family as he knelt to worship God.

"I thank you for all my personal blessings. I always sense Your presence when I pray. This day impresses me as especially sacred."

Jonah talked with God about his future. Then God spoke to him about His call on Jonah's life.

"Get off your knees and go to the great city of Nineveh. You must announce My judgment against those wicked people."

The rumble of thunder sounded in the distance.

"To Nineveh? The despised enemy of Israel? Why do You care about wicked heathens?" Jonah paused to catch his breath. "You are a God of mercy and kindness, so I doubt You plan to destroy them anyway."

Silence.

The prophet discerned no response from God.

Nineveh ranked as the largest city in the world and the capital of the ungodly nation of Assyria.

"I recognize Your voice, but I possess no knowledge of *any* prophet who warned a heathen country of God's punishment, and I resolve not to become the first!"

No response from God.

"LORD, you know my life plans focus on Israel."

Again, no response.

The young man, named to exemplify the gentle temperament of a mourning dove, did not think or care that he might now be known as a prophet who refused to obey God's instructions. That day, Jonah revealed his true spirit.

As fast as wildfire burns through dry sagebrush on a windy day, he made plans to leave his family and country and plotted how to remove himself from the range of God's voice.

"Three large wooden wagons contain the wine harvest and Father always gives his sons the duty to deliver the produce to market. Two wagons are headed to local towns and a third to the seaport at Tyre. I will make plans to ride with Jemuel to Tyre and then board a ship heading south."

Jonah's brothers never learned of his plans, and he refused to share them with his father. His decision remained closed to discussion.

God did not debate the subject with me, so why talk with my father? I want to get away as far as possible from God's voice.

Jonah said to himself, "My stubbornness surprised even me; but nevertheless, I refuse to preach to the ungodly people of Assyria."

He said less than ten words on the trip to Tyre. Jemuel tried to converse with him but without success.

"I will stop the wagon under those trees up ahead and we can enjoy the bread and figs my wife prepared for us."

Jonah responded, "Not hungry."

"But you didn't eat yesterday."

"Still not hungry."

"Where do you want to camp for the night?" Jemuel asked.

"Anywhere," said Jonah.

Jemuel understood the message. Jonah did not want to talk.

When they arrived in Tyre, Jonah jumped down from the wagon without hesitation or a word of farewell. He found the largest ship headed south and paid the fare to Joppa.

Later, he boarded a Phoenician freighter scheduled to arrive at the port of Ezion-geber at Tarshish. The distance from Tyre to Tarshish measured over twenty-three hundred miles.

Jonah hoped, *Surely, Tarshish is far enough from God's voice.*

However, Jonah still had much to learn about the ways of God.

~ 5 ~

The captain warned, "This looks like the biggest storm I have ever seen. We must get prepared!"

The strong gale increased in velocity.

"Unload the less valuable freight to navigate easier," the captain shouted.

The calm blue-green waters of the Great Sea always presented a welcome invitation to sail in autumn because stormy conditions would not develop for several months. However, a strong northeastern wind blew three days after the ship raised anchor. A wintry storm arrived with godlike fury. The worried sailors watched a wild tempest develop in the distant sky.

Their efforts accomplished nothing. Next, he ordered *all* the cargo and supplies overboard. As experienced mariners, they understood their perilous situation.

The captain said, "We all need to pray for mercy!"

The sailors originated from various countries and each one prayed to a different god, but their prayers prompted no change in the stormy conditions.

"Where is Jonah?" A deckhand noticed the man who wore a prophet's robe did not join them topside.

The captain found him asleep below deck. As a paid passenger, Jonah enjoyed the privilege of no responsibility on the ship. However, the captain understood the grave danger and forced him on deck.

"Everyone must pray to their god, or we are doomed!"

Jonah reasoned, *I have not spoken to God since I left home and do not plan to pray now.*

"Who caused this storm?" The navigator shouted as they talked among themselves.

The seasoned captain yelled over the sound of the wind. "This storm has the presence of evil. The guilty man must repent before it is too late for all of us."

To eliminate the innocent, the crew agreed to cast lots.

The captain said, "We will use the wheat stocks I found in the storage bin. He who chooses the shortest one is guilty of causing this storm."

Jonah pulled out the shortest one. The sailors gathered around him as they threw questions at Jonah.

"Who are you?" demanded the steward.

"What country are you from?"

Another sailor asked, "Why are you on board?"

Jonah's voice trembled. "I am a Hebrew who serves the living God, creator of everything and everybody. I am His prophet, but I have disobeyed God and now I run from His voice."

Horrified by Jonah's story, the captain posed a question to his crew, "What will Jonah's God do to us because of *his* disobedience? Will we be punished also?"

As they discussed their grim situation, the storm raged even more violent.

A crewman hollered above the roar of the storm, "Captain, the water level on deck increases and the ship will probably capsize very soon. We must take action now!"

The desperate captain pointed his finger in Jonah's face. "What shall we do to save ourselves and my ship?"

"I am to blame for this storm. Throw me overboard and

the storm will cease." Jonah's proud spirit showed in his posture—head held high and hands on his hips.

At first, the crew refused his suggestion and continued to row with desperation toward land. But their strenuous efforts brought them no closer to safety.

Jonah whispered to himself, "As a long-distance swimmer, I have no fear of the sea. No obstacle stands in my way. I will take my time to float and swim to conserve my strength. My goal to reach Tarshish will still be accomplished."

Finally, the sailors accepted their best course of action. They pleaded with Jonah's God, "O Great God in heaven, please do not punish us because of Jonah's sin."

The captain begged God, "Forgive us for what we are about to do. You must have a good reason for this storm. I beg You not to hold us responsible for the death of Your prophet."

When the sailors threw Jonah off the stern of the ship, the vile storm stopped in an instant.

"Look! The sea is calm again! The one true God has been revealed to us. We must sacrifice to Him." The captain's voice rang with joy. "Bring wine for a sacrifice."

All the sailors knelt on deck and vowed to serve the God of the universe forever.

The captain and his crew learned the power of God. However, Jonah had more to learn.

~ 6 ~

I expected the storm to calm down when they threw me overboard. I am certain my plan will work. Now I will take my time as I swim to shore and board another ship headed south.

An hour into his swim/float routine, Jonah had a definite reason to panic.

I see a gray fantail rising high above the horizon. It is enormous!

With his eyes focused on the frightful sea monster, Jonah continued to watch as the tail fell gracefully under the waves of the blue expanse of the sea. The giant fish continued its approach.

I better swim in a different direction and stay out of its path!

A frightful sea monster with a wide jaw full of jagged teeth headed straight for Jonah. His effort to swim faster than the monster proved useless, even though he held the champion record at school.

I cannot swim any faster. I think the monster will catch me!

The unthinkable happened. The creature overtook Jonah and swallowed him.

"O God! You chased me and caught me. I deserted You, but You found me. Now I am locked in your dark dungeon!"

Its huge stomach cavity allowed him to breathe,

although a horrible stench made the effort difficult.

I never smelled anything so rotten. I know I shall either suffocate or drown any moment.

The young man found it difficult to identify what floated around his chest and his legs in the cold darkness.

This mess feels like seaweed but moves like a thousand tiny fish on a mission. Are they going to suck my blood?

He spoke his thoughts. "How long can I take in air? Maybe I am already dead. This must be my judgment day. Is it too late to pray? Maybe I am already in the darkness of Sheol."

I am so thirsty. When I swallow this horrific water, I need more water, so maybe I am not dead yet.

Sometimes the rhythm of his ride changed. From time to time waves of water rushed in, then receded.

It feels like the monster swims upward, then takes a deep dive. I am getting dizzy!

Jonah had trouble keeping his head above water in the small cavern, but his air supply did not fluctuate.

I must keep the water from sloshing up my nose.

Time passed, but in his present position, Jonah was unable to discern the duration.

I possess no power to change my circumstances.

Eventually, he became brave enough to talk to God.

"O God of Israel, can You hear me? I think I am still alive." Jonah hesitated, then because his circumstances demanded honesty, he said, "God, I am so scared!"

He inhaled a deep breath before he continued.

"Even in this black well, I cannot hide from You, O God. Darkness and light are both alike to You. You saw me before I was born, and You see me now in this frightening water-logged tomb."

The young prophet memorized the law years ago, so he

quoted the lines to himself and his audience of one—his captor. He concentrated on every word to help take his mind off the raw seaweed stew in which he floated.

"I am the LORD your God. You shall have no other gods before Me."

"You shall not make for yourself a carved image."

It is so hard to concentrate!

"You shall not take the name of the LORD your God in vain."

"Remember the Sabbath day and keep it holy."

He paused to take a deep breath. *I must continue talking or I shall lose my sanity.*

"Honor your father and your mother."

I love to quote the law. LORD, I really do love Your laws.

"You shall not commit adultery, covet, lie, murder or steal."

Jonah continued to recite the sacred law and soon sensed Jehovah's holy presence.

Not brave enough to eat whatever accumulated in the fish's stomach, his communion with God became bread for both his body and his soul.

If I am not dead, death must be close.

He cried out and pleaded with God. "O LORD, I am more wicked than the heathen that You wanted me to warn of judgment. I am without excuse. Can I be forgiven?"

The prejudice prophet repented and acknowledged the shame brought on himself by his act of rebellion. His guilty feelings eventually changed to a spirit of praise. Loud and full of emotion to God, he sang the song of Moses that he memorized as a child, though he suffered with a raw throat and hoarse voice.

"The LORD is my strength and my song,

My God has become my salvation,
I shall praise Him with many songs."

He recited parts of the law and sang King David's songs. His weak voice echoed in the dark water-filled cavern. Using his scratchy voice, Jonah sang Miriam's song with sincere affection for his God.

"Who is like You, glorious in holiness,
Fearful in praises, doing mighty wonders?"

His repenting heart generated quietness. Quietness became trust. Confidence in his God gave him strength to endure God's unknown agenda.

Again, thoughts flooded Jonah's mind. *I accept this watery grave. But I also perceive God might not withdraw my assignment or my calling as His prophet.*

"God, my heart is heavy, and my eyes burn like fire. Though I am in the blackness of this monster's belly, You dwell both in the depths of the sea and on the highest mountaintop. All creation belongs to You which includes both me and this gigantic fish."

His song became his sacrifice of praise.

"O Lord, I am Your servant!
I want to fulfill my vow!"
O Lord, I am Your servant!

"Lord, I cry out to You from the depths of this sea. I know You hear me. I ran from your presence, but I know I will look once again toward Your holy temple."

Jonah's obedience to God's call would take him on a long journey.

~ 7 ~

Jonah's prison began to move much too fast and the churning water inside the fish's belly tossed him from side to side, then forward and backward. He coughed and choked as sea water went up his nose and down his raw throat. The young prophet sensed a heavy feeling of anticipation.

Now what is this fish doing? Jonah held his breath as he waited.

The runaway prophet did not really expect his nightmare to end. Jonah learned a first-class lesson of obedience plus experienced the ride of his life.

He and the giant fish landed on the eastern shore of the Great Sea. With its last breath, the fish beached itself with mouth wide open and ejected the prophet onto the sandy beach.

Jonah, with his heart pounding, laid on the beach gasping from shock. The young man breathed in and out with shallow quick breaths. His lungs filled with clean fresh air. The exhilarating scent intoxicated him to the extent he did not trust himself to rise to his feet.

Eventually, Jonah stood on his wobbly legs. "Jehovah, what just happened?"

Then he collapsed to his knees, face in the sand. He whispered, "Does this mean You forgive me?"

The prophet remained on his knees for a long time. His

mind whirled with a hundred questions and ideas.

Jehovah, I do not have any words to say!

Later, an old familiar song formed in his raw throat.

"I praise You with all my heart.
I shall tell people all the
marvelous things You have done.
I praise Your name, O Most High!"

Though his voice sounded weak from lack of fresh water, he again rejoiced singing songs written by King David.

I still have my memory. The sea did not rob me of that. He clapped his hands with joy and appreciation to God.

When Jonah's voice no longer could sing, he stood with caution again and examined himself. His skin, bleached from acid in the fish's stomach, hung wrinkled and waterlogged.

He chuckled to himself. *I must look a hundred years old.*

After that life-threatening experience, Jonah still wore his prophet's robe. The cherished coat, no longer clean, but faded and out of shape, hung from his shoulders covered with green stain and smelled sour beyond description. He found a fresh-water stream nearby where he washed seaweed and other unknown debris from his body and his clothes.

After a thorough scrubbing, the weary man sat on a boulder on the beach to rest and meditate about his precarious situation. Drained of all emotion and not knowing where he landed, Jonah experienced extreme hunger pangs. He watched the snowy white seagulls fly overhead and dive into the sea to scoop up small fish to eat.

One large seagull flew at him several times, then dropped a fish on Jonah's head. The attentive seagull returned three separate times. Though not delivered by a raven as Elijah experienced, Jonah accepted this meal of fresh fish as from God. Later, that same friendly seagull bombarded him with fresh bread from an unknown source.

God is feeding me just as He did Elijah. Me and Elijah. Elijah and me—prophets of God!

Overwhelmed with emotion, the young man could manage neither to sing nor speak. He dropped to his knees once again and remained there until he recognized God's thundering voice.

"Jonah, rise and go to Nineveh, and deliver that message I gave you."

God must be giving me a second chance.

Without delay, the young prophet stood tall, shoulders pushed back, and shouted to the heavens.

"I shall obey!"

He headed for the nearest town. Not knowing where he came ashore, his two obvious choices suggested north or south along the coast.

"God, direct my steps."

Jonah chose to travel north.

"I see a seaport ahead. It looks like the port of Joppa—right back where I commenced my voyage of disobedience."

God, how shall I pay the fare for my journey north? I *need money for food, lodging, and travel expenses.*

On the hills above Joppa, he noticed something familiar—field after field and row upon row of vineyards. Over-ripe grape clusters still hung from the vines. The white grapes in Philistia were harvested later in the season than the red grapes in his hometown of Gath-hepher.

Jonah approached the first vineyard on the road and asked to speak to the owner.

"I am Samos, the owner. What can I do for you?"

"I noticed your grapes are ripe for harvest. My father owns the famous Amittai Vineyards, and I am very experienced in making wine. I need to earn money for an emergency trip north."

"I am aware of the excellence of Amittai wine. You are a god-send, my son. I am desperate for pickers."

Samos hired him the same day. Jonah worked long hours for three weeks as he harvested and pressed the grapes.

"Jonah, you have more than proved your efficiency. I am so pleased that I will pay you a large bonus before the wine goes to market."

Once again, God provided for Jonah. He earned enough money for his expenses to Nineveh and later back home to Gath-hepher.

With money in his pocket, he went to the dock to purchase passage to Tyre. Very hesitant to board another ship after his dreadful ordeal, he prayed to overcome his fear.

"God, this time I vow to follow *all* Your instructions. I believe You will give me an uneventful sea journey this time."

He located a ship headed north and the first mate allowed him to board the ship early. Three sailors recognized him even though his appearance revealed a drastic change.

With panic in their voices, they approached the captain. "Sir, we recognize the passenger in that ragged robe, and we want no part of him. He is nothing but trouble!"

The stocky captain went below deck to talk to Jonah with the sailors following close behind. They were eager to hear Jonah's explanation.

"Is it true you caused a great storm at sea?" The skeptical

captain waved his finger at Jonah.

"Yes. My God sent a storm because I refused to obey Him."

One excited sailor interrupted, "How did you get back to Joppa?"

"It is an unbelievable story. Are you sure you want to hear it?"

The captain demanded, "If you want to travel on this ship, you better tell us everything."

Jonah shared his story with the sailors, though he found it difficult to believe his own adventure.

"When you threw me overboard, I planned to swim to shore except my God planned another experience. He sent a sea creature to swallow me."

The sailors stood with their mouths open in shock.

"I lived in the depths of the ocean in a wet, slimy cavern long enough for me to repent. My God showed mercy and allowed me to live and tell my story. Now I will do what He told me. I am confident we will all experience a safe voyage today."

The captain said, "I doubt the truth of your tale, but the explanation satisfies my curiosity and I agree to let you stay on board."

"We sailors believe his story because we witnessed the drama of the storm, and we agreed to throw him overboard."

The full crew wanted to hear more about Jonah's adventure. His story impressed a captivated audience for the entire trip to Tyre. He also told the crew stories of God's dealings with the Israelites.

"God ordered me to go to Nineveh and warn them of God's coming judgment. The people maintain an extreme and wicked lifestyle, and they will be destroyed."

The crew members suffered heavy conviction of their

own sinful lifestyle.

"What can *we* do? We are just as wicked as the people of Nineveh."

"Bow your knee to God and repent. Stop your evil ways. Jehovah might forgive you as He forgave me."

The voyage by ship from Joppa to Tyre proved uneventful, except for thirteen sailors who repented of their sins and swore to follow the one true God. Their decision of faith amazed Jonah.

"Jehovah, I am astonished that You used me to speak to Gentiles even before I reached my assigned destination."

Jonah would continue to have more opportunities to experience the goodness of God.

~ 8 ~

After Jonah disembarked from the ship at Tyre, he located a caravan leader named Hamata in the town square. "Sir, I am Jonah from Gath-hepher. I am looking for a caravan that travels east to Nineveh."

The overweight old man with a dirty turban and long bushy beard studied him with contempt, eyeing Jonah's bleached robe. "Why are *you* going to Nineveh? You do not have the appearance of a merchant."

"I am going on important business, a mission from God." Jonah rubbed at his robe to smooth his wrinkled garment.

Hamata smirked at Jonah's last comment. "It is going to be a long trip, over four hundred miles. My next caravan will leave in five days, and I expect full payment in advance."

"What route are you taking?" the prophet looked off into the distance, still full of dread of his assignment from God.

"We travel east to Damascus, north to Tadmore, further east to Mari where two roads cross. At Mari, we backtrack to cross the Euphrates River at its shallow point, then straight north to Haran. At that point, we connect to the northern route toward Nineveh. Normally, the trip will take four to five weeks."

"I will be ready." Jonah said as he paid Hamata the required fee. The young prophet remembered when

Abraham left the land of Ur, he traveled west through Haran, Tadmore, and Damascus.

Jonah reflected. *I will take the same route going east. This will be the longest trip I have ever made through Gentile country. This journey might take a month just to get to Nineveh.*

"We travel through mountainous terrain with weather unpredictable this time of year. Be prepared for freezing temperatures."

"I shall. Now, can you direct me to a place of lodging?" Jonah inquired. He still tried to smooth his faded robe with his hands.

"You will find a respectable inn on the left beyond the market."

The innkeeper wanted payment for the room and meals in advance. Jonah was relieved when the owner and the guests did not ask too many questions.

The prophet sighed to himself. *My nerves scream with tension. I want to avoid any discussion with strangers regarding my mission.*

As he waited for time to pass before the next leg of his journey, Jonah searched for a tailor to replace his faded prophet's robe. He located a gruff-looking weaver in the marketplace. Jonah instructed him to make his mantle plain and simple, patterned after his original prophet's robe.

"Your new robe will be ready in two days, and I want payment in advance." The shop owner held out his oversized hand.

What is it with these Gentiles? I look trustworthy. Jonah examined his tattered robe once again. *Well, I suppose not.*

The tailor fashioned the new robe as ordered.

"I will keep the old garment in case of chilly weather as

we travel northeast to the high country. My sandals float somewhere in the open sea. I prefer to travel barefoot, but this long trip justifies a pair of new sandals."

The tailor said, "You will find leather footwear next door to my shop."

God, thank you for providing for my needs.

He spent his free time visiting with various vendors as he strolled through the marketplace. At the wine shop, he paused to admire the inventory. As he expected, shelves lined with wine in clay jars and skins displayed the large "A" for Amittai wine. He remembered his family's vineyard as a dreaded question struck him hard.

Should I tell my family about my rebellion? Jonah paused to consider this critical issue. *No, I cannot bring dishonor to them. I shall tell no one. Besides, I would be too ashamed. Or am I too proud?*

"LORD, do I have any pride left?" He whispered aloud.

He heard no response.

The day of departure dawned with cloudy skies and cold temperatures. The caravan of over one hundred growling, smelly camels, dozens of donkey-drawn wagons, and large flocks of sheep and goats assembled east of town. The wealthy, well-dressed merchants rode groomed horses. The average merchants rode camels. The camels, a valuable source of milk for the trip, carried about five hundred pounds each of goods to trade with merchants in Damascus, Tadmore, and Nineveh.

Jonah learned no one walked on those trips due to the distance and the rough terrain. Hamata assigned Jonah a large camel since he owned no transportation.

"Guess I did not need these sandals after all." Jonah chuckled to himself. "Though I am sure I will need them someday."

Jonah estimated the number of people on the caravan at one hundred merchant men and a handful of brave women. Everyone kept to themselves, even at mealtime.

Arseen the cook prepared two meals a day for the travelers. Based on the bulk of the man, Jonah recognized that Arseen must enjoy his own cooking.

I would not trust a skinny cook. Jonah smiled to himself.

Jonah and Arseen established a friendship on the first day of the journey.

"Hey, Jonah, would you like to help me prepare food for the travelers? This way you could earn your meals."

"Sure." Jonah responded.

Jonah took advantage of their time together. "Abraham traveled this same route one thousand years ago. God called him to form the nation of Israel."

Arseen showed interest in Jonah's God, and many evenings they talked late into the night.

Eight days into the trip, Arseen revealed his curiosity. "So, Jonah, why do you go to Nineveh? It is a rough city."

"You are right about that. Nineveh is known as the largest city in the world." Jonah lowered his voice, "and the most wicked. God will destroy this city, and He told me to warn them."

Arseen raised an eyebrow and smiled. "They will laugh you out of town."

"Well, maybe so, but I have already learned I must do what God says." *Someday, I will share my sea adventure with Arseen.*

"I am dying to hear the end of *this* story."

"Maybe you will. I shall return in forty days after I enter Nineveh."

The route to Damascus, capital city of Aram, took them

across one of the shallow tributaries of the Jordan River. They traveled around the base of Mt. Hermon that rose nine thousand feet in elevation. Its three rugged mountain peaks glistened with snow.

Arseen described Damascus. "It is my most favorite city. The mountain water is the purest you will find to drink anywhere. The air hangs enchanted with the scent of jasmine. It is the most beautiful garden city I have ever seen."

Jonah anticipated the well-known charm of Damascus, the oldest inhabited city.

"Abraham's servant Eliezer lived in Damascus," Jonah enjoyed sharing Hebrew history with Arseen.

The long caravan arrived in Damascus a week after they left Tyre. To the west, Jonah observed rugged Mt. Qassioun.

I am glad we are not climbing that snow-covered mountain, but it does not appear as high as Mt. Hermon.

Arseen said, "Damascus is packed with noisy caravans that travel east and west loaded with wares to sell. No wonder it is the most important trade center in the region."

Mountain snow water flowed into ancient canals and meandered through the city to nourish the lush gardens.

The caravan rested east of town in the desert oasis of Ghuta by the Barada River. The large fertile oasis glowed with beautiful flower gardens, fruit orchards, and meadows.

"This country makes me think of a paradise when compared to the long dusty road we traveled to get here. Too bad we leave tomorrow," said Jonah while preparing meals.

"Yes, Ghuta would be a perfect place to live," said Arseen.

All too soon for Jonah, they prepared to depart. Three roads led out of Damascus. The driver chose the eastern road to Tadmore, their next stop.

Between Damascus and Tadmore, the caravan experienced a horrific storm that delayed them for two days. The camels had no problem with sand in the air due to their long curly eye lashes on two of their three unusual eyelids, but the travelers suffered. Rationing food and drinking water became necessary.

Jonah waited for the blinding sandstorm to blow away, *"I am not sure what is worse for me, sitting out a desert windstorm or floating in the sea monster. My eyes burn blistering hot, and breathing is difficult in either place."*

On the third day, the storm ceased, and the caravan leader rode his camel up and down the line shouting, "Next destination, Tadmore. Move out!"

The people of Tadmore inhabited the small oasis one hundred miles northeast of Damascus. Because of its strategic location centered on both the east-west and the north-south trade routes, Tadmore developed into an important commerce center.

The caravan continued through the small village of Mari without a rest stop. Traveling north, they arrived in Haran to purchase more supplies for their journey.

The grueling trip with its adverse weather conditions, difficult terrain, and long days between stops depressed Jonah.

He said to himself, "I wish this trip was over and I was returning home now." Jonah experienced painful tension as Nineveh drew near.

Hamata, the caravan leader, rode up beside Jonah with information. "Nineveh sits about two hundred miles south of Haran. The day of our arrival depends on the uncertain weather."

The prophet whined as Hamata rode off. "God, why did You send me to a city so far away?"

Once again, no response.

Jonah understood the most difficult part of the trip remained ahead. He wandered off by himself because he needed to talk with God in private.

"God, I need You more than ever as we draw closer to Nineveh. Sometimes I want to run in the opposite direction again. I am so unprepared. Will You tell me what to say to those Gentiles?"

The young prophet continued to question God's ways, but God in his great wisdom allowed Jonah to discover the answers for himself.

~ 9 ~

The slow-moving caravan descended the mountains of northern Assyria. A fertile valley glowed in the warm sunshine. The towns of Rehoboth-Ir, Calah, and Resen shared the valley with the larger city of Nineveh, the capital of the Assyrian empire. Hamata led the camel train along the bank of the Khoser River that flowed eastward from the Tigris River and through Nineveh. These two rivers provided water for drinking and irrigation for thousands of people on the plains.

After their morning meal, Jonah and Arseen discussed Nineveh.

Arseen said, "The town is located on a trade route between the Great Sea and the Indian Ocean. Nineveh became one of the wealthiest cities on the continent. The capital city developed into the hub for many business transactions."

Jonah asked, "Where is the headquarters of their military?"

Arseen answered, "The dreaded Assyrian military established their headquarters in Nineveh."

As the caravan approached their destination, Jonah guided his camel to the head of the line and asked the leader a question. "Hamata, you have visited Nineveh many times. How big is this city?"

"The biggest I have seen. Maybe more than a hundred

thousand people."

"Are they religious?" Jonah raised an eyebrow.

"Not really, but they follow several gods as we all do. They also worship their king Shalmanezer." Hamata chuckled with that bit of information.

Jonah wiped nervous sweat from his brow. He wanted Hamata to know his plans to depart soon. "I am leaving the caravan before we reach the city. I shall walk the rest of the way on foot."

"Traveling alone, you should beware of robbers," Hamata warned.

Jonah frowned. *Robbers should beware of my God.*

The day arrived when Jonah saw the ancient city in the distance known to the early Israelites as the land of Nimrod. The brick dwellings and winding water canals were visible for miles. He hurried his camel to the head of the caravan.

Jonah announced, "Hamata, I leave your caravan now. Maybe I will meet you again in forty days."

He said farewell to his new friend Arseen and returned his mode of transportation to the camel driver.

The young prophet crouched on the roadside with a full pouch of water and his original prophet's robe draped over his arm.

Why am I keeping this faded robe? This garment reminds me of my frightful experience, not the blessing of a prophet!

He listened to the music of the camel bells grow faint in the distance as the caravan continued without him. Not eager to stand and move toward town, Jonah wasted time as he considered Nineveh.

I know Nimrod built this city. That makes Nineveh ancient.

Jonah sighed with apprehension, worried about the

outcome of his mission. *O God, why am I here so far from home?*

Once again, thunder rolled in the distance.

"Jonah, get up! You must warn the people of Nineveh now! Preach against their wickedness. Warn them of destruction in forty days."

God's instructions vibrated loud and precise in Jonah's ears. The prophet jumped to his feet and tossed his old, weathered robe in a ditch half-full of water beside the road. Ready to accomplish his dreaded assignment, Jonah sprinted down the long, dusty road and located housing at the edge of town.

The owner quizzed him. "How long will you stay?"

"Forty days." *A grueling forty days!*

Though fearful of the peoples' response, Jonah preached the warning on the first day he arrived.

"I bring a message from the one true God who created you. You became a wicked and violent people. In forty days, you will be destroyed! God will judge Nineveh!"

As he walked the streets, people opened their windows and doors to hear the foreigner who shouted a threat of impending disaster. Their startled expressions showed concern and fear for their safety. They listened with respect to Jonah's message.

Jonah delivered this brief and concise warning day after day for forty days, and every night when he returned to the lodge, he marked off the day on a clay calendar that he designed with forty small boxes. The young man wore his new robe and preached the same message as he traversed every street in that wicked city. The assignment took Jonah three days each time to systematically travel throughout every section of the city as he shouted God's prediction.

He returned to the inn exhausted every evening, yet

unable to rest because people brought their friends and neighbors who had not yet listened to his message. They arrived by the hundreds to hear the unknown prophet.

No one caused a riot, no one threatened to stone him. The crowds believed the words of Jonah, much to his amazement. Thousands fasted and repented of their wicked ways.

All violence stopped and a peaceful atmosphere reigned in the city. Young people no longer fought each other nor roamed the streets at night creating terror; the elderly made peace with their long-time enemies; soldiers refrained from killing for no reason. All acts of adultery, lying, and stealing ceased.

On a knoll in the middle of the city, Jonah observed the golden royal palace, the residence of King Shalmanezer IV. The bright sunlight glistened on the moat that circled the king's headquarters. Colorful flower gardens surrounded the palace.

Shall I go preach to the king? Jonah asked himself. *Well, why not?*

Twenty days of the forty-day period had passed when Jonah approached the gate to the palace and proclaimed the same warning. "In twenty days, God will destroy Nineveh because of your wickedness!" The prophet shouted God's forewarning as loud as his hoarse voice allowed.

To Jonah's complete surprise, word reached him that the king was quick to step off his throne, replace his royal robe with a burlap mourning garment, and repent on a pile of ashes. People on every street corner discussed the king's response. The display of remorse shocked even Jonah.

King Shalmanezer issued a declaration to all the citizens. "Every man must wear burlap clothing and fast and pray to the true God in heaven. Put burlap on your animals. We must all turn from our evil ways. Stop all your violence. Refrain from food and drink and pray in earnest to the one true God. Everyone, repent! Maybe God will turn from his anger and show mercy on Nineveh."

Jonah did not pay attention to the beauty of the city nor its water fountains.

I am only here to do God's business. I have neither compassion nor pity for these wicked people. When God destroys this city, I shall be safe watching from a distant mountain top.

On the evening of the fortieth day, the prophet checked off the last day on his calendar, ended his message to the people, and moved out of the inn. In haste, he left town with his robe flapping in the wind. A young lad in a short burlap garment watched Jonah leave town and followed him.

"Prophet, where are you going now?" he shouted.

Jonah pointed north. "I will climb that mountain and wait for God's judgment to fall," Jonah muttered as he quickened his steps.

"Can I come with you, sir?" the boy begged.

"No! Go home to your mother."

"But I want to watch what your God does," he pleaded.

"If you insist. But stay behind me." He turned his back to the boy. "I do not want to talk to you, understand?"

"Yes, sir!"

He stayed ten paces behind Jonah in case he wanted to ask more questions about his God.

~ 10 ~

Jonah's head throbbed as he squatted on the hillside and waited for disaster to strike. He demonstrated no patience. His breath came in short pants and sweat dripped off his forehead, burning his eyes.

"Why am I so tense?" Jonah tried to relax his tight muscles. "Okay, God, now do not prove me wrong!"

He waited for the great devastation of an earthquake or fire from heaven. Exhausted from preaching day and night for forty days, he nodded off to sleep before the full moon set in a sky twinkling with bright stars—a beautiful picture of God's creation.

The boy awakened hours before Jonah did and inched closer to the sleeping prophet. "I want to hear Jonah's conversation with his God," he thought to himself.

Jonah awoke squinting in the glaring morning sunshine. Every direction he turned his head, Jonah assessed a peaceful Nineveh.

"Do I hear music? Are people dancing in the streets?"

The boy answered, "It looks that way from here."

Jonah raised his voice heavenward. "LORD, just as I thought. You did not destroy them. I told You when I left Gath-hepher that You would show mercy to these heathens. God, kill me now. I must die if my prophecy does not come true!"

Jonah's body suffered—his breath shallow, his hands in tight fists, his jaw tense.

Jehovah responded to Jonah's selfish attitude. "Why are you angry? They made sincere prayers of repentance. I am pleased to show mercy on the people of Nineveh."

"But the Assyrians are heathens! Enemies of Israel!" Jonah displayed his proud and annoyed spirit.

After that conversation, the prophet relocated to the far east side of the city. The boy followed him.

He pulled on Jonah's robe. "Why do you want your God to kill my people?"

"I told you not to talk. You should go home now. There is nothing to watch anyway. Go home!" Jonah had lost patience with the boy and with God.

Disappointed in his missed adventure, the boy hung his head and walked back to the city.

As the sun rose high in the sky, the intense heat from the rays made Jonah sweat. He needed shade, so he built a shelter from branches off a pine tree.

Jonah bragged to himself, *Now I shall be cool and comfortable while I wait to see God's drama unfold.*

God showed kindness to the unhappy Jonah and created a towering plant with extremely large leaves to grow beside his makeshift hut. Jonah smiled with appreciation for the much-needed shade.

"This must be a sign God will grant my desire for judgment on those Ninevites," Jonah said to himself.

Early the following morning, a large spotted worm chewed through the thick stem of God's gift of shade. Right before Jonah's eyes, the plant wilted and died within minutes. As the glaring sun shined on Jonah once again, a violent east wind blew his hand-made shelter down the steep hillside. The morning did not progress well for Jonah.

The extreme heat and lack of food stressed the young prophet. Life was not going as he expected.

Sand blowing in the air irritated his eyes. Jonah raised his voice over the sound of the wind. "Lord, I think I will faint in this blazing heat. I would rather be dead!"

"Jonah, is it right for you to show anger when the plant I grew for you died?"

"Yes! I have that right." Jonah suffered from a twinge of guilt. *Did I really say that?*

God's words sounded slow and distinct as usual. "But *you* did not plant it."

"I am not going to win this argument." He gritted his teeth. *Am I disgusted with myself or with God?*

"Will you now favor the people of Nineveh more than us, your chosen people?" Jonah was not in a congenial mood.

The pause in God's conversation with Jonah made the young prophet uncomfortable. He dropped to his knees. "What am I supposed to learn here, Lord?" Jonah's voice was not audible.

Thunder rumbled behind him.

God said, "In this great city, thousands of children are unaware of the difference between right and wrong. Why not show mercy on them and their animals when the sincere people and their king repented? As you said earlier, Jonah, I am kind and slow to show My anger."

"But, but . . ." Jonah stammered.

"Jonah, have you forgotten the mercy I showed you recently?" God's question was gentle but pointed.

Humbled and still on his knees, the prophet offered no response.

Epilogue

Almighty God demonstrated His mercy as He spared the animals and the people of Nineveh from judgment at that time in history (862 BC). Jonah exposed his true character as a prejudiced prophet when he showed lack of compassion for the heathen. An unknown amount of time passed before he demonstrated enough courage to record his testimony of disobedience.

Repentance and a change of heart brought peace to Jonah's soul. Later, Jonah experienced fellowship with God as a prophet to His chosen people. His fulfilled prophecy that concerned Israel is recorded in 2 Kings 14:25-27.

God's patience with the Assyrian empire expired. Under the rule of Sinsharishkun, the people of Nineveh rejected God and enlarged the Assyrian empire through violence and cruel oppression. Assyria destroyed Damascus and Tyre.

About one hundred fifty years after Jonah's warning, the prophet Nahum foretold Nineveh's destruction again. That time they did not repent. God fulfilled Nahum's prophecy. Nineveh fell captive to and was destroyed by Babylonia and its allies in 612 BC. No one ever rebuilt the city of Nineveh.

In Matthew 12:38, Jesus spoke of the prophet's length of time spent in a great fish and compared Jonah's experience to His own destiny. Jesus said the people of Nineveh repented after Jonah's warning, even though Jonah gave no call for them to repent and change their ways. As instructed, he only preached judgment.

Six hundred years before Jonah's mission, God instructed Moses that obedience influences the blessings of God. His requirements are fourfold: fear God, walk in all His ways, love and serve God with all the heart and soul, and keep His commandments. Every people and every nation will prosper when they follow these instructions given by Almighty God, Creator of the universe and Creator of Jonah's gigantic fish.

Juanita Turner Paslay

Mercy in Phoenicia

Azita

A desperate Gentile woman encounters Jesus.

A story based on Matthew 15; John 4;
Isaiah 40, 45; 1 Kings 17, 18, 19

~ 1 ~

"Must you leave again so soon? It seems you returned only moments ago." Azita sighed.

She directed her eyes away from Shaheem as she struggled to hide her tears of loneliness. Her husband's occupation took him away from home for weeks at a time.

The subject of conversation focused on Shaheem's next business trip. As a successful merchant, he traveled by caravan as far north as Tarsus and east to Damascus. Last week he traveled along the eastern coastline of the Great Sea to Alexandria, one of the largest cities in Egypt.

"Azita, I hope to return in three weeks. I wish it were three days, but you know that is not possible. Tomorrow's journey will take me into Jewish country. I will travel to Capernaum in Galilee and maybe as far south as Jerusalem if I have not sold all my merchandise in Galilee."

Shaheem and his wife Azita reclined in the shade of their garden courtyard as they enjoyed a special time together.

Beautiful varieties of flowers and sedums thrived in the sandy soil of Phoenicia. Azita spent hours tending her garden of vegetables and colorful flowers.

Azita said, "I love the beauty of my sea daffodils as they glow in the morning sun. They are my favorites."

"I would rather see the early morning sun highlight your hair." Shaheem adored his wife. "I always cherish our quiet times."

"I agree we experience far too few such occasions." Azita smiled at her husband.

Shaheem, Azita and their two children—Flora, age eight and Omeed, age twelve—lived in the coastal city of Tyre in Phoenicia.

Tyre, known for its fabulous silks, also produced the most desirable purple dyes available in the world. Tropical sea snails lived among the large rocks on the shoreline of Phoenicia where dye makers extracted the prized purple from the murex's secretions.

The family experienced many pleasures afforded them by Shaheem's profitable business. Their well-furnished brick and stone house was built on a hill that overlooked the busy seaport. Their son attended a prestigious school for boys, and Azita's wardrobe held beautiful gowns that she loved to wear on social occasions.

"Oh, Shaheem, listen to the loud roar of the surf. I love to hear the waves crash on the rocks below. They create such relaxing music for me."

Azita tried to concentrate on the beauty of nature before she changed the subject.

She wrinkled her brow as she spoke again. "Lately, our daughter is becoming more agitated and more distressed. I wish your business did not take you out of town so often. She talks to herself in a strange voice and makes me afraid for her."

"What did the physician say on your last visit?"

"He suggested she might outgrow the symptoms or maybe she has an evil spirit. Either way, he offered no help."

"Physicians always say that when they fail to heal someone. Azita, do not worry. I am sure Flora will improve as she gets older. I am sorry I cannot be home every night, but you know I must travel with my type of business."

Shaheem refused to admit his own concern over his daughter's behavior.

"I am trying not to worry, but it is more difficult when you are not home."

"Does Omeed help you care for Flora?"

"He avoids talking to Flora. He stays with her when I leave to purchase food at the market, but he is not happy watching her."

Shaheem rose to his feet and leaned over to hug his wife. "I love Flora, too. When she was a small child, she acted so sweet and playful. We must hope she returns to our precious Flora."

The following morning, the family gathered in the living room for final hugs and goodbyes.

"Flora, come give your father a kiss." As Shaheem kissed his daughter goodbye, he noticed a strange, faraway expression in her eyes that unnerved him.

Shaheem hugged his wife again and whispered, "Azita, keep a close watch on Flora."

"I shall." Azita held her breath for a moment as Shaheem walked toward the front door. *I wish he would stay home with me. I am not sure I can manage Flora by myself.*

"Omeed, I expect you to take care of the family while I am gone."

"Yes, Father." Omeed exhaled loudly and left the room.

Azita wanted to end their conversation on a pleasant topic. "You make a handsome impression in your new silk robe. I am sure you will sell many garments on this trip."

"When I wear what I sell, it creates good advertising. All the town elders find my exquisite robes difficult to resist. They can well afford them, too. Only royalty can afford the purple robes, but I have robes of many colors." He smiled at the prospect of more wealthy customers.

"I visited the silk shop last week. The women mixed a beautiful new shade of purple. I adored the unusual dark hue." Azita hinted with a twinkle in her eye.

"If this business trip meets my expectations, I shall buy you a purple scarf when I return." He hugged Azita close and affirmed his promise with a long kiss.

"I will miss you, Shaheem. Please hurry home." They embraced again, then Shaheem closed the door behind him.

~ ~ ~ ~ ~

The caravan gathered at the south end of town. Rafa, the local caravan driver, greeted Shaheem with a welcome smile. "I see you are on your way again. Where are you headed this time?" Shaheem traveled with the Jewish caravan leader for the last ten years.

"I am headed for Capernaum first. I might go on to Jerusalem. When does your caravan depart?"

"At the third hour. I have told everyone to choose their position in line as soon as possible. Shaheem, you will need to join a different caravan at the seaport of Ptolemais to travel east through Galilee."

Long before departure time, Shaheem chose a place close to the head of the caravan to avoid eating dirt. Wagon drivers in the rear found it necessary to cover their nose and mouth with their head scarf if they did not want to breathe dust kicked up by the horses and camels.

Before the caravan moved out, Rafa, riding his spirited camel, approached Shaheem. A young boy sat behind with his arms around the man's waist. "Shaheem, want to indulge in the company of my son Simon for a few hours? He joins me on his first trip south."

"Sure!" the merchant extended his hand. "Simon, jump

up here and sit beside me. You look about the age of my son Omeed. Ever drive a team of donkeys?"

Simon's freckled face exploded with a grin. "Nope, but I can learn."

"I am sure you will, if your father approves."

Rafa nodded his approval.

Simon added proudly, "I am eleven."

When the caravan had traveled an hour out of Tyre and entered the southern valley, Shaheem said, "Simon, how is this for beautiful scenery?"

"Those dreadful lilies make me sneeze. I can smell them from here." The boy wiggled his nose and sniffled.

"My wife Azita would love to see those wildflowers." He lowered his voice and spoke to himself. "Someday she will travel with me when our children are grown."

Young Simon raised his voice over the blaring noise of the camels when he recognized the tall cedar trees on his left. "Did you know that Israeli King David and King Solomon constructed their palaces with cedar from Phoenicia?"

"I am not surprised because everyone knows the wood grain is exquisite. I wish I could afford cedar instead of brick for my house, but I am no king."

Shaheem shifted his position to face Simon. "Are you ready to manage the reins?"

"Oh, yes sir!"

The young boy and the merchant enjoyed their day together on the road south. The donkeys responded with obedience as Simon held the reins for several hours.

The price to travel with the caravan included the evening meal. Merchants gathered around the food wagon to eat and share stories.

Certain men, famous for their exaggerated tales, loved

to entertain. Shaheem, a sociable man, always enjoyed mealtime with his fellow travelers.

"Hey, Arif, good to see you again. Do you have a new story to tell us?" Shaheem challenged the merchant.

The men acquainted with Arif and his exaggerations chuckled to encourage him.

"I bought a new camel last week. You ought to see him spit. He hit me at twenty feet, so do not ride too close to me."

Salim, a new merchant with the caravan, spoke to Shaheem. "I am carrying fine wines from Gath-hepher in my wagon. What is your merchandise?"

"My crates are loaded with handmade silk robes and scarves crafted by the women of Tyre. Royalty and other wealthy people account for most of my return customers. I also sell small clay jars filled with the purple dye in great demand by the professional weavers."

Shaheem's valuable containers, packed with care to avoid damage from the rough roads, sat in sheepskin bags for their long journey to Capernaum in Galilee. An extra wheel, his bedroll, and other necessary supplies hung secure on the sides of his wagon.

The thirty-mile journey south along the eastern shore of the Great Sea proved uneventful but beautiful as usual during the spring months.

Shaheem considered the terrain. *I always enjoy this part of the trip when the wild lilies are in full bloom and cover the fields this time of the year. The coastal grasses show off their green shades and the forest of cedar trees on the mountain range grow so tall.*

At the ninth hour the following day, Shaheem waved goodbye to his young friend Simon, paid his account with Rafa, and joined another caravan headed east through Galilee.

"Two years ago, I delivered my silk garments and purple dye to the Jewish town of Capernaum. I anticipate a prosperous trip again this year," Shaheem said to himself.

Shaheem could not imagine the extraordinary experience that awaited him in Israel.

~ 2 ~

The day after Shaheem's departure for Capernaum, an uninvited visitor arrived at their home in Tyre. Soft, strange cries brought Flora to the living room out of curiosity. As she opened the front door, a wagging tail replaced the whining. A puppy with sad brown eyes stared up at her. When Flora leaned over to pet him, the dog's tail spun in a circle like the wheel of a runaway oxcart.

"Mother, Mother! Come here!"

Azita rushed to the door and discovered why her daughter jumped up and down with excitement. "Flora, do not touch that dirty cur. They bite children. Shut the door quick!"

As soon as Flora closed the door, the black long-haired dog whined again. She peeked out the open window. "Oh, Mother, he looks hungry. We must feed the puppy."

"I admit the puppy is thin. Maybe a piece of dried bread will satisfy him." Azita opened the door a crack to observe the dog. "At least I think it's a male."

Flora ran to the food pantry and returned with a piece of stale bread and gave the food to her mother. Azita threw a morsel out the window into the front yard. The little dog devoured the treat and licked all the crumbs off the ground in a matter of seconds. He raised up his short-pointed ears and wagged his tail again.

"He wants another piece, Mother. Please?"

"Give him one more, then tell him goodbye. The dog must go home where he belongs. Close the window so he does not jump inside."

Flora tossed out another piece, then closed the window shutter. The puppy settled down for the evening in the shade under their large fig tree.

"Mother, today has been a good day. The puppy made me happy." Flora smiled. *I did not hear those scary voices scream in my head.*

Flora said, "I want to sit by the window and watch the sun disappear. Where does it go when I cannot see it?"

"The sun hides below the sea until morning." Azita brought her chair close to Flora. "I will sit beside you, dear. The setting sun makes a beautiful picture of orange and reds, my favorite colors."

"Mine, too, Mother."

The following morning, the rejected animal remained camped in their yard. Omeed noticed him first.

"Mother, shall I chase him away?" Omeed asked.

Flora responded, "No, Mother, we must feed him breakfast. He waited all night. Please?"

Azita sighed. "I wish your father could examine the dog. But I will let him stay outside until your father returns. The pup reminds me of a young sheep dog." She smiled. "Too bad we do not own sheep."

Flora giggled as her small feet skipped to the kitchen and returned with food for her new friend. "I brought two pieces for Happy this time."

Omeed watched the scene from the kitchen. He frowned and sounded jealous. "Happy? That is a silly name for a dog. Besides, he looks dangerous to me."

"He is not dangerous. He is just a little puppy and he

makes me so happy. His name *must* be Happy. Okay, Mother?"

"Do not get attached to him because I am sure your father will chase him away," Azita warned. "Dogs are usually sick and dangerous and not meant to be a pet." She inspected him from the window. "But I admit this one has bright eyes and appears healthy except he looks so thin and hungry."

Time passed, and the puppy continued to beg for food and sleep in their front yard. The young dog did not behave as a wild animal and earned the trust of the family. Happy survived a soapy bath at the hands of Flora and made himself at home. He worked his way into their hearts until Azita allowed him to sleep inside on an old pillow at the foot of Flora's sleeping mat.

~ 3 ~

By late afternoon, the caravan entered the outskirts of Capernaum, a fishing village on the northwest shore of the Sea of Galilee. Travelers from southern Israel and as far north as Tyre and Sidon filled the city streets. Shaheem drove to the center of the market and parked his wagon beside a merchant named Adiem who sold wine. As the sun disappeared behind the rolling hills, carts and shops covered their wares with heavy tarps and prepared for an evening of quiet conversation and aged wine.

The main topic of the night centered around a small boy ill with a high fever. All the local merchants were well-acquainted with the family. The boy's father, Albus, held a prominent position as a nobleman under King Herod Antipas.

Shaheem's business neighbor repeated all the known facts. "The physicians failed to reduce the fever. The delirious child is unable to stand, so the father left this morning for Cana to implore the help of a traveling healer named Jesus."

His last statement aroused Shaheem's curiosity. "Adiem, I am not aware of this Jesus. Who is He?"

"Hundreds of people follow this Jewish man. He heals diseases and casts out demons. He travels throughout Judea and Galilee teaching about God and telling people to repent of their sinful ways. He claims to be the Son of God. Some say he *is* God."

"Your Jewish people have the strangest beliefs. How can a man be a god? How does one person heal another person?"

Adiem ignored Shaheem's pointed questions and asked him a question. "Where are you from?"

"Phoenicia."

"Do your people have gods?"

"Well, if we do, I have never met one." Uncomfortable with the topic, Shaheem raised a hand to straighten his head scarf as he forced a chuckle.

"I am from the hill country of Judea. I have never encountered a god either, though I hope to." Adiem turned his head as his voice trailed off and ended the conversation.

Shaheem shared no further comments. He returned to his wagon and retrieved his bedroll and pillow, cleared away the larger pebbles on the ground, and smoothed out his mat. Sleep did not come as he hoped.

His mind rehearsed the ending of the story of the sick child with a high fever. *Will the young boy die or live?*

During the night, a strong wind blew in off the lake and rain drenched the town. Shaheem awoke to the sound of water pelting his tarp. He crawled out from under the wagon to check the knots and made sure the canvas held secure. Confident, Shaheem returned to his mat, but sleep evaded him. His mind dwelt on the nobleman's son and his own daughter.

The unexpected storm passed, and the skies were clear the following morning.

Shaheem told himself, "Time for breakfast. I smell the aroma of fresh baked bread. I am in the mood for warm twisted Jewish bread."

Shaheem followed the tempting scent and located a

baker down the street and around the first corner where he purchased three loaves. As he chewed on the hard crust, he strolled past other merchants as they uncovered their wares. He noticed no other sellers of fine silk robes.

Shaheem smiled to himself. *That is a good sign. No competition means more sales for me.*

The first day ended as a profitable day for business. The women preferred purple scarves over the other colors. Many ladies returned in the afternoon to purchase robes of various shades for their husbands.

On the third day around the sixth hour, a well-dressed Roman approached Shaheem's wagon. He dismounted his well-groomed horse wearing a fancy leather bridle and requested a small robe.

"Sir, may I show you a size perfect for you?"

The smiling nobleman shook his head. "I will not buy a robe for myself. I want the best robe you have for my son. He deserves the finest. When I returned from Cana last night, he greeted me at the door standing straight and healed of his dreadful fever."

The man's enthusiasm and commanding voice attracted attention from several local merchants and shoppers. They gathered around him, excited to learn the full story.

"When I located the prophet Jesus in Cana, many sick people and hundreds of townspeople surrounded him. Everyone desired his attention. I held back for about an hour and watched the people's response to the healer. They pushed and shoved to get close to him. When Jesus noticed me, he sent a welcoming smile my direction. I guided my horse through the crowd and knelt before Him. Bowing was the reasonable thing to do. I told Him my son lay dying and pleaded with Him to make the thirty-mile trip to Capernaum to heal him."

"What did he say?" Adiem asked.

"Jesus squeezed my hand and lifted me to my feet. 'Go home. Your son lives.' That is all he said."

The crowd pleaded, "Tell us more!"

"One smile from Jesus and anyone will believe what He says. I have never met a man like this man. I believe God walks in Galilee."

One bystander moved in closer and asked what others wondered. "You saw God?"

"That is what I believe. My horse galloped home in record time. I found my healthy son on his feet, waiting for me. Now, my family and my household staff believe in Jesus."

The Roman man's story touched Shaheem's generous side. The merchant from Phoenicia selected a short bright garment. "Sir, please take this robe as my gift to him."

"Oh, no. I shall pay you double. My son is worth more to me than any price."

Business slowed after five days and Shaheem broke camp and joined a caravan south through the Judean hills. He stayed three days in Magdala known for its beautiful woolen garments. The men in the wool business were eager to buy Shaheem's supply of dyes, especially the shades of purple and red. From Magdala, Shaheem traveled south to the marketplace in Jerusalem.

Jesus and his followers traveled north to Capernaum.

Their paths never crossed.

~ 4 ~

Azita marked off the days on her clay calendar as she waited for her husband to return from Israel. The days developed into a nightmare as her daughter became increasingly agitated. At times, her physical actions were uncontrollable. Sleep eluded both mother and daughter during those long nights.

One early morning, the family awoke to screams from Flora's room—eerie enough to make a person's heart stop. As Azita pulled back her daughter's curtain over the doorway, Happy ran out. The dog raced across the living room, jumped out the open window, and ripped the beautiful lace curtain as he escaped.

"Flora, dear Flora. What makes you cry?" Azita knelt beside her daughter to calm her as she held the child's small body against her breast. The girl continued to sob and scream unrecognizable words. Azita cried too, not knowing what else to do. She called to her son for help. No response. Omeed did not want to be in the same house with his sister.

Flora's sobs changed to a soft whimper.

Azita held her close. "What can I do, Sweetheart?"

"Mother, tell those mean voices to go away." Flora gasped for air as she spoke. "Where is Happy? I want to hold my puppy."

"Do not worry, my sweet. Happy went outside. I am sure he will return soon."

~ ~ ~ ~ ~

As the morning sunrays shined over the eastern hilltops, Omeed knocked hard on the door of his teacher's residence. The half-hour run made him short of breath.

Jason open the door with caution to his uninvited guest.

"Omeed, we do not have classes today. Why are you here?" Jason frowned a puzzled expression.

"My father travels out of town and I cannot live with my mother anymore. My little sister acts crazy. She scares me. Can I stay with you?"

Jason glanced up and down the street. He saw no one to witness the boy approach his property. He whispered. "No, Omeed. Best you go home where you belong." Without hesitation, he closed the door and left the boy standing alone on the porch.

Omeed threatened, *I am not going home. Never!*

~ 5 ~

Diane followed her favorite trail to climb the hill that overlooked the Great Sea. The view of the surf below and sea gulls flying overhead fascinated her as usual, giving her inspiration for another charcoal drawing.

"Fresh salty air always revives my spirit and helps my mind dwell on pleasant things. This view is most comforting during the times my husband drives his caravan out of town."

Her husband, Rafa, sold her charcoal sketches when he traveled. Artwork signed by Diane became a popular treasure for wealthy patrons from Tarsus to Alexandria.

The atmosphere was not calm that day. Diane approached the bluff with her drawing supplies tucked under her arm. Horrible screams sounded from the last house on the road.

Something terrible is happening in there! Diane walked faster to quickly pass the house.

Diane loved walking in the fresh air. That was her time alone to meditate on God and draw her favorite scenery. At the end of the trail, Diane relaxed on the boulder she called her creation bench. She sketched a rough drawing, then completed a dramatic ocean scene with storm clouds on the horizon using charcoal from her kitchen fireplace.

With the sun high overhead, Diane unpacked her grapes

and bread for her noon meal. After she ate the last grape, she covered and rolled her picture on the dried sheep skin, taking care not to smudge the charcoal, packed her supplies, and headed down the trail. Diane sensed a calm atmosphere now as she approached the last house, but she could not forget the awful sounds that had resonated from inside.

A distressed woman now stood on her front porch calling, “Omeed, Omeed!”

Diane hesitated, then approached the gate. “Can I help you?”

“My son Omeed ran away. Have you seen him?”

“I have not seen a child on the trail this morning.”

The distraught woman collapsed to the ground and her tears flowed again. Diane unlatched the ornate metal gate, entered the yard, and placed her drawing supplies on the ground.

“My name is Diane. Why did your son leave?”

“He is afraid of his sister, and . . . and . . . so am I!”

Diane knelt beside Azita to comfort her. “As I headed for the bluff this morning, a child screamed.”

“That was my Flora. Her seizures happen most every day now. The doctors cannot help her.”

“I am sure you worry about her. Does she scream because she hurts?”

“It might be pain. She looks frantic, makes a terrible face, and waves her arms. You know, Diane, sometimes I feel she might have a demon in her head.” Azita rubbed her hands up and down her arms. “But please do not tell anyone what I told you. I do not want people to talk about us.”

The two women stood and embraced each other. Diane held Azita’s hands in hers. “I will keep your secret, but I will ask my God to help Flora. The God of Israel has performed many miracles for His people.”

"Oh, thank you. I have begged the gods for help, but so far, they ignore me."

"Azita, there is only one true God. We will have faith together." Diane hugged her again.

"I am so glad you came today. You encouraged me." A frown of worry crossed Azita's forehead. "Now I pray Omeed will return home. He is twelve. Much too young to live by himself."

"At that age, the only job he could acquire might be a cabin boy on a sailing ship," Diane said.

"I hope he comes home before his father returns."

As the days passed, Azita and Diane became close friends. Whenever Diane went to the bluff to enjoy the scenery, she knocked on Azita's door to check on the family.

Demons tormented Flora every day and neither Omeed nor Happy had returned home.

~ 6 ~

Wherever Jesus traveled in Israel, reports of His miracles and teachings preceded Him. He walked many miles as He healed sick people, cast out demons, and upset the Pharisees—all accomplished in the will of His Heavenly Father.

Jesus and His disciples arrived two miles outside Capernaum as the setting sun painted the sky with red hues. The hot, dry wind blew all day and covered the men and their supplies with a layer of dust.

"Master, can we camp here for the night?" Peter eyed a grove of olive trees beside a meandering creek. The weary men welcomed the cool shade.

Jesus raised his arm to wipe sweat from his forehead with his dusty sleeve. "This is the perfect place. I am ready for a drink of cool water. How about you, Andrew?"

"Drink? I am ready for a swim. We have traveled too many miles today." Andrew, the youngest in the group, dashed to the creek.

Everyone dropped their packs under the closest tree and raced down the bank. Andrew disrobed first and jumped in, followed by Philip and Nathanael. They behaved like young boys—splashing and dunking each other. The loud, exuberant voices of James and John echoed across the stream like thunder in a storm.

Jesus joined His friends in the cool water. He raised His

voice over their excitement. "Hey, John, you have the loud spirited voice of your father. I am sure everyone in Capernaum can hear you from here."

John's face beamed. Jesus and John cherished a close relationship.

Before dawn the following morning, the men broke camp and walked the short distance into Capernaum.

"I am eager to join the faithful in the synagogue today. My Father God has designed a special day for someone, a blessing of deliverance," Jesus whispered to John.

A few empty seats in the men's section remained available as Jesus and His disciples entered the building. The women's section had filled in record time. Jesus, the famous teacher, had arrived in town and no one wanted to miss hearing Jesus explain the Kingdom of God.

A guest speaker always increased the attendance of the less faithful ones at the synagogue. The local Pharisees did not hold people's attention the way Jesus did with His soothing yet authoritative voice.

James leaned toward John and asked, "Have you noticed every time He accepts a scroll to read in the synagogue, He looks into the eyes of His audience and speaks? His eyes do not need to stay on the scroll because He knows all the words."

John nodded. "His wisdom is definitely beyond my understanding."

The Pharisees failed to comprehend that Jesus illuminated and personified God's Word in the flesh. The common people drank in every word as if they experienced certain Scriptures for the first time.

Jesus chose a seat in the row reserved for visiting rabbis. After the traditional formal prayers, the synagogue leader invited Jesus to read the Scripture. When Jesus ascended the platform, the leader opened the holy chest used to store the scrolls and handed Jesus the next scroll for the scheduled reading of the day. Jesus unrolled it, stood at the podium, and spoke His Father's message recorded in the book of Isaiah.

"For there is no other God but me, a righteous God and Savior. There is none but me.

"Let all the world look to Me for salvation! For I am God; there is no other.

"I have sworn by My own name; I have spoken the truth, and I will never go back on My word. Every knee will bend to Me, and every tongue will confess allegiance to Me.

"The people will declare, 'The Lord is the source of all my righteousness and strength.' And all who were angry with him will come to him and be ashamed.

"In the Lord, all the generations of Israel will be justified, and in him they will boast."

When Jesus finished reciting, He rolled up the sacred scroll and handed it back to the leader. Silence hung suspended in the room. Spellbound, no one moved in their seats, no one whispered. Their personal plans for the rest of the day became unimportant. All eyes were fastened on Jesus. The only sound in the room was a baby fussing in the women's section. Once again, God communicated with Israel through His Son.

Jesus walked toward His seat when, without warning, an old man disrupted the silence and stumbled down the center aisle as he screamed and waved his arms.

"I recognize You. Go away and stop bothering me. You . . . You . . . Holy One of God!"

Before the worried demon revealed more personal information, Jesus raised His commanding voice and pointed a finger at him. "Be silent!"

People sitting near the aisle scattered against the wall as the unexpected drama unfolded.

Jesus positioned himself right in front of the man, stared into his eyes and demanded in a firm voice, "I command you to leave Asher at once. Now!"

The man's body stiffened, then slammed onto the floor as the demon uttered a sharp piercing cry and left his body. Asher trembled and gasped for air. Jesus knelt and gathered him in His arms and held him close for several minutes to calm the elderly man's nerves.

Asher wept and thanked Jesus repeatedly. "That demon destroyed my life for many years. Now I am free! Thank you, Jesus. I even feel young again."

Jesus kissed Asher's wrinkled forehead with love. Holy tears dropped on the old man's cheek as Jesus rejoiced with him.

Asher, well-known in the community, shared the story of his healing with everyone who traveled in and out of Capernaum. The miracle amazed all who listened to his testimony.

After the morning session, Jesus sat outside the synagogue and again taught the crowd about living in God's Kingdom. Two young children stood in the crowd with their mother. Jesus grinned at them and held out His arms of love and they dashed toward Him. The girl climbed up on Jesus' lap. The little boy sat on the bottom step and grinned up at Him.

Jesus stared at the Pharisees standing near Him and said, "Unless you turn away from your sins and become humble as these children, you will not enter the Kingdom of Heaven."

James whispered to John, "Watch those Pharisees. They stand in the background, but still close enough to listen for

Jesus to say something they think is false."

"Yeah, the Pharisees burden us with teachings that Moses did not authorize. No wonder Jesus calls them hypocrites, plus most of them do not follow their own rules."

~ ~ ~ ~ ~

Peter invited Jesus and the disciples to his home for their evening meal. His wife, Dayna, greeted them at the door with disturbing news.

"Peter, my mother is in bed with a high fever and refuses any food or water. She says large ugly spiders crawl on her blanket. I have never seen Mother delirious. Will Jesus help her?" Her eyes pleaded with the Master as He entered through the doorway.

Jesus responded at once. "Take me to Leah's bedside."

Dayna led Him into the darkened room and leaned against the wall next to Peter. Jesus approached the bed and held the elderly woman's hand in His and helped her sit upright. Her head cleared, her eyes opened and Leah, with tears in her eyes, directed a big smile toward Jesus. As Leah stood to her feet, the fever left her.

"Thank you, Jesus, for Your amazing gift of strength today. Now I have energy to fix dinner for everyone." Leah's face beamed as she bowed her head to Jesus.

Dayna hugged Peter and Jesus in one big embrace. "Thank you, Jesus! I believed You would heal her. Men, please relax in the garden while Leah and I prepare fish and fresh bread for your evening meal."

The ladies exited the sleeping room singing the words of an ancient prophet as they retreated to prepare food for their special guests.

"He gives power to the weak
And strength to the powerless.
We who trust in God find new strength."

After supper, Peter detected the sound of excited voices outside his front door. He pulled back the curtain to reveal a crowd of people gathering in the yard.

"Master, we have company." Peter chuckled and motioned for Jesus.

"I see many crippled and sick people outside. I must help them," Jesus said as He opened the door and entered the front yard. Peter and Andrew followed Him.

Jesus healed every sick person who came to Peter's house that night. He blessed them and taught the people until sunset.

Jesus told them, "I teach only the truth. My words give eternal life with God our Father if you repent of your sins and follow My teachings."

The next day before the morning sunlight sparkled on the Sea of Galilee, Jesus slipped on his sandals, left Peter's guest room, and disappeared before the others awoke. He loved to walk the hill country He had created eons ago. He found a quiet place outside Capernaum to communicate with His Father God.

"Father, guide my steps according to Your will. My limited time on earth gives Me a sense of urgency. I desire Your blessing on Your chosen people of Israel."

After searching for two hours, Peter located Jesus. "Listen! I hear Him singing."

"I will praise You, LORD, with all my heart;
I tell the marvelous things You do.
I am filled with joy because of You.

I sing praises to You, O Most High."

Peter and his brother, Andrew, paused a moment to listen to Jesus sing, then interrupted Him.

"Master, everyone is looking for You. Please come back to town now. The women have prepared our breakfast."

Jesus placed both hands on their shoulders and announced, "We will travel to other towns soon. More people must learn about the Kingdom, and hundreds need healing."

Jesus spent the following night again by Himself in prayer. In the morning, He revealed their next destination.

"I travel to the Great Sea. Who wants to go with me? It is time for a leisure walk and relaxation away from the crowds."

Peter leaned in toward Philip. "Why does He want to travel so far?"

"Jesus always has a plan. Do not question Him," whispered Philip as he shook his head.

After their breakfast of grapes and dates with Leah's fresh bread, they headed west to Cana, passed through the province of Galilee, and reached the coastal plain in four days.

Peter enjoyed sharing his knowledge of the terrain. He raised his hand and pointed south. "Mt. Carmel—where Elijah challenged King Ahab with fire."

Jesus could not resist another opportunity to reveal His true self. Smiling, He shared part of the story. "Too bad you were not there. Elijah's confrontation with the Baal prophets achieved a major victory that day. Four hundred and fifty bodies slain by Elijah's sword filled the Kishon Valley. And that is not counting the evil prophets of Asherah.

The disciples raised their eyebrows at each other. They all wanted to hear more of the story.

John asked Jesus, "What happened after that?"

"Remember, there had been no rain for three and a half years. You should have seen Elijah outrun King Ahab's chariot in the sudden rainstorm. Wicked Jezebel was very unhappy that day!" Jesus nodded his head and laughed.

"Her threats on Elijah's life caused him to flee in fear for his life. Two times, My Father sent an angel to feed and encourage him. The miracle food gave him strength for forty days while he hid from Jezebel in the wilderness."

They enjoyed their time away from the crowds. Jesus explained to His friends the expansion of the Kingdom of God, what part they played, and what it meant to follow the Son of Man. In between the serious times, they fished for their meals, raced on the beach, and relaxed under the coastal palm trees.

The third night on the beach, storm clouds rolled in off the Great Sea bringing heavy rains and intense winds. The waves rose higher than normal and crashed loud on the rocks near where the men slept. All the disciples were awakened in the middle of the night by distant peals of thunder and moved their bedrolls thirty feet up the bank for fear of being washed out to sea.

By daylight, the storm pushed eastward, and the men awoke to the pleasant sounds of seagulls flying overhead. They were startled to see Jesus still asleep in his original location on the beach.

Thaddeus showed his concern for Jesus. "I thought we *all* moved up the bank. Someone better check on Him."

Andrew and Peter dashed down to make sure Jesus survived the storm. "Jesus, are You awake?" Peter raised his voice and shook Jesus by the shoulder.

"I am now." Jesus grinned, then stood to His feet and stretched both arms over His head. "Is breakfast ready?"

"Did You hear the storm last night? We moved our beds up the bank. Did the high waves concern You? Are You soaked?" Andrew was full of questions that morning.

"I confess," Jesus said, "I slept through it all. My Father is all-powerful over the mighty waves of the sea and the noise of a storm. God is our protection and our refuge."

"But Master . . ." Peter did not continue, though it proved a difficult challenge for him.

"He will provide shelter in your storms of life. Always remember that." Jesus smiled and gave Peter a friendly slap on the back. "Shall we catch some fish for breakfast?"

Peter hollered over his shoulder to the other disciples still on the high bank. "Guys! Bring the nets. We are going fishing."

The disciples learned a great lesson of Jesus trusting His Father God. The LORD is mightier than the mighty waves of the sea.

The following morning as the sun reflected on the waves of the Great Sea, Jesus rolled His sleeping mat and lifted the load to His shoulder. Andrew noticed and whispered to his brother. "We must be moving on."

"Yep, looks that way." Peter said while they all rolled up their blankets.

Traveling the Coastal Road, they left the bay at Ptolemais and headed north to the town of Tyre in the Gentile land of Phoenicia—unfamiliar territory for the disciples.

Father, guide My steps as we travel through this land. I desire to accomplish Your will. Jesus communicated daily with His Father.

Jesus again focused on His mission and the disciples

followed, though with slight hesitation.

Peter glanced over his shoulder toward the sea. He sensed an uncomfortable excitement as they left the familiar terrain and traveled to a country that might not welcome Jewish fishermen.

~ 7 ~

Rafa returned home from his five-day caravan trip to Ptolemais. Young Simon was excited to tell his mother about their adventures during the journey.

"Mother, I am ready to travel with Father again. It was a fun trip. I never counted so many animals. The long camel train went on forever." Simon's voice rose higher as he talked faster. "Camels are sure noisy!"

"Now, Simon, I am sure you exaggerate!" Laughing, Diane tousled her son's hair.

"No, I tell the truth, and I drove Shaheem's wagon. Father said I can travel with him again real soon."

Diane glanced at Rafa and he nodded his head in agreement.

After lunch, Diane and one of her kitchen staff, Suzanna, headed for the market. While Suzanna inspected the vegetable section, Diane noticed a group of men she did not recognize. She, the curious type, listened to them converse with one another and concluded they must be Jewish. She made her purchases and hurried home to share the information with her husband.

"Rafa, I noticed Jewish travelers at the market today. Can we invite them to stay with us? I would love to prepare a meal for them."

"What a great suggestion! We do not often experience an

opportunity to meet our distant Jewish neighbors. How many?"

"I saw at least ten or twelve men."

"Simon and I shall walk to the market and invite them to spend the night here."

"I am excited! Too much time has passed since we have entertained Jewish guests. I will tell the staff to prepare the meal."

Rafa located Jesus and His disciples resting under an oak tree in the center of town. Everyone introduced themselves and they all accepted the invitation to supper.

Within the hour, Simon and Rafa returned from the market with over-night guests for the evening meal. The kitchen servants busied themselves making plans for a feast as if for a special holy day. Soon they would learn just how special.

Rafa escorted his guests to the sitting room. "Welcome to our home. We are honored to receive guests from our home country. Come in, take off your sandals and rest. My servants will wash your feet before supper."

Eli, the head servant, brought a stack of towels and three basins of water.

Rafa addressed one of the men who had the poise of a respected leader. "Sir, allow me to wash Your feet."

Jesus nodded. "You may. We traveled long dusty roads this week. God bless you for your kindness."

With the men comfortable and the washing ceremony completed, Rafa and Eli gathered the cleaning supplies and returned them to the kitchen.

Rafa spoke in private to his wife. "Diane, I experienced a most unusual impression as I washed Jesus' feet. This man must be well-known. Why did I dare to even touch Him?"

"Now you have made me curious. After they have eaten,

please introduce me. I would love to meet Him."

The staff prepared a Jewish meal and served the lamb and vegetables as the sun dropped into the sea. While the disciples and Jesus reclined around the table after supper, Rafa slipped out of the room to locate his wife.

"Diane, come and meet our guests, especially one man named Jesus. I noticed one of the men referred to Jesus as the son of David. When I washed His feet, I sensed I attended to royalty. You must come and meet Him."

"Royalty? I am not sure I am dressed for a king." Diane said with raised eyebrows.

"You look beautiful to me. Come, my dear."

Holding hands, Diane and Rafa entered their formal dining room. "Men, I want you to meet my wife, Diane." Each one introduced himself.

Diane held her breath waiting to learn the identity of Jesus. *I see one who looks like a son of a king—so humble but has the proud posture of a leader. Why does He travel to a Gentile country?*

Jesus smiled at Diane. "Thank you for the delicious meal. Please join us for a time of conversation."

As the guests, along with Rafa and young Simon, relaxed on rugs scattered around the room, Diane leaned against the wall. She stood enthralled with their stories—amazing stories that touched her heart. The guests retold story after story of their adventures with Jesus from making superb wine out of plain water to casting demons out of young boys and old men. Jesus talked about loving people, helping the needy, and worshiping God.

Diane pondered every word Jesus spoke. *Am I back in the synagogue hearing the Scriptures read aloud? His words amaze me!*

Five years ago, Diane and her family moved from Cana

in Israel to Tyre. Her husband made the move to increase his caravan business.

She moved in closer and sat on the floor at Jesus' feet. She did not want to miss one word or one story that Jesus shared.

Diane listened to Jesus talk about God's Kingdom. "Our heavenly Father knows your needs. If you live a holy life, He will bless you in His Kingdom. Be generous with your resources. Our Father will reward you if you follow My teachings."

After long days on the trail and a good home-cooked meal, the Jewish guests retired for the evening. Rafa and Diane went to their sleeping room, but Diane could not sleep. Her mind lingered on her friend Azita and her daughter.

First thing in the morning, I shall go to Azita's home and tell her about Jesus and the miracles He performs.

The morning hours slipped away as Diane slept. She did not awake in time to join their guests for the morning meal before they traveled north.

~ 8 ~

Diane, alarmed to see the bright sun so high above the trees, dressed in haste and joined her servants in the kitchen. "Where is Jesus and His men?"

Her cook Ella responded, "They left right after breakfast."

Diane gasped as her hand flew to her mouth. "Where do they plan to go next?"

"They mentioned something about Sidon."

Without delay, Diane left the kitchen and ran out the front door. *I need to talk with Azita as soon as possible!*

She ran all the way to Azita's home and pounded on the door. "Azita, Azita! It is Diane. I must talk to you."

When Azita opened the door, Diane surmised Azita had not slept much the night before as she yawned and rubbed her eyes. "Come in and sit down. Why are you so excited?"

Diane sat on the edge of the couch. "Azita, I have wonderful news! Last night I met Jesus, a Jewish man called the son of King David."

"You mean the ancient king of Israel?"

"Yes, and He heals sick people and casts out demons wherever He goes."

"Oh, I wish He could heal Flora." Azita leaned forward in her chair and laid her hand on Diane's arm.

"He and His disciples left our home about an hour ago."

"Oh, no!" Azita raised her voice in anguish.

"But maybe you can find them. They might have stopped at the market to buy supplies. I heard they will continue north to Sidon."

Azita jumped to her feet. "I shall leave right now. Will you please stay with Flora? She was awake all night but is sleeping now."

"Okay, but you must hurry." Diane pointed to the open door.

"A son of a king! Will He allow me to talk with Him?"

"I never met a more compassionate man. He has more wisdom than King Solomon. He will know what to do for Flora."

Azita, excited but nervous, chose her newest clothes. "I shall wear my prettiest robe, my most expensive perfume, and my new sandals. I have a gold necklace from Ophir that looks proper to wear in the company of royalty."

After Azita quickly changed her clothes, the two friends hugged. Azita ran out the gate and down the road toward town.

Diane entered Flora's bedroom to rest on a cushion. She hoped Flora would stay asleep until her mother returned, but that did not happen. Before noon, Diane sensed a strange, heavy presence in the room. Flora stirred awake, then sat up in bed. Her eyes bulged wide and she pulled hard on her hair as she screamed and cried at the same time. The young girl tore through the house as if chased by wild animals.

Diane had never witnessed one of Flora's attacks and did not know how to respond. Afraid, she guided the child back to her room and closed the curtain. "God, please help Azita find Jesus soon!"

~ ~ ~ ~ ~

When Azita arrived at the market, she paused at the first shop and asked if any Jewish men had shopped there that morning.

"Yes, about a dozen men purchased dried fish and a bag of figs, but they left town." The man pointed north. "They headed that direction."

Azita did not take time to thank him. She spun around and continued running. *If they are walking and I am running, I shall find them soon. O God of Israel, help me find this man Jesus!*

After an hour, Azita slowed down and walked to catch her breath. *I must find water to drink.*

She noticed a large grove of trees in the distance. *There should be water nearby. I hope it is clean water. I am getting dizzy.*

She staggered through the trees, knelt at the creek, and drank handfuls of cool water.

She rested in the shade. *Men's voices!* Azita's heart pounded in her throat. *Have I found Jesus?*

She stood and approached the voices. When she saw a small group of men, her heart almost stopped. They carried their bedrolls and were walking away from the shady area. She had no time to waste.

Azita's weary legs trembled. *Imagine me in the presence of the son of David, the famous king of Israel!* Her beautiful silk robe now hung limp with dust, her sweaty hair stuck like tree pitch to her neck, and the scent of her favorite perfume had evaporated. *Will He allow me to talk with Him? I know I am not worthy.*

Azita whispered His name. "Jesus, Jesus!" *I feel like a stray dog, a pariah. I am not sure if I am brave enough to ask Him for help. But I must for Flora's sake!*

When Azita called His name louder, several of the

disciples looked over their shoulders.

"Jesus, how did that woman recognize You?" Andrew asked.

"Keep walking. Maybe she will go away." Peter voiced his lack of patience.

Jesus paused for a second, then continued walking. *Her precious child is the reason I came to the town of Tyre. I shall never travel this far north again. Thank You, Father, for this opportunity to show Our love to her and her daughter.*

"Mercy! Jesus son of David. Please show mercy!" *I must not give up hope. This is a life or death situation for my daughter.*

Jesus gave the appearance of ignoring her as He continued His pace.

Peter noticed a slight smile on Jesus' face. "Master, tell her to go away. We do not want to deal with crowds today. This is our time of relaxation." Peter, the whiner in the group, tried to take charge.

Azita, running faster than the men walked, overtook them. "Jesus!"

They all stopped and faced her. She recognized the one named Jesus by His expression of compassion. Sobbing, she fell at His feet.

"Jesus, a demon tortures my daughter. She is a small child. Please have mercy on her."

She raised her perspiring face, considered His brown eyes and recognized immense love. Her spirit celebrated with hope.

Jesus saw tears run down her dusty cheeks and recognized faith. His smile broadened, but His voice sounded stern. "My mission brings nourishment to My own people. Their food does not belong to dogs."

Azita, desperate but brave, said, "Jesus, I can sympathize with dogs. I had a stray puppy named Happy. He appreciated all the crumbs and stale bread I fed him because he was starving. We let him eat under our table and he became part of our family."

Jesus' smile changed into a hearty laugh. He reached down and lifted her off her knees. "Dear woman, you gave the perfect answer. Enjoy my blessing! Go home and you will find the demon has left your daughter, never to return."

Azita dropped to her knees again and kissed the feet of the son of David. "Thank you, thank you, my Lord!" Her face beamed through her tears. She stood tall and attempted to push her stringy hair off her face.

"Lord, You could have walked away from me, but You did not. You listened to my cry for help." She bowed again and kissed His feet.

Azita continued, "I am overwhelmed by Your wonderful love and kindness. May I honor You?" Azita removed her gold necklace and held it up to Jesus. "Please accept my gift of gold."

Jesus understood the value of gold. The woman offered something of great worth to herself. Jesus leaned over and accepted her upheld treasure. *This is My second gift of gold from a Gentile – the first when I was a little child. He was a wise man, and this is a wise woman.* Jesus smiled at Azita and hung the shiny necklace around His neck.

Azita stood up one more time to leave as the men walked away. Looking back over her shoulder, she called out, "I shall tell the whole town of Tyre that I met the mighty God of Israel today and He healed my daughter!"

The woman hurried home to celebrate her daughter's healing. Full of joy, she sang loud praises to God on her return trip.

"The God of Israel showed mercy today.
Praise the son of David!
I shall sing His praises every night and day.
Praise the son of David!"

Now Azita understood what Happy experienced when her daughter welcomed the stray puppy with food. The little dog was loved and accepted.

~ 9 ~

"My business trip to Israel was profitable, as usual. I left Jerusalem with a depleted inventory of robes and scarves. Only three clay jars of dyes remain in my wagon," Shaheem said to himself.

He breathed a sigh of satisfaction over the results of his sales. Eager to return home to his wife and family, he joined a caravan traveling north.

Shaheem separated from the caravan on the outskirts of Tyre. He drove his donkey cart up the familiar lane to the top of the bluff. *Besides missing my family and my comfortable bed, I welcome the distinctive smell of the fresh salt air blowing in off the Great Sea.*

He walked through the front door with his promised gift of a purple silk scarf draped over his arm. He was greeted by an unfamiliar woman reclining on the couch. "Where is Azita?" Alarmed, Shaheem raised his voice.

The woman was quick to stand to her feet. "I am Diane. You must be Shaheem."

"I said where is Azita?" Shaheem set his satchel and Azita's gift in the corner and approached the stranger.

"She should return soon. She asked me to watch Flora while she located a Jewish man named Jesus."

"Jesus? His name was mentioned in Capernaum." Puzzled, a frown crossed Shaheem's forehead.

"We met Jesus and His men yesterday. They spent the night in our home. You have business dealings with my husband, Rafa, a caravan driver."

"Oh, yes, I have traveled with him many times." The tension in his voice relaxed. "Now, why are you here?" Shaheem made himself comfortable on the couch.

Excited, Diane talked fast. "I told your wife about miracle healings performed by Jesus. She was desperate to take your daughter to meet Him, but I slept late this morning, and Jesus already left town. Azita wanted Him to heal Flora, so I agreed to stay here in the house while she tried to locate Jesus."

Diane paused to take a breath at the same moment Azita burst through the front door.

"Azita, you look exhausted! Come and sit beside me." Shaheem rose off the couch and greeted her with a hug.

Diane grasped her friend's trembling hands. "Did you find Jesus?"

"Oh, yes! What a marvelous man! He told me Flora is healed!"

"Healed?" Shaheem frowned, unable to grasp her meaning. "How?"

"Jesus just said she was healed. I have been singing praises to the God of Israel all the way home."

Shaheem straightened his posture. "Where is Flora now?"

"Let me tell you," Diane offered. "Azita, after you left, Flora suffered another attack. She screamed out of control, pulled her hair, and ran around the house. Frightened, I guided her to her room and closed the curtain. I did not know what else to do. Now she has been asleep for the last hour or so."

Unable to hold back her excitement any longer, Azita

squirmed, then stood to her feet. "I want to talk with her. Is she still asleep?"

The three of them went to Flora's room and Shaheem opened the curtain with caution.

"Hi, Mother." Flora was sitting on the edge of her mat, twirling her feet. "Father, when did you get home?"

"Just a few minutes ago, my sweet Flora," Shaheem whispered.

Laughing and crying, Azita ran to Flora and hugged her daughter. "Look at me. You are beautiful! How do you feel?"

"Mother, the scary voices in my head are all gone. I am so happy!"

"I believed Jesus when He said you were healed. Oh, Shaheem! Look in her eyes. See how they shine!" Tears streamed down Azita's face.

Diane cried with her. "Another wonderful miracle by Jesus!"

"Mother, my heart is happy inside!"

At that exact moment, a dog barked in the front yard.

"Mother, Happy wants to come in. May I feed him bread?"

"Yes, sweetie, you may feed him all the food he wants."

When Shaheem opened the door, a dog with a spinning tail bounced into the room. Young Omeed stood in the doorway looking dusty and hungry.

Azita saw Omeed from Flora's open curtain and ran to give him a big hug. "Oh, son, I am so glad you came home. I worried every night and day about you."

"Mother, I am sorry I left without telling you. I was scared after Father left." Omeed held his arms out to his mother.

"I am going home," Diane announced with joy. "I am sure you all have much to talk about."

"Bye, Diane. Please come for another visit real soon." Azita embraced Diane as she went out the door. "I want to tell you about my conversation with Jesus."

Shaheem closed the door, put his arms around his family and squeezed them tight. "Now we shall sit in the garden and talk. I believe you all have much to share with me about Jesus and this dog, Happy."

JUANITA TURNER PASLAY

His Ambassador

Ari

Meet a hopeless young man possessed by demons.

Meet his Deliverer.

A story based on Mark 4, 5

~ 1 ~

The children of Gadara feared Ari. When he ventured too close, they shouted at him.

"Go away, crazy kid!"

"Go home!"

Most children ran from him and some taunted him because he talked aloud to himself in a strange voice.

Ari never enjoyed a happy childhood. When children gathered in his village to run races or play games, he watched their fun from a distance.

He wished, *I want to play with the other kids, but they never let me. They think I am crazy.*

In Gadara, boys his age attended reading classes. Ari had to discontinue the lessons when convulsions hindered his concentration.

As a thin child with unkempt hair, he often acted as wild as his hair and ran around in circles screaming. Ari told no one, except his mother, about his fears.

"Mother, voices in my head shout at me all day, even at night when I try to sleep. Sometimes I am so scared I hide my head under my pillow."

"Son, I will talk with your father. I am sure he can chase away the noise." *I feel so helpless!*

Ari was afraid of himself. *The shrill voices in my head frighten me. I know my father loves me, but I wish he would help me.*

Ari's parents, Agatha and Damien, worshiped the Greek goddess Artemis. They took him to the Greek temple to pay the priest to cure their son, but there was no improvement.

"Father, please do not take me to the temple anymore. When I go, the voices in my mind grow louder causing my head to throb even harder."

His father loved him very much, but soon found that neither he nor his wife could change Ari's mental situation. When Ari was not within hearing distance, his parents discussed the seriousness of their son's condition.

Agatha whispered, "Damien, I know something is terribly wrong with Ari. He scares me when I am alone with him. His screams will drive me insane if he does not stop. What can we do with him?"

Damien shared his worries with his wife. "I believe our son is beyond help. We have tried everything, but he only gets worse. Sometimes when Ari is so violent, I think he has a demon living in him. I am afraid of the boy myself."

As Ari grew older, his condition worsened. His parents tried to keep their uncontrollable son in the house away from the neighbors, but that plan proved impossible to maintain.

Damien made a major decision.

"Agatha, the time has come for me to talk with our town elders. I do not see what more we can do with Ari."

Damien met with the leaders and everyone agreed Ari must stay confined with shackles to prevent him from hurting anyone. Scared, Ari broke the chains with his unusual strength. Ari's mental condition continued to deteriorate.

"Agatha, we need to take drastic measures."

"It hurts me to agree, but we must."

Damien said, "We will make plans to take Ari to an old cemetery by the cliffs of the Sea of Galilee's eastern bank. It is only about fifteen miles from Gadara."

"You will need several strong men to help you transport Ari." Agatha wiped away her tears.

Damien, his two friends, and the demon-possessed young man left Gadara before sunrise in a wagon pulled by Damien's donkey. Ari uttered violent screams every hour and broke away four times, making the long journey difficult for everyone.

In desperation, one of the men hit the young madman on the head with a board, putting him in a semiconscious state. Then, Ari stayed in the wagon until they arrived at the tombs.

"I gave Ari a basket of bread and dried fish. We must leave before my son becomes aware that we chained him to the wall of this tomb," the father whispered.

Damien returned home after dark, put the donkey in the shed, and went inside his house.

Agatha needed to talk. "Tell me about your trip. Is Ari okay?"

"I am too exhausted to talk now. I need to go to bed. All the details must wait until morning." He turned and left the room.

Sleep evaded Agatha as she imagined her son isolated in a cold, damp cave. When she drifted off to sleep a few hours before daybreak, scenes of guilt dominated her dreams.

The following day dawned with fierce winds and black clouds. Agatha's spirit weighed heavy with depression. Before Damien left for his carpenter shop, she begged him to talk about Ari.

"Agatha, we must not feel guilty that we moved him to the cemetery. Remember, we both believe there is no hope for Ari. How many times did we take him to our temple priests and even to witch doctors? Once, I took him in secret to see the Jewish rabbi. We must forget him, even if he is our only child."

"But how can I forget him? I love him so much."

She remembered their tender mother-son relationship that had deteriorated to only brief conversations. As a teenager, Ari told her about his tormenting dreams. Now as a young man, he communicated with no one, not even her.

With Ari away from her watchful eye, Agatha continued to worry about him. She asked herself, "Will Ari stay warm on these cold nights? Where can he find food to eat? How long will my son live?"

~ 2 ~

As the fog in Ari's mind cleared, he remembered part of the trip to the tombs but not the final hours. Cold darkness had descended on the cemetery.

Ari asked himself, "What is that rancid smell? This must be the place of the dead. I am so weary of trying to live a normal life, I wish I were dead."

When dawn arrived with fierce winds and a heavy downpour, Ari discovered his precarious situation—staked to the wall of a tomb. Two hours passed before he broke free of the heavy chains. His efforts caused his ankles and wrists to swell and bleed as he used the rough links to grind against the shackles.

Ari climbed the hills around the cemetery in search of wild berries to eat. He added them to the fresh bread and fish left for him in the cave.

I know this is my mother's woven basket. Mother, thank you for the food.

Ari experienced a strange consolation in the cemetery as if he belonged there.

This dreadful place for the dead gives me the feeling of the perfect place for torment. Now, when my screaming attacks come, no one restrains me. But there is no one here to offer sympathy either.

Ari now became more afraid of the countless voices

screaming in his head.

Why did my own family desert me? I am all alone and rejected now.

With the bread and dried fish from home gone weeks ago, food was scarce. Dead fish that washed ashore became his next meal. Sometimes hunger overwhelmed him.

"As I watch the sea from my cave on the hill, I have a sense of contentment," Ari said aloud.

When the young man noticed a sailboat or fishing boat in the distance, his eyes followed the craft as it sailed out of sight. *I wish I would disappear.*

Greeks lived in the vicinity around his hometown of Gadara. They raised swine, unlike Jews who raised sheep and goats. Their herds grazed on the hill near the tombs. Occasionally, a hog separated itself from the others and Ari tried to approach the animal, but he soon discovered even strays wanted nothing to do with him. The pig squealed and disappeared into the brush.

I am sure everyone talks about me—the crazy, naked man of the tombs.

He endured isolation except when devious teenagers came to harass him.

They shouted at Ari, "Devil-man! Devil-man!"

When they ventured too close, Ari screamed and ran after them.

I do not want to chase them, but something forces me.

On certain days after sunset, a compassionate person placed a basket of food near the cemetery. Days when he was in his right mind, he wanted to thank them for their thoughtfulness, but Ari never saw them.

Did my mother bring me food today?

~ ~ ~ ~ ~

One night in late autumn, a fierce storm developed on the Sea of Galilee. High winds arrived on shore about midnight with flashes of lightning and loud, crashing thunder. Storms invite an audience to participate. Ari awoke with the sound of waves crashing onto the rocks below.

Ari experienced fear. *I feel the rumble vibrate in my chest and hear the winds howl through the rocks. What keeps me from sleeping? Is it the fierce storm on the lake or the violent storm in my head?*

That night, screaming voices in his mind generated more fear than usual.

This might be my last day in the tombs, and even on earth.

Part of him wanted to end that nightmare any way possible. But, in his heart, a faint spark of hope ignited.

An unforgettable experience awaited Ari.

~ 3 ~

"Jesus, I have never seen so many people come to hear You. People have arrived by the hundreds." Peter raised his voice and shook his head in amazement.

The white clouds reflected on the calm Sea of Galilee—a perfect day for a walk to the lake. People from villages around Capernaum followed Jesus and His disciples down to the shoreline.

While the crowds walked around to find an unobstructed view of Jesus, one man pushed his way to the front. He carried a young girl in his arms.

"Master, I know you can heal every disease. My daughter cannot see. Please have mercy on her," he pleaded.

Jesus placed his hand over her eyes. "I love to show mercy." He whispered in her ear, "Sweet child, open your eyes!"

The girl giggled and opened her eyes. "Daddy, I can see you! I can see everyone. I can see Jesus. Thank you, Jesus!"

The man put her down on the sand. The young child raised her arms to Jesus and gave Him a big hug around His legs. Jesus leaned down and squeezed her. She hugged Him again, crying with happiness. The people clapped their hands and raised their voices to praise God for the miracle.

Jesus walked among the people for several hours, touching and healing the lame and the sick. He healed everyone who asked, and everyone wanted His attention.

As more people gathered closer, John whispered to Jesus. "Master, if You stood in my fishing boat docked at the pier, the people would not crowd around You." John was always concerned for Jesus' safety.

"Clever idea. My voice will carry on the waters and everyone will be able to hear me." Jesus gave John a shoulder hug.

All twelve apostles climbed into the boat with Jesus. It was large enough for them to rest and stretch their legs from their walk to the lake.

As Jesus stood in the boat, everyone on shore stopped talking and turned their attention to Jesus. They had walked many miles that day to hear the famous Teacher and did not want to miss a single word.

"When you use a candle to illuminate a room, do you place it under a bed? No, you put it on a stand where everyone can see it glow. Everything hidden now will be seen in time. Pay attention to what I say, and you will understand its meaning. If you do not listen, you will learn nothing."

Someone in the crowd shouted, "Tell us more about the Kingdom of God." Others echoed the same request.

"The Kingdom of God is among you now. It is beginning small and will continue to grow and expand like yeast in a bowl of flour when a woman makes bread for her family.

"There is much to learn about the Kingdom." Jesus paused as the crowd became quiet again. "It is like a pearl merchant who looks to buy the largest, most beautiful pearl. When he finds one, he will sell everything he owns to buy that one special pearl.

"The Kingdom of God is also like a treasure. When a man finds a treasure in a deserted field, he will cover the prized possession, and go into the city to purchase the land. Then he will become the owner of the hidden treasure. Living in the Kingdom must be your greatest desire."

Jesus spoke several hours describing the Kingdom as a pastureland sown with good and bad seed, a fishing net that gathers both righteous and evil people, and a small mustard seed that grows into a large plant that shelters and protects the nations.

He encouraged people to open their hearts to what He said. "Do not be like the unbelievers. Some people worry about what they will eat or drink or what they will wear. Our Father knows all our needs.

"Do not worry or fret about your finances. Store your treasures in heaven. If you confess your sins and forsake them, you will receive mercy from our Heavenly Father and live in His Kingdom."

As the sun set behind the hills and painted a reddish glow in the horizon, the people folded their blankets and began their long journey home. When the disciples were alone, Jesus reminded them what Isaiah said more than seven hundred years ago.

"Isaiah prophesied that these people will hear My words but will not understand because their hearts are hard. You have been permitted to understand the secrets of the kingdom, though you have much more to learn when the time is right." Jesus paused and looked at each one in the boat as He spoke.

John, on the verge of asking a question, wanted to know more but held his question.

"We must pull up anchor now and head to the other side of the lake. Someone waits for Me there."

Once again, John wanted to ask for an explanation but did not want to appear ignorant in front of the other disciples.

"Matthew, you and John pick up the oars and row. I will distribute bread and dried fish for our evening meal," Peter said.

Jesus moved to the stern of the boat to rest. Soon the disciples listened to Jesus snoring as He rested His head on a comfortable but old tattered cushion. Jesus missed supper.

When the men approached the middle of the lake, they secured the oars to enjoy the cool breeze and the bright moonlight on the water. Within an hour, all the disciples fell asleep.

Sometime just after daybreak, a strong wind arose, and black clouds hid the moon from view. The change in the weather and the pitching and rolling of the boat woke John and Peter. The sudden storm made them uneasy.

"John, do you think we should head back to Capernaum? I know the dangers of an unexpected storm on the lake from past experiences."

"No, Jesus said He wanted to cross over to the other side of the lake. We will wait out the storm." As soon as John made that decision, he regretted it.

The wind increased to a gale. The waves intensified and washed across the boat. A severe storm had developed. Thunder cracked and lightning flashed in the distance. John was concerned for their safety.

"Peter, you must wake Jesus and the other men. I think we are in trouble, *big* trouble!" John raised his voice over the roar of the wind.

Peter shook Jesus awake, causing the pillow to fall to the bottom of the flooded boat. "Jesus, Jesus! Wake up! Do something before we drown. The boat is filling with water."

Jesus sat up and said, "I rebuke the wind and command the waves to subside!"

The sound of the storm changed from loud violence to peace and calm in an instant. The Sea of Galilee once again became smooth and quiet in the early morning hour. The sky cleared as the sun appeared and a beautiful double rainbow overhead reflected on the water.

"Why were you afraid? Where is your faith?" Jesus looked into Peter's eyes. The fisherman had no answer.

Father, my disciples have so much to learn. Open their eyes.

Jesus looked at John and grinned. "Do you think My Father sent me here to drown? You still do not know who I Am."

First John, then the other apostles dropped to their knees in the water-filled boat and looked at Jesus in amazement.

James turned to John and whispered, "Even the waves obey Jesus. Do we know who our Teacher *really* is?"

John shrugged his shoulders. "God listens to Him. Could He be God Himself? Only God can calm a storm in a second."

"Man the oars! Jesus said He has an appointment on the eastern shore." Andrew took charge after Jesus stopped the storm.

Andrew gave Peter the extra bucket. "Bail water!

~ 4 ~

What a terrible night! I hardly slept because of that fierce storm. Why am I screaming? I cannot control my shrieks.

Violent voices in Ari's head shouted at one another and he yelled back at them with his weak, frail voice. In that early morning hour, an unknown force made the demon-possessed man fall continually on the sharp rocks and caused his thin arms and legs to bleed.

After that last attack, I am exhausted. I can barely breathe.

The rising sun warmed his back as he rested on the grassy bluff overlooking the Sea of Galilee. He tried to quiet his dazed mind as he regained his strength.

What a beautiful rainbow!

The sea was now calm and peaceful.

I see a large fishing boat coming toward the pier. Now they are docking and about a dozen men are climbing ashore. Why they are here?

One fisherman captivated his attention. Ari's eyes fixated on Him and noticed how He walked with definite purpose and energy in every step. Ari's heart raced with anticipation as the man's deep, contagious laughter floated uphill toward him. Ari engaged what little strength he possessed and descended the hill to the rocky beach and fell at Jesus' feet.

I have neither worshiped a statue nor another man. I cannot understand why I am kneeling before this stranger.

Instantly, the young man perceived his heart-stopping fear that bound him for years had disappeared.

I feel so safe. I shall never leave this man!

Horrific screams from deep within him sounded again. The serene stranger grasped Ari's hands, lifted him to his feet, and focused on him with immense compassion. No one, not even his mother, captured his attention with such amazing love in their eyes.

Jesus spoke with His usual authority. "Evil spirit, come out of this man! I demand you to come out, now!"

Loud, ungodly voices echoed out through Ari's mouth. "Why have You come to these tombs? We know who You are. You are Jesus, the Holy Son of Almighty God!"

Everyone on shore, except Jesus, backed off and kept their distance from the naked man. The frightening, shrill voices created heavy tension in the air. Every man, including Ari, held their breath, not knowing what to expect next.

Calm and unafraid, Jesus addressed the demon. He demanded, "What is your name?"

"My name is Legion. Many of us live in this man. Is it time for our judgment?"

"We beg You, do not torture us yet!" The next voice sounded pathetic.

Another scary voice shrieked, "Do not send us back to our dreadful world, that hellish abyss!"

"May we go into that herd of swine above the tombs?" Another demon begged.

Jesus looked over at the pigs and allowed all the demon spirits to go where they requested. The frantic herd ran in circles with their curled pigtails unwinding, then chased and attacked each other. In a matter of seconds, the pigs ran squealing and kicking off the cliff and drowned in the sea below.

Ari dropped to his knees and looked up at Jesus. "Those wicked demons called you Jesus. Is that your real name?"

"Yes, you may call me Jesus." His Deliverer smiled.

"You have changed my life! I have no way to thank you, but to say, 'thank you'. What more can I do?"

"Worship God. He is your heavenly Father who loves you."

Peter squatted in front of Ari. "I have an extra robe on the boat. I shall run and get it for you."

Tears filled Ari's eyes as one of the fishermen removed his sandals and gave them to the young barefoot man delivered from demons.

Another disciple came running back from the boat. "My name is Andrew. Please accept this bread and dried fish. I know you must be hungry."

"I have never experienced such love and kindness from strangers. Jesus, you all must be filled with God."

Herdsmen on the hillside, unaware what happened to Ari on the beach, saw their swine chase each other into the sea. Afraid, they ran to town and told everyone about the devastating incident. Hundreds of people came to look for the hogs. Not one animal survived.

The townspeople walked into an unforgettable scene. Ari, the infamous crazy man, sat clothed and in his right mind at the feet of a stranger.

The crowd had neither met Jesus nor His disciples, and the whole situation terrified them. They asked questions among themselves.

"Why did the swine run off the cliff?"

"What magical power did He use on the man from the tombs?"

They saw their profitable swine business destroyed. An older man demanded that Jesus and His friends leave their country.

The angry crowd agreed. “Leave at once! Whoever You are, You are not welcome here.”

A moment ago, the unexplainable happened. They feared what the man named Jesus might do next.

Jesus addressed His disciples. “I have completed my mission here. Now, we return to Capernaum.”

His disciples untied the rope from the pier and got into their boat.

Ari ran after the fishermen and shouted, “Jesus, wait for me. I must go with You.”

“Ari, you have a special mission now. I send you as My ambassador to the towns on this side of the Sea of Galilee. Tell everyone about your healing. Declare how Almighty God showed mercy on you today.”

Instead of leaving with them, Ari stood on the shore and waved farewell to Jesus and his new friends as they sailed back across the sea. The young man ran along the beach laughing, singing, and clapping his hands. Jesus replaced Ari’s fear, his violent headaches, and the screaming voices with joy, joy, and more joy!

Ari shouted to everyone on the beach, “This is the best day of my life. I am a new person! I am going home!”

~ 5 ~

Jesus gave Ari a mission to accomplish as His ambassador and he began without delay.

First, I will go to Gadara to tell my parents what Jesus did for me.

The young man glanced over his shoulder at that dreadful cemetery one last time and remembered again the amazing look of compassion on the face of Jesus.

As Ari tucked his new robe in around his leather belt and set out for home, comforting thoughts of Almighty God filled his soul.

My heart is about to burst with thanksgiving. I cannot help but sing to God.

He worshiped as loud as he could.

"Almighty God,
You are so good to me!
Almighty God,
I shall always praise You!"

Ari experienced such amazing strength and energy that he wanted to run all the way home to Gadara. He made excellent time traveling and arrived in town early the following morning.

Shopkeepers had opened their booths in the

marketplace to begin their day of buying and selling.

Oh, how I love that aroma of fresh baked bread and smoked fish.

The exotic scents of cinnamon, anise, and coriander blended with the local herbs. Mixtures of fragrances and sounds of the market brought back many memories to Ari.

"Praise God, I am home at last!" Ari shouted.

Jason the weaver recognized Ari and whispered to his partner Jerome. "Is that Damien's crazy son? What is he doing in town?"

"That is him all right. You better warn his parents."

News of Ari's arrival reached Damien and Agatha in record time. Someone pounded on the door as Agatha washed her vegetables and prepared their noon meal. She opened it to see Jason gasping for breath.

"Agatha, your son has returned! You must tell your husband. Hurry!"

"He cannot be back. Are you sure it is him?"

"Oh, yes! But he does not look like the same person."

She ran to Damien's carpenter shop located behind their house.

"Damien, Damien! You will not believe what Jason told me. Ari is back. What shall we do?"

"Now calm down, Agatha! I shall take care of this."

They both ran the short distance to the market and found Jason's story correct. Their son Ari was talking with the merchants. When Ari saw his parents, he held out his arms. Damien and Agatha hesitated at first, but in a matter of seconds, the three of them hugged and danced in circles, singing.

"I have returned!"

"Our son has returned!"

Both his parents spoke at once. "Son, tell us what

happened. You look and act so different. So calm!"

The people of Gadara, including the children, assembled in the town square and listened to Ari describe everything Jesus said and did. He told how compassionate men from the boat gave him food and clothing. The report of two thousand swine running off the cliff into the sea fascinated the children.

Agatha, Damien, and their son Ari enjoyed an amazing day of unexpected celebration and reunion. Agatha was thrilled to serve a family feast at her table.

With mixed feelings, Ari said farewell to his parents the next day.

"I shall return when I complete my God-given mission to visit all the towns and villages in the Decapolis region. I have wonderful news to share with our people."

~ ~ ~ ~ ~

With a rejoicing spirit, Ari told everyone willing to listen about the incredible gift of peace Jesus gave him.

"For years, I endured the horror of being controlled by demons. Jesus, the Son of God, rescued me from a living nightmare and transformed my life."

The incredible story about a man from Gadara delivered from evil spirits preceded him as he traveled to tell of God's mercy. Everyone looked forward to hearing the story directly from him.

Other demons tried to harass and prevent Ari from sharing his story of victory, but no demon from hell possessed enough power to keep Ari from giving glory to God. People, young and old controlled by evil spirits, listened to his amazing story. Using the name of Jesus, he told evil spirits where to go. Many demon-possessed people received deliverance from their tormentors.

Ari said to the people, "I am thrilled to tell my story of amazing love and mercy everywhere Jesus sends me."

Everyone acknowledged Ari's healing as a special gift from God. The man, once controlled by demons but now healed, remained faithful to proclaim his message of healing.

"The promised Deliverer has come!"

Juanita Turner Paslay

A Young Widow

Sarah

Her world turns upside down.

Jesus turns her life right side up.

A story based on Luke 5, 7

~ 1 ~

"Nathan is older than my father. Is he too old for me?"

"Well . . ." Lila paused. "I would not want to marry him. But, remember Sarah, I do not want to marry anyone."

"Lila, your parents will find your perfect man sooner than you expect."

"I am too old to marry now."

"Remember, not every girl is as young as I when my marriage was arranged." Sarah said.

"Well, I still feel old." Lila frowned.

"My friend, you always encourage me. Now let me remind you that God has a plan for your life, just as He does for mine. So, we will trust God together for His blessings on our lives. That is what friends do."

"Oh, I love you, Sarah!" Lila laughed. "But I am serious now. Tell me, do you believe Nathan will make you a good husband?"

"I hope so." Sarah paused. "But I know so little about him. As a traveling merchant residing in Nazareth, he has not spent much time with me nor my family here in Nain. However, Father assures me that Nathan maintains a successful business. He sells rugs at local markets as he travels to towns in Galilee and Judea. He should be a good provider."

Lila covered her face with her long sleeve. "Your

marriage has a mysterious air of an unknown adventure!" Since childhood, Lila loved to tease her best friend.

Sarah smiled at Lila's comment, but an unwelcome frown clouded her heart as she acknowledged to herself how little she knew about Nathan—a man more than twice her age. His first wife died five years ago and left no children.

"Will you come to my wedding in Nazareth?" She pleaded, "You must."

"Sarah, you know I will be there. Nain is only ten miles from Nazareth. We will always be best friends wherever you live, so stop worrying."

"I will miss you so much after I move. Promise you will come to visit me." Sarah could not hide her concern as her eyes filled.

The two friends reclined near the creek that flowed south into the Jordan River. The grassy meadow along the bank was a special place to discuss life and all its challenges. They rode donkeys less than a mile from their hometown of Nain to reach their destination. The donkeys grazed among the tall grasses and cattails while Lila and Sarah reclined in the warm sun on their blankets.

"I brought a loaf of Mother's fresh bread for our treat today." Lila tore the warm loaf apart and passed the sweet, crushed grapes to Sarah.

"Thanks. I love your Mother's grape jam!"

Lila frowned as she confessed, "My mother tries to teach me the importance of kneading bread the correct way, but handling flour is so boring. When I am finished, white covers everything. The flour dust in the air makes me sneeze so loud I scare the pigeons."

Sarah laughed as she drenched her share in the purple fruit. "Eventually, I learned the knack. So, do not despair, Lila. My mother said that every good wife must learn to make bread."

"Your wedding happens next month, so you *had* to learn. I do not plan to get married—ever!" Lila was emphatic as she tossed her long hair over her shoulder.

~ ~ ~ ~ ~

The wedding ceremony of Sarah and Nathan took place in Nazareth. Everyone wished the couple happiness and enjoyed the wine and fruits served during the three-day celebration in Nathan's impressive courtyard. Beautiful flowers with a sweet scent filled the air. Talented musicians arrived mid-day and played every hour until sunset.

After the wedding feast, Sarah spoke with her best friend. "Lila, I am so glad you came. My parents said they enjoyed your company on their trip from Nain."

"You are a beautiful bride! Nothing could keep me away from my friend's wedding, remember? Your parents were a delight as we traveled together. I love your father's humor. He loves to tease me. Your mother said that she was so proud of you designing your own gown."

"Two things I have learned to make. Bread and my clothes." Sarah grinned. "My mother has given me hours of training."

"I am so glad I came." Lila whispered and pointed toward a shady area. "We can sit on the bench under that olive tree. Later, you must give me a tour of your new home."

"My mother taught me the advice King Lemuel's mother taught him." Sarah held both of Lila's hands in hers and spoke in a serious tone. "I want to become the wife and mother she described, the perfect woman—kind and thoughtful to family and neighbors, full of wisdom, an excellent cook, and a successful businesswoman. Her children adored her, and her husband showed pride in her. I asked God to help me follow her example."

"Oh, Sarah! What a beautiful desire. I am sure you will be the best wife and mother in Nazareth."

Sarah would need strong faith in God to endure the tragic events in the coming years.

~ 2 ~

Summer arrived and the purple crocus bloomed in abundance. Sarah wore a slight frown despite the warm sun and gentle breeze that waved the palm branches in her yard.

Two soft knocks sounded at Sarah's front door. Her frown changed to a smile when she opened the door to her best friend with a large bouquet of fresh field lilies.

"Lila, I am so happy to see you. Please come in." Sarah greeted her with a big hug.

"Please forgive me for not coming sooner. I was helping Mother take care of my sick brother, but he is healthy now."

"I am glad Joseph recovered. Oh, I love these flowers. What a beautiful gift! And so special for my announcement. I must tell you that I am expecting a child this winter."

"A baby?" Lila exclaimed. "Have you told your parents yet?"

"No, you are the first person I told. I have not seen my parents for several months."

Sarah stood up to place the flowers in her prettiest clay vase and admired them. "You remembered lilies were my favorite. Come and sit with me in the garden. You must tell me all the gossip of Nain. I miss our long talks together."

They held hands and headed for the courtyard.

"I miss sharing with you, too. Are you busy with wifely duties?" Lila's hand covered her mouth as she giggled.

"No, Nathan travels more than he lives at home."

"I was not aware he traveled so much."

"When the baby comes, I will enjoy more responsibilities to occupy my time. I am so excited God has answered my prayers for a child. God is so good to me. Last Sabbath, our ruler of the synagogue read the writings of David. I memorized his words. 'Take delight in the LORD and He will give you the desires of your heart.' I asked God for a son."

"I am sure He will give you a son that will make both you and Nathan proud."

"I committed all my talent to the LORD. I trust God for a happy life, but, between you and me, there is little joy in my marriage to Nathan. When he returns from his business trips, he treats me like a slave, always demanding constant attention until I am exhausted. He plans large banquets for his friends and requires that I prepare all the food by myself. He never shows me kindness. I am more content when he is gone, but please do not tell my parents. I do not want to burden them with my problems."

Lila placed her hand over her heart. "I promise." A tear escaped Lila's eye.

"You are a good friend." Sarah reached for Lila's hand and brought her close for another hug.

~ ~ ~ ~ ~

The blessed day came when baby Aaron arrived as a healthy, happy child.

"Mother, I appreciate you traveling here to help me deliver my baby."

"Oh, that is the privilege of a grandma. I am pleased to show you the ways of a nursing mother," said Adina. "I know you will be an excellent mother."

"I am afraid I will not receive much help from Nathan. He is so involved with his rug business."

"Sarah, I am sure Nathan will be an attentive father. Remember, your father and I love you both. We wish the best for Nathan's business." Adina hugged her daughter.

~ ~ ~ ~ ~

Sarah traveled to her hometown of Nain to celebrate Aaron's tenth birthday with her parents while Nathan was away on a business trip. After the party with friends and family, Sarah and Aaron returned to their home in Nazareth to await Nathan's arrival.

"Four weeks have passed, and your Father has not come home as I expected."

"Do not worry, Mother. I am sure Father will return soon."

"I am trying not to worry, son."

The next day, Lila arrived for an unexpected visit. Sarah shared her concern about her husband's long absence.

"Lila, when you return to Nain, please talk to my father. Tell him Nathan has been gone a long time. I am worried! I do not want to leave town to tell my parents because I must be home when Nathan returns."

"Oh, Sarah, now I am worried, too! I shall tell your family as soon as I get home. Remember your vow to trust God. He promised to always help us."

"Lila, thanks for your encouragement. Aaron and I have prayed for Nathan's safe return."

They hugged and shed tears together. Early the following day, Lila joined a group of travelers and left Nazareth on her donkey and returned to Nain.

~ ~ ~ ~ ~

The setting sun painted the sky with hues of gold and orange. Sarah, weary with concern for Nathan, retired early and missed the beautiful sunset. Before she fell asleep, a loud knock sounded at her door. She hurried to wrap her night robe around her.

"Sarah! Open the door." She recognized her father's voice.

She was quick to unbolt the door. "Father, what is wrong? I am surprised to see you so late tonight. Come and sit on the couch with me."

"I came as soon as I received the news."

"What news? Is Mother sick?"

"She is fine. Is Aaron asleep? I want to talk with both of you."

Aaron entered the hallway rubbing his eyes. "Hi, Grandpa Reuven. Did Grandma come, too?"

"No, Grandma stayed home. Aaron, come sit with us on the couch."

Reuven held out his arms to the child as he ran to embrace his grandfather. Reuven gathered his daughter and grandson in his arms and brought them close to his chest.

"Sarah and Aaron, I bring heartbreaking news. The authorities discovered thieves attacked and robbed a caravan last week near the foothills of Chorazin. Nathan was one of the merchants killed. I am so sorry, my dears."

The young mother slid out of her father's arms and dropped to the floor in shock. The three of them cried together until they drained all their tears.

"Father, what shall I do? I do not want to stay in this house alone. May I come home?"

"Of course. Your mother and I shall be blessed if you and

Aaron would live with us. You may stay as long as you want." Reuven embraced his daughter and grandson again.

~ ~ ~ ~ ~

The authorities brought Nathan's body to Nazareth for burial. Many of the townspeople attended the long procession out of town to the cemetery. Young Aaron held his mother's hand in a firm grip as they walked behind the bier. Sarah's parents walked beside them with their arms entwined around the young family.

After Nathan's funeral, Reuven and Adina helped Sarah load their household furnishings and personal belongings into two large carts and brought Sarah and Aaron home to live with them. Her friend Lila waited at Reuven's house to welcome Sarah back to Nain.

Lila dashed outside as soon as she saw the family approach the front gate. "Sarah, I am so sorry you lost your husband. God has not deserted you. He promised not to!

"Oh, Lila you are a devoted friend. What would I do without you?" Sarah embraced her friend as salty tears flowed down their cheeks.

Sarah's mind held unanswered questions. *Will my years always be filled with sadness? Does God see my pain?*

~ 3 ~

"My father wants to arrange another marriage for me."

"And . . .?" Lila poured them a fresh cup of water and waited for a response from Sarah.

They relaxed with their feet in the water and splashed each other. Young Aaron played and swam in the shallow creek. As usual, the young women's discussion switched to a serious topic.

"I explained I am content without a husband. Raising Aaron brings me such joy and my parents adore him. We feel welcome in their home and we get along so well together."

"So, you do not want another husband?"

"It took time to convince my father I did not want the stress of another husband, but he finally conceded."

Sarah and Lila continued to enjoy their close friendship after Sarah moved back to Nain. They returned often to their pleasant habit of long conversations in the meadow near the creek.

"Lila, I see a sparkle in your eyes today. Are you keeping a secret from me?"

Lila giggled.

"Okay, tell me everything." Sarah gave Lila a friendly nudge in the ribs.

"Oh, someone placed a bouquet of red flowers on my window ledge yesterday."

"Flowers? Lila has an admirer. Lila has an admirer!"

"My friend, you better keep this to yourself."

Now it was Sarah's turn to giggle. "What has God planned for *you*?"

They remained silent on the return trip, absorbed in their thoughts. When they approached their neighborhood, Lila remembered an important question she had.

"Sarah, are you aware of a healer from Galilee?"

"No, who is he?"

"His name is Jesus. My father says He teaches about the kingdom of God and heals sick people. Some people say Jesus is the Son of God."

"He sounds amazing! I would love to meet Jesus and listen to His teaching." Sarah nodded.

"That would be an exciting experience, for sure. We will plan to hear Him together."

"Do you think Jesus will come to our small town?" Sarah asked.

"I believe He will."

~ ~ ~ ~ ~

A severe winter storm arrived early that year. Record-breaking temperatures brought snow and ice to the hills. Sleet blew across the valley for days. A strange sickness spread throughout the village of Nain. People said the illness arrived on the fierce wind. The affliction showed no mercy on the elderly. Both Sarah's parents succumbed to the sickness on the same day. Adina died first, then Reuven.

Lila was the first person to visit Sarah. When Sarah opened the front door, she almost collapsed in Lila's arms.

"Thanks for coming, my friend. My heart is broken! I do not know what to do first."

"My parents will be here soon to make the burial arrangements. Leave everything to them."

"I must sit down before I fall. I know God promised to care for the orphans and widows. That is me in both circumstances now."

Lila sat beside her friend on the couch. "I know you are feeling deserted, but you must determine to remain strong for Aaron's sake."

After his grandparents died, Aaron, one of the few young people to contact the illness, became extremely sick. Delirious and refusing to eat food or drink water, he stayed in bed with a high fever. Most children recovered within a week but not Aaron.

Sarah stayed by his bedside, cooling him with wet towels. Lila came to their home often and sat with Sarah. Holding hands, they hoped and prayed for Aaron's recovery.

"Sarah, your father named you after Abraham's wife. Your name means princess and that is what you are to God," Lila reminded her. "He blessed Sarah with a child, and He will bless you and Aaron also. God has a good life planned for you."

"I believe that, too." Sarah was desperate to agree with her friend. "I am trusting Aaron will be better tomorrow."

Young Aaron did not recover. He died the following morning in his mother's arms.

~ 4 ~

All Jesus' followers enjoyed spending time with Jesus and loved to hear Him teach about the Kingdom of God. The group laughed and talked as they drew near the village of Nain.

"I am shocked Jesus healed that Gentile's servant. He is *our* promised Messiah, not theirs." Peter complained to his brother Andrew.

"Peter, why do you talk that way? Jesus cares about everyone. The Roman officer showed faith in Him and was desperate for help."

Andrew and Peter walked a short distance behind Jesus and the other disciples. At that moment, Jesus stopped and looked over His shoulder at Peter. Their eyes met for a moment, then Jesus resumed His pace.

Peter whispered, "Do you think He heard what I said?"

"Maybe not, but I am sure He knows what we think. Remember when the Pharisees were upset after Jesus forgave the sins of that paralyzed man?" Andrew reflected, "In their minds, they accused Him of blasphemy. Jesus read their thoughts. He explained to them that He possessed power both to heal the cripple and forgive his sins. Neither action presented a challenge for Jesus."

Peter exhaled, then said, "I agree. He read their minds more than once and told them so."

He left Andrew and slowed his pace to mingle with the

noisy crowd that followed Jesus. *Hopefully, Jesus will not know what I am thinking if He cannot see me. There is so much about Him I do not understand.*

As Jesus and His followers came in sight of the city gate, a solemn funeral procession made its way out of town. In respect for the dead, they hushed their conversations as the funeral crowd approached them. The disciples stepped aside to allow the mourners to pass.

Jesus came face to face with Sarah behind her son's bier. *I understand why tears blind her red, swollen eyes. I read her breaking heart and know her tragic story.*

He stepped forward out of the crowd to walk beside Sarah, then touched her arm.

This woman needs her son. Death shall not keep him now! "Dry your eyes, Sarah. Trust Me," Jesus said.

The chilly air blew against Sarah's face and whipped at her robe. She was cold, but His expression of love warmed her whole body.

Sarah thought to herself, *Oh, how I need His comfort. How does He know my name? I do not recognize Him.*

The procession stopped as Jesus walked over to the bier. He laid both hands on Aaron's cold body.

"Young man, sit up! Your mother needs you."

After Jesus spoke to the boy, Peter whispered to his brother. "Are we expecting a storm? I think thunder rolled over those southern hills."

"I did not hear thunder, but Jesus spoke to that dead boy on the bier. Look, he is sitting up!" Andrew whispered.

"Another miracle!" Peter said as he slapped his brother on the back.

Aaron opened his eyes. Jesus grinned at him. The boy slid off the wicker frame and shouted, "Mother, Mother!

Holding hands, Jesus and Aaron went to Sarah who now

sat collapsed on the ground, laughing and weeping. She held her arms out to Aaron.

Lila ran forward to join the circle of celebration. "Sarah, I always believed in God's promise to show you His love. But not in *this* way!" Together they shed tears of happiness.

The disciples mingled with the crowd who now were rejoicing instead of mourning. One of them referred to the healer's name as Jesus.

Lila leaned over and whispered to Sarah still on the ground. "He is Jesus, that prophet I told you about!"

Sarah lifted her eyes to Jesus still standing over her. "Praise the holy name of God! Jesus, You have given me reason to live again." Sarah kissed His feet as her tears mingled with the dust on His sandals.

Jesus put His arms around the boy in a big hug and whispered something in his ear that made Aaron laugh. Then the boy gave his mother another hug.

After several minutes, Jesus stepped back and addressed the crowd. "I have come down from heaven to do the will of My Father God who sent Me. Follow me and I will lead you away from the darkness of sin, for I am the light of the world."

Sarah whispered, "Lila, did you hear what Jesus said? He must be our Messiah! I committed my ways to the God of Israel and look what He did for me!"

Andrew whispered to his brother, "I have never known a man who shows love as Jesus does."

"He cares so much for hurting people," said John.

The townspeople marveled for days over Aaron's healing. People shared their opinions with each other.

"Someone greater than a prophet has visited us today," insisted Elizabeth, one of Lila's neighbors.

"Thank God for this amazing miracle," said Asher.

"I have never attended a funeral like Aaron's," exclaimed Eli. "Now it is a celebration!"

The people of Nain all agreed that only God, the Creator of life, possessed power to raise the dead. Aaron's story spread throughout Galilee like a fire in dry brush.

Sarah and Aaron never forgot their miracle of life and their special warmth of love from the Son of Man, the Eternal Son of God.

Juanita Turner Paslay

A Friend of Nicodemus

The Other Joseph

Joseph hears Jesus teach.

Joseph sees Jesus perform an amazing miracle.

Come with Joseph to meet Jesus.

A story based on Matthew 21; Mark 15;
John 3, 7, 11, 12, 19; Acts 1;
1 Peter 1; Revelation 19

~ 1 ~

My close friend Nicodemus, a fellow Pharisee in the Sanhedrin, met with me early one morning at sunrise. I still remember the excitement in his voice.

"Joseph, I encountered our Messiah the other night!"

I raised an eyebrow and tilted my head. "You must explain yourself, Nicodemus. Who is the Messiah *this* time?"

I had exposed too many false messiahs to count on one hand since I became a member of the high council.

My devout Jewish father named me after Joseph son of Jacob. Father taught me all the desirable characteristics of Jacob's eleventh son—forgiveness, honesty, and trust in the God of Israel. Father told me the Messiah will demonstrate the same qualities as Joseph of old.

Nicodemus rested his hands on his hips and asked me a straightforward question. "Have you listened to Jesus teach in the temple? He is surrounded by more people than Caiaphas draws. When He is in Jerusalem, crowds gather early every morning to hear Him."

"No, I have not listened to Jesus. Most of the Sanhedrin distrust Jesus after He threw the money changers out of the temple. I traveled home to Arimathea that week, but I understand Jesus released the sacrificial sheep and cattle that the merchants sold, and even let the doves fly away."

I learned about this incident in detail from Simon, one

of our more outspoken Pharisees. We leaders agreed to closely monitor this man's actions. We must prevent any temple riots.

"I stood there in the crowd and observed the whole scene." Nicodemus smiled. "He caused a huge commotion that morning."

"Tell me, friend, how did you react to this teacher's dramatic behavior? The temple guards almost arrested Him that day."

"Well, at first I said to myself, *how dare He disrupt business?* But I was close enough to see the fury in His eyes. He showed unusual zeal for the temple, calling it *His* Father's house. Not our Father's but His! The noisy buying and selling of the animals and merchandise in the temple area before Passover offended Him."

Nicodemus talked so fast he had to pause to catch his breath.

I interrupted him. "I hear this man heals blind eyes and cures diseases. Is that true?"

We walked over to an olive tree and stood in the cool shade because the rising sun now glared in our eyes.

"Jesus attributes His miracles to His Father God. I was drawn to Him, but His strong teachings required more explanation to satisfy me. The other night after dark, I met and spoke with Jesus. So many questions plagued me, but they no longer matter in His presence."

"So, what did Jesus say?"

Nicodemus had captured my attention. I adjusted the belt around my waist and reclined on a stone bench under the tree. Nicodemus stood over me and grinned his wide smile that I have seen so many times.

"We must have conversed for over an hour, but most of the time, we spoke about the Kingdom of God. He explained if I wanted to live in *His* kingdom, I must be born again—a transformation of my spirit by God's Spirit. Jesus said He came from heaven to provide salvation and then will return to His Father in heaven."

He paused, then spoke with even more excitement in his voice. "Joseph, now I wish I had invited you to come with me. His words brought real meaning to my life. The Messiah has indeed arrived in our day!"

I found the idea hard to believe that my friend became a follower of this man Jesus. I did not know how to respond to his unexpected decision.

I pointed a finger at my friend. "So, you actually believe Jesus is our Messiah?"

"Yes, I do. Jesus looked deep into my eyes and said if I believed in Him, eternal life belonged to me, not eternal death."

"Eternal life?" *How could Jesus do that?*

My friend Nicodemus continued. "The moon hung low on the horizon when I returned home. Sleep avoided me, so I laid awake for hours repeating in my mind all the words Jesus privately spoke to me. I pondered His phrase 'born again'."

"The law does not mention that term." *Does Jesus plan to rewrite our law?*

Nicodemus said, "I sense a new spirit about me now. I feel I belong to Him. I am not sure where this new life will lead me as a Pharisee. All the religious leaders in general disapprove of Him."

I stood up and placed my hand on my friend's shoulder. "I imagine most of them hate Him."

I had overheard Caiaphas the high priest voice serious charges against Jesus, but I did not want to quote them to Nicodemus right then. The threats would give him further cause for worry.

"I have noticed their attitude also." Nicodemus whispered as several men passed in front of us. A frown marked my friend's forehead.

"Do you believe Jesus feels threatened by us religious leaders? How brave is this healer?"

Nicodemus straightened his shawl and showed me a broad smile. "No one threatens the Son of God!"

"My friend, I suggest you keep this experience to yourself. You might find your honored status with the Pharisees in a precarious condition."

~ 2 ~

I held serious concerns for the commitment Nicodemus made to follow this Messiah.

As a faithful Jew and Pharisee, every Sabbath I left my home in Arimathea to worship at the temple in Jerusalem. Since learning of Nicodemus' decision to believe in Jesus, I made a point to listen to Jesus teach at the temple at every opportunity because I wanted to learn all about His message for Nicodemus' sake. But the more I listened, the greater my interest in His message grew.

At first, I looked for errors that disagreed with our Scripture. Instead, I learned amazing truths about Him, His Father God, and His future kingdom.

One rainy day on the temple steps, Jewish Sadducees—known for their disbelief in life after death—took advantage of an opportunity. I witnessed them ask Jesus a ridiculous question. The subject centered around a widowed woman who had married seven brothers after each man died. Jesus used our Scripture to reveal their ignorance. The Teacher impressed everyone within hearing distance with his answer, including myself.

Jesus said, "There is no marriage after the resurrection."

I stood next to Ethan, a fellow Pharisee, and whispered to him, "Which commandment does He believe is most important?"

"That is a good question. I shall ask Him." Ethan stepped forward to get Jesus' attention and asked our question.

I saw Jesus turn His face up at the falling rain, then gave a double answer centered around love. "You must love the LORD your God with all your heart, your soul, your mind, and all your strength. This is the greatest commandment."

If that explanation was not difficult enough to obey, Jesus paused, then added, "Love your neighbor as much as you love yourself."

We Pharisees always care about ourselves. Religious teachers I know act as though they love *only* themselves. When a leader celebrates with a feast, we scramble over each other to sit at the head table. Even I stand guilty of desiring a place in the first rows of the synagogue when the holy Scripture is read.

Jesus was impressed with Ethan's serious question and encouraged him with His answer. "You are close to the Kingdom of God."

Did He mean me as well—since I was first to think of the question? Probably not. I did not have the courage to ask my question in front of everyone.

I know the complex teachings of Jesus challenged the belief of every Pharisee, whether we admitted it or not. Most of us refused to examine our attitudes, but in time, He touched and changed my heart. I found myself desiring His approval of my thoughts and even my actions.

Whenever Jesus taught in public, we received our assignment from the high priest to follow Him and observe what He said and what He did, particularly on the Sabbath day. I labeled our secret mission as spying. I took advantage of every occasion to listen to Him. But in a perplexing way, I believe Jesus almost compelled me to listen.

One spring afternoon, I joined the crowd as Jesus

climbed a nearby bluff with His disciples. The wild lilies in full bloom created a perfect setting of vibrant color and pleasant perfume. Hundreds of people from Galilee and Judea and many from Samaria east of the Jordan River traveled by donkey cart and on foot to hear Him teach. The fact that people came from as far away as Tyre and Sidon on the west coast impressed me. I spied on Him in an official capacity, but my heart listened to encouraging words of blessing at the same time.

He taught profound truth. "God blesses people who have a pure heart. God blesses the merciful with mercy."

One blessing I found hard to understand. He told us, "My followers who suffer persecution because they live for God will be blessed to live in My Kingdom."

That statement recalled the decision my friend Nicodemus made. I contemplated the same decision, but who wants persecution from the Sanhedrin? Not I.

I admit we act unrighteous most of the time, and exert more power than Moses gave the first Levites. Once we threw a man out of the synagogue because Jesus healed his blind eyes on the Sabbath. I was one of the few who disapproved of that decision but said nothing.

~ ~ ~ ~ ~

I reside in Arimathea, near Bethany, and was acquainted with Lazarus. When I learned he died, I grieved for him. Four days after he died, I traveled to Bethany to console Mary and Martha. Their prestigious home and garden courtyard overflowed with people who mourned and wept—a sad time for everyone. I waited in the garden because the air inside weighed too heavy with grief. Mary and Martha were not home, so I rested on a bench in the shade and waited for them to return.

When the sisters came home, Jesus accompanied them. *Why Jesus?* Then I remembered Nicodemus told me that Jesus and Lazarus trusted each other like best friends.

I heard the Teacher ask, "Where did you bury Lazarus?" He showed a look of determination about Him, a certain posture of control, though His eyes looked red from mourning.

Lazarus' sisters led the way to his burial cave. I followed along with a crowd of family members and friends. The unexpected happened. I saw Jesus cry! Hearing Him weep made tears come to my own eyes. We both lost a dear friend that week.

I listened to Mary and Martha's narrow-minded neighbors say to each other, "This teacher heals blind and demon-possessed strangers but refused to heal His friend when he was sick."

Others grumbled. "Why is Jesus here now? He is too late to heal him."

Now, as I look back on that day, I asked myself if Jesus' tears showed His joy of knowing Lazarus would live again in a few minutes. Did He cry in anticipation of Mary and Martha's joy or did He recognize the looks of doubt and unbelief in those neighbors' eyes making Him shed angry tears? Maybe He was angry with the presence of death.

"You two men, remove the stone from the entrance." Jesus ordered two young, strong men to roll the stone.

Jesus looked up to the sky and spoke loud enough for the people in the rear of the crowd to hear. I observed thunder rolling in the distance when Jesus spoke again.

"Father, I thank You for always hearing Me." Then Jesus shouted, "Lazarus! My friend, come out of that cave!"

That is exactly what Lazarus did, though with difficulty.

The burial linens were tied so tight around his body that he struggled to put one foot in front of the other. With his face bound by the napkin, he could not see where he stepped.

Most people stood frozen in place as they watched Lazarus reappear. Some backed away as fast as they could.

Someone asked, "Is that his ghost?"

A few neighbors said, "Praise God!"

I sensed joy in Jesus' voice when He ordered Lazarus to be unwrapped. I did not hesitate for that privilege! I almost tripped over my own feet as I ran toward the tomb.

"Lazarus, please stand still while I unwind these linen strips. Someone sure did an excellent job wrapping your body for burial." I laughed and cried at the same time.

I removed the cloth napkins from his smiling face.

After I freed him, I greeted my friend with a big bear hug. Mary and Martha joined me as we jumped up and down rejoicing together.

I turned to face Jesus standing behind us. Within a matter of seconds, I found myself kneeling at His feet. Mary, Martha, and Lazarus joined me. Worshiping Him was our most natural response.

On that day, Jesus' miracle for Lazarus cinched the matter for me.

"He is the Son of God! I believe God sent our long-awaited Messiah and King," I said to a man next to me.

Without delay, I headed back to Jerusalem to tell Nicodemus my experience. Imagine me—a believer in Jesus!

~ 3 ~

The humid air hummed with excitement. People anticipated another opportunity to see the Galilean teacher named Jesus, the prophet who brought a man back to life after four days in the grave. They also spoke of hoping to get a glimpse of Lazarus, the man who experienced that miracle of new life.

Jesus, His disciples, and many believers began our walk toward Jerusalem to celebrate our most sacred festival—Passover week, the annual observance of our deliverance from Egypt.

As we passed through Bethphage, Jesus told Peter and Matthew, "Hurry ahead to Bethany and bring back a colt for me to ride."

I volunteered to accompany them on the errand.

"You will find a donkey with her colt tied to a hitching post near the entrance of the town."

"But, Master, I am sure the owner will object." Peter tried to conceal his frown as he turned his head away from Jesus.

"Just inform him that I want to borrow the animals for the day. I shall take proper care of them." Jesus grinned.

The three of us jogged on ahead and found the donkey and colt just as Jesus said. The owner reclined on a bench in the shade and objected when Peter untied the animals.

"Do you want to buy a donkey?"

Matthew stepped forward to explain. "Jesus needs them just for today."

The man said, "I know about Jesus. I will be thrilled to see Him today. The colt has never been separated from its mother. Even though the colt is full-grown, the animal has never been ridden, is very wild, and does not like being led by the rope." The owner chuckled, expecting an unpleasant scene.

The owner's son asked, "Is Lazarus coming too? I heard what happened to him."

Peter nodded his head to avoid a lengthy conversation with the lad.

The colt bucked and kicked as we led the animals back to where Jesus waited for us.

Peter reminisced, "Jesus always walks wherever He goes. Why does he want to ride a wild donkey into Jerusalem this time?"

"Jesus knew right where we would find them. He always knows everything!" Matthew endeavored to explain to Peter.

Matthew told me later that he himself struggled to understand how Jesus was always right.

Peter said, "It will be a miracle if He can ride this colt. He has not stopped kicking and braying."

Jesus was resting in the shade of an oak tree waiting for us to return. He laughed as we came around the bend in the road. I am sure Jesus listened to the animal's uproar a mile away.

"Jesus, here are the animals you wanted, but beware, this over-sized colt has never been ridden and is very unhappy with the whole situation. I am fortunate it did not kick me in the head," Peter said.

Jesus walked over to the colt, rubbed its nose, and whispered in its hairy ear. The colt snorted once, pawed the dirt, then relaxed. Jesus had calmed another storm, this time on dry land. I removed my outer robe and laid it across the colt before Jesus mounted the animal. Matthew strapped the disciples' bedrolls on the donkey, and we continued our journey to Jerusalem.

The crowd had witnessed Jesus heal the diseased and demon-possessed, and talked of seeing more miracles from the one who called Himself the Son of Man. As the people left Bethany, our numbers increased. Shouts of praise to God and songs to our promised King of Israel echoed as everyone, young and old alike, expressed their enthusiasm.

"Bless the one who comes
in the name of the Lord.
Praise the King of Israel!
Praise the Son of David!"

They danced, shook timbrels, and laid palm branches on the route to honor our King. The palm branches also helped to control the dust stirred up by people who walked and ran on the road.

Men and women removed their outer garments and laid them on the trail. I never saw such an unusual display of honor.

Near Jerusalem, Nicodemus joined me as we blended in with the crowd walking into the city. The local and visiting Jews entered the city by the thousands. Nicodemus and I were positioned close to Jesus riding the colt.

For the second time in a week, I witnessed Jesus cry. Jesus raised His forearm to wipe His eyes with His sleeve. I walked several paces to the left of my Lord and noticed He looked up to the clouds, moved His trembling lips, then dropped His eyes to the colt on which He sat.

"Nicodemus, see how tears mingle with the dust on Jesus' face. Why this visible sadness? He should be happy to hear the people praise Him as our King."

"He must know something we do not."

Everyone celebrated as if going to a wedding, everyone except Jesus, the Honored One, and the Pharisees.

"Do you notice all the stern Pharisees in the crowd?" I turned to question Nicodemus.

"Yeah, they stand out like broken crutches. I would say none of them are pleased with this crowd's demonstration."

I agreed. "Our fellow religious members act extremely worried. Jesus presents no small crisis. The anger and hatred in their cold eyes sends chills down my back."

They muttered among themselves and kept their attention fixed on Jesus. I am sure they feared what Jesus might do next.

"I expect Jesus to go to the temple and declare Himself king today," I told Nicodemus.

Nicodemus lowered his voice and whispered, "During a recent meeting of the Jewish high council, we Pharisees discussed killing Jesus and determined He must die. I tried to defend Him, reminding them that our laws required a legal hearing before any conviction. They rejected my protest and changed the subject saying that no real prophet ever came from Galilee."

"I see they ignored the fact that both Jonah and Elijah grew up in that same northern province." I reminded my friend.

Nicodemus admitted, "I am so tense today. It is hard to breathe, let alone smile and rejoice with this excited crowd."

My mind was confused. "More than once, Jesus declared

He would die and then come back to life. I do not understand what He means because our Scripture says the Messiah will live and reign forever."

A few days after the grand parade from Bethany to Jerusalem, Jesus made another unexpected visit to the temple. I witnessed Jesus chase out the sacrificial animals and knock over the table of the dishonest money changers for the second time in three years.

"Listen to Me, you religious leaders! You made My Father's temple nothing more than a den of thieves. You have rejected this sanctuary of prayer and dwelling place for the presence of our Father God!"

As a Pharisee myself, I understood they lost control of what Jesus did and said. They believed their only alternative was to make definite and immediate plans to kill Him.

Those hypocrites talked of doing away with Jesus, but now they applied action to their threats. The priests and teachers of our law looked for an opportunity to capture Jesus in secret. They plotted to put Him to death after Passover which they hoped might prevent a riot of opposition.

Toward the end of Passover week, the Pharisees' plans accelerated. Prophecy was fulfilled in a matter of hours.

~ 4 ~

One of twelve disciples made the arrest of Jesus easy and sooner than expected. He revealed to the high priest the location of the secluded grove of olive trees where Jesus spent evenings alone with His disciples.

It is a known fact that hundreds of Roman troops and temple guards acted without delay to capture Jesus. Thus, began the actions that led to a series of illegal trials.

As a member of the high council, I attended the illegal trials of Jesus but was given no opportunity to defend Him. Then the high priest and eventually the enraged mob seized control of the hearing with Pilate.

Judgment was pronounced before daylight. Dawn came all too soon as the sky displayed grey hues, turned pale blue, then azure.

By nine o'clock, our Messiah hung crucified on a cross.

We will never forget what event developed at noon that ignited fear in the heart of every man and animal. Something or Someone caused complete darkness to fall over Jerusalem for three hours in the middle of that afternoon while Jesus hung on the cross.

Days later, I learned caravans brought news that darkness covered the entire land of Israel, not just the holy city of Jerusalem. I neither saw nor heard of an event like this lasting three hours. Three eerie hours.

My Savior died around three o'clock as the darkness

slowly faded away.

Our country rarely experiences an earthquake, yet in the blackness of that afternoon, a series of violent tremors shook the ground under my feet. In fear for my safety, I quickly moved from the marketplace to an open area to escape danger as shops crumbled around me. Why an earthquake now, of all days? An innocent man had already been tortured and hung dying on a cross like a helpless lamb. What more could go wrong?

The quake caused more damage than destroying buildings. The religious leaders on duty in the temple panicked as they tried to escape through the nearest window. A mysterious Power unknown to them invaded our temple. The double thick sacred curtain between the holy place and the most holy place ripped apart from the top band to the bottom hem. It sagged open on the golden hooks overhead. The priests told me that they shook with fear as they fled. It was unlawful for them to stare upon the exposed, most sacred place in our temple.

Our high priest accesses that special room once a year to present a blood sacrifice. Now with the curtain torn apart like old fragile parchment, did all the Jews have permission to approach God's presence in the most holy place or did the Spirit of God abandon our temple forever?

I tried to contemplate, without success, the significance of Jesus dying the same time as that destruction. Much later, I fully understood Jesus' death gave us all the privilege to enter God's holy presence and seek forgiveness for our sins.

Joel, a shepherd I know, described how large boulders on the hillsides of Jerusalem cracked apart from the impact of the earthquake and rolled down to the level fields.

Seals on the burial caves in local cemeteries crumbled and some graves split open by the pressure of the rolling ground. We heard reports that three days after the quake, bodies of resurrected saints were seen walking the winding streets of Jerusalem. People talked about the damage to the graves; none tried to explain the meaning of that mystery. Acquaintances whispered their concerns to me.

Jared asked, "Did the bodies return to their graves or did they ascend into heaven?"

"When?" Tobiah wanted to know.

The apostle John and women who adored Jesus remained on the hill of Golgotha during and after the crucifixion. One woman reported that four soldiers stood guard over the three crosses. When the afternoon sky became dark as midnight and the ground shook with violence under their feet, the fearful armed soldiers crouched close to the ground to avoid falling on their face. I am sure they never witnessed an execution like that one.

The grieving women said the centurion in command that day confessed, "Jesus must be the Son of God. Too many unusual events happened today for Jesus to be an ordinary man."

When the Romans crucify a criminal, the guards post his crime on a rough board and hammer it to his cross. I read the sign nailed to Jesus' cross. "This is Jesus of Nazareth, the King of the Jews". It was written in Hebrew, Latin, and Greek so all the travelers in town for the Passover could understand it without any confusion. That was no ordinary proclamation and it infuriated the high priest. I was aware the Jewish leaders were upset with the wording of the inscription and they demanded that Pilate change it, but he refused.

"It shall stand as I have written." Pilate told them.

That might have been Pilate's first and last correct decision.

I agreed with the townspeople who confided in me. Someone may have upset God in a horrific way! Not just one, but most of our religious leaders, the Roman rulers, Herod, and Pilate, plus an unruly mob of men and women were all guilty of condemning an innocent man to death.

I refused to watch Jesus suffer on the cross. I climbed the hill after Jesus had died.

He died that day with a common thief hanging on both sides. Jesus died on the center cross where Barabbas was supposed to hang. Where was Barabbas now? He ought to kneel at the cross and thank Jesus for dying in his place!

Was He not the Son of God as His own words declared? His life was not supposed to end that way. Nothing made sense to me. I wish I admitted sooner my belief in Jesus as our Messiah. As a believing Pharisee and a member of the Sanhedrin, could I have prevented this nightmare?

~ ~ ~ ~ ~

I resolved to accomplish one final good deed for Jesus, this man in whom I believed and chose to follow. Pilate took charge of his Roman crucifixion; therefore, I needed his permission to claim the body for burial. I experienced no fear entering that pagan's palace or even handling a dead body. Jesus needed a decent burial—a burial fit for a king. By this time in my life, the opinions and rules of my fellow Pharisees mattered little to me.

"He cannot be dead already. Bring me the centurion!" Pilate shouted at me when I entered his residence with my request.

I sensed fear in his voice. Did he regret his decision to crucify Jesus?

After a soldier, weary from the day's tragic events,

verified Jesus' death, Pilate issued a written order that allowed me to remove His body. As I climbed the rocky execution butte outside the city, I hardly possessed enough emotional strength to put one foot in front of the other. The closer I got to the crosses, the heavier dread weighed down upon my soul like an iron ball chained to my ankle. The frightening darkness ended, daylight returned, and the infamous hill in the shape of a skull looked almost deserted.

I noticed women sitting on the rocky ground a short distance from the center cross. I recognized Mary Magdalene, Mary, the mother of young James and Joseph, and Salome. Looking tired and exhausted with tears dried on their faces, their arms encircled each other as they whispered. I placed my shaking hands on their shoulders as I passed the women who moaned in anguish.

Near the cross, John squatted with his trembling arm around Mary who could not take her swollen eyes off her precious Son. They were in a state of unbelief regarding the travesty that had transpired.

I lifted my eyes, hesitated, then approached the middle cross. I was not prepared for that appalling scene. My heart asked a difficult question. Did Jesus die from the severe beatings *or* the crucifixion? I stared at Him—black with immense bruises and mutilated from the cruel whippings. Dark, dried blood covered His entire body. Jesus' swollen, disfigured face was unrecognizable.

I believed our Messiah did nothing wrong. Why had God allowed this crucifixion to happen? There must be a reason for this ugly tragedy. There had to be!

I am strong, but I groaned under the stress of trying to lift the red stained cross out of its deep hole. This was not a job for one man. I refused to cut down the cross and allow it to fall to the ground with Jesus still nailed to it. I left the hill to locate my friend Nicodemus. After thirty minutes of searching the city streets, I found him praying alone on his knees in the temple. I hesitated to disturb him.

"Friend?" I leaned over and whispered in his ear.

Nicodemus raised his head to look at me, then whispered with trembling lips, "Joseph, did you hear what happened to the holy curtain? Torn in two! The room stands exposed for all to see."

"Yes, I know the Pharisees look for someone to blame."

"I am sure they will accuse the followers of Jesus." Nicodemus stood and adjusted his wide strip of leather around his waist.

"Nicodemus, I need your assistance. Pilate gave me authority to take Jesus off the cross, but the cross is too heavy to lift up out of the hole by myself."

Nicodemus responded like a devoted friend. "I would be honored to help you. First, we will purchase myrrh and aloe for His anointing. We need strips of linen to wrap around His body."

As we quickened our steps toward the market, Nicodemus placed his hand on my arm to slow my pace. "Did you hear about one of Jesus' followers?"

"Which one?"

"Judas son of Simon Iscariot. He managed the money for the disciples."

"What about him?" Only slightly interested, my mind already held too many distressing thoughts.

"He was the traitor who told our leaders where they could capture Jesus at night away from the crowds."

I exhaled with emphasis. "I bet he is sorry now!"

Nicodemus turned to face me. I saw anger in his eyes. "Yeah, really sorry. He threw the silver coins at the feet of the priests and then killed himself."

"Well, that is one pathetic way for him to handle his guilt." I could not keep my sarcasm to myself. If it was not for Judas' betrayal and greed, Jesus might still be alive.

~ ~ ~ ~ ~

Within the hour, we returned to His place of execution and trudged side by side keeping our thoughts to ourselves. The dreaded task to remove Jesus from the cross took a long time. Between our tears and sobs, we struggled to pull the spikes from His hands and feet. We carefully wrapped Him in linen.

"He was so beaten, I hope His body does not fall apart in our hands." I held my breath.

Nicodemus exhaled. "I hope not, too."

A handful of women watched as Nicodemus and I removed Jesus' body from the cross and wrapped Him in linen. I listened to Joanna whisper to the other women, "We will go with the men to see where they bury Him. When the Sabbath has passed, we must come back and anoint our Lord's body as our final act of worship."

With that emotional undertaking completed, we remained seated on the ground for several minutes to gather our thoughts, rest our backs, and dry our tears.

Before we left the hill, the disciple John spoke to us. "The legs of the two thieves were smashed to hasten their deaths before sundown, but thankfully Jesus died without that added torture."

When we choose a lamb for a sacrifice, it must be an animal without any broken bones. I almost mentioned the connection here, but too many thoughts already whirled around in my head.

I broke the silence with another painful sigh. "The

Romans showed Jesus no mercy. They beat Him and spit on Him. The prophet Isaiah wrote we would be healed because of the Messiah's injuries." I changed my position to stretch my legs. "This is too difficult to understand."

A faint smile swept over Nicodemus' distraught face and his voice was soft. "I remember Jesus described Himself as a good shepherd who would lay down His life for His sheep."

I whispered, "This situation looks so final." I was unaware I held my breath. I exhaled slowly.

My friend added, "Jesus said that He possessed the power to take back His life. I see hope here."

"Jesus is dead! Just look at Him."

Nicodemus offered no further discussion. Weary from the ordeal, he groaned. "Joseph, where do you plan to bury Jesus? Since today is Preparation Day, we must bury Him before sunset."

Years ago, I purchased a burial ground outside the city of Jerusalem. The area is filled with caves large enough for the resting place of generations of my family.

"We will take Jesus to one of my empty caves. The location is a short distance from here."

As I spoke those exact words, I recalled that Isaiah prophesied the Messiah will lay buried with the rich. That fulfillment brought no joy to my heart. I wished this day had never happened.

What tragedy might tomorrow bring?

Are Jesus' disciples safe from the Romans?

Or from the Pharisees?

Lazarus is now a living example of the power of Jesus. Is his life also in jeopardy?

~ 5 ~

I saw Jesus exemplify God's love in so many ways. In towns like Capernaum, I know he delivered every sick person from their disease. Everyone. He enjoyed healing the blind and the crippled. Even the dead were brought back to life. Jesus encouraged the young children and elderly alike. He loved them all.

Jesus went from an acclaimed king to a condemned criminal in a matter of days. Our elders and the priests challenged Jesus' authority and rejected Him; the Roman soldiers mocked and whipped Him.

No one defended Jesus. Witnesses received money to lie about Him. His private trials in the homes of Annas and Caiaphas exemplified our Jewish justice gone violently awry. One of the trials before the Sanhedrin was unlawfully held in secret before daylight. The high priest issued the judgment of death before the lawyers officially accused Jesus during the final trial.

I remember the day Jesus called us Pharisees hypocrites. In fact, He accused us more than once. That day they retaliated—they killed Him! Jesus was a man filled with amazing love for everyone. Why did He have to suffer?

I knew Jesus died because Nicodemus and I buried Him. The day He died, my heart nearly stopped from the stress of losing Him. I had placed all my hopes in Him and who He said He was—the eternal Son of God.

When the shouts to crucify Him ended, the evil deed completed, and the darkness at high noon silenced the vicious crowds, fear cast a heavy shadow over everyone, both Jew and Roman alike. Most people could not comprehend their own feelings, but, in my mind, the crucifixion was unjustified.

After Nicodemus helped me bury Jesus' body, I returned home on foot to Arimathea. Every minute dragged into hours. My next twenty-four hours became a blur. Would every day be as depressing as that one? Even breathing became difficult.

I dreaded falling asleep. I did not want to wake up to another day without Jesus—another day, another week, an uncertain lifetime.

Later, John told me that the disciples experienced the same distress, but they also feared for their lives. They huddled together behind a locked door for safety from the religious leaders. They remained secluded the entire Sabbath day.

Our normal activities stood suspended. The Sabbath was always a day of rest, but on the day after my Lord's crucifixion, none of us followers wanted to do even what was allowed by law.

Despair hung over Jerusalem like a thick gray fog drifting in off the Great Sea. Every citizen was affected, though many unbelievers would not admit their feelings to anyone. Most faithful Jews, including myself, sensed no desire to attend the Temple for Sabbath prayers.

My body trembled, my head ached, my vision blurred. I had no interest in living my life as a Pharisee or as a man. I had no purpose now.

My friend Nicodemus hurried his donkey to Arimathea the hour he received word that Jesus rose from the dead. He pounded on my door, shouting my name.

"Joseph! Open the door!"

I was not in the state of mind for company, but I slowly opened the door.

"Joseph, He did it! He is alive! Jesus rose from the dead!"

I was speechless for a minute. "Jesus said He would. Why did I doubt? Tell me everything!"

After I recovered from the amazing announcement, I said, "Now the Pharisees will *really* be upset if Jesus teaches in the temple again!"

We both laughed at that comment. We praised the LORD and laughed with joy again.

~ ~ ~ ~ ~

The events transpired as Jesus predicted and as Isaiah prophesied – a dreadful, horrific death followed by His glorious resurrection after three days in the grave. That third day dawned as the greatest day ever!

The women who remained at the cross with Jesus until the end were the first to see and talk with Him on the day after Sabbath. They instantly recognized Jesus and saw He was alive. John told me the disciples voiced their disbelief. They believed Jesus' ghost visited them when He entered the room through their locked door.

I shouted praises to God when He rose from the dead. From *my* grave! Someday I shall rise from the same grave, just as a dead man who came back to life when he was buried in Elisha's tomb centuries ago. Maybe Jesus will return to set up His kingdom *before* I die. Then I shall shout my praises even louder.

In the beginning, my eyes and heart were not open, not

understanding the purpose of His life and death. It is true that people comprehend more after facts become history. Now I know why Jesus left His heavenly home and why He died on a hill outside our holy city, the city that brought tears to His eyes more than once. He died for my sins, giving me eternal life.

Months after His crucifixion, I learned the reason Jesus cried the day He rode a colt into Jerusalem. A disciple who walked beside Jesus overheard Him speak about the future destruction of our beloved holy city. Jesus described how Israel's enemy would surround us on every side and scale our walls. Our buildings and the people would be crushed into the ground. Why would God allow this destruction? No wonder Jesus cried that day. Now I am heartsick and scared for our future.

After Jesus ascended and returned to His Father in heaven, I recalled the prophet Zechariah said our King would ride a colt into Jerusalem. That is why Matthew, Peter, and I borrowed the animal. We helped fulfill prophecy that day.

~ ~ ~ ~ ~

Luke, a follower of Jesus, recorded the events during the forty days *after* Jesus' resurrection. His disciples received additional teaching on the Kingdom of God. They wanted to know when He planned to deliver us from our Roman enemies and set up His Kingdom.

Jesus' answer became our mission. "Only My Father knows the answer to that question. Until then, the Holy Spirit will give you the joy and the power to be My witnesses to the entire world."

I learned the apostles followed Jesus to Bethany on the eastern slope of the Mount of Olives one last time. As He raised His hands over them with words of blessing and comfort, all eleven witnessed His glorious return to heaven. They watched Him rise slowly out of sight into the most beautiful cloud formation ever seen. Two unknown men mingled among them and spoke with godly authority.

They announced to the apostles, "Jesus will return to set up His promised kingdom."

~ ~ ~ ~ ~

I was acquainted with Peter the fisherman *before* Jesus returned to heaven and I know him today. During Jesus' earthly ministry, Peter was full of doubts. Now, he declares the message of salvation with boldness everywhere he travels.

Peter, filled with the Holy Spirit, explained Jesus' death this way. "God paid a ransom to save everyone from their empty life you inherited from your ancestors. The ransom He paid was the precious blood of Christ, the sinless and spotless Lamb of God.

"God chose Him as your ransom long before the world began, but He has now revealed Jesus to you in these last days. You have placed your faith and hope in God because He raised Christ from the dead.

"You are cleansed from your sins when you obey the truth. You have been born again, but not to a life that will end. Your new life will last forever because it comes from the eternal, living Word of God."

Jesus was beaten without mercy and then died on a rough wooden cross to pay the price for my salvation from eternal punishment and for everyone else who accepts Him as their King and Messiah. Now I understand the real purpose of *my* life. Before Jesus returned to His Father, He gave instructions to share this gospel of salvation with everyone. The first people on my list are my fellow Pharisees.

As a member of the high council, I had never experienced contentment. Now I have peace with God because Jesus is my Lord, my *risen* Lord! Now I can enter heaven's Most Holy Place to worship Him because Jesus died for me and became my High Priest.

I shall never fully understand the depth of His amazing love for me. He gave me a purpose to live; the greatest joy and contentment; peace of mind that I do not deserve. I shall never stop praising Him.

Jesus rode a young donkey on the day Nicodemus and I watched Him enter Jerusalem. The crowd, including little children, shouted praises as we proclaimed Him our King of Israel. The next time Jesus returns to Jerusalem to establish His earthly kingdom, I can visualize Him, the King of all kings, wearing a golden crown sparkling with diamonds and a magnificent robe flowing behind Him as he rides a prancing white stallion in victory. He will lead a conquering army of valiant warriors riding large white steeds. What a grand victory celebration *that* parade will be.

I eagerly await my Lord's return!

Signed,

Joseph

from Arimathea

The suffering of the Messiah was prophesied in Isaiah 53.

Who has believed our report?
And to whom has the arm of the LORD *been revealed?*

For He shall grow up before Him as a tender plant,
And as a root out of dry ground.
He has no form or comeliness; And when we see Him,
There is no beauty that we should desire Him.

He is despised and rejected by men,
A Man of sorrows and acquainted with grief.
And we hid, as it were, our faces from Him;
He was despised, and we did not esteem Him.

Surely, He has borne our griefs and carried our sorrows;
Yet we esteemed Him stricken,
Smitten by God, and afflicted.

But He was wounded for our transgressions,
He was bruised for our iniquities;
The chastisement for our peace was upon Him,
And by His stripes we are healed.

All we like sheep have gone astray;
We have turned, every one to his own way;
And the LORD *has laid on Him the iniquity of us all.*

He was oppressed and He was afflicted,
Yet He opened not His mouth;
He was led as a lamb to the slaughter,
And as a sheep before its shearers is silent,
So, He opened not His mouth.

He was taken from prison and from judgment,
And who will declare His generation?
For He was cut off from the land of the living;
For the transgressions of My people He was stricken.

And they made His grave with the wicked —
But with the rich at His death,
Because He had done no violence,
Nor was any deceit in His mouth.

Yet it pleased the LORD to bruise Him;
He has put Him to grief.
When You make His soul an offering for sin,
He shall see His seed,
He shall prolong His days,
And the pleasure of the LORD shall prosper in His hand.

He shall see the labor of His soul, and be satisfied.
By His knowledge My Righteous Servant
shall justify many,
For He shall bear their iniquities.

Therefore, I will divide Him a portion with the great,
And He shall divide the spoil with the strong,
Because He poured out His soul unto death,
And He was numbered with the transgressors,
And He bore the sin of many,
And made intercession for the transgressors.

About the Author

Juanita Turner Paslay and her husband Craig of fifty-four years reside in the Pacific Northwest. They have two sons, two daughters-in-law, and three grandsons. Juanita loves gardening on their two-acre property, spray painting art for their garden, and writing a blog. Juanita attended Bible Standard College in Eugene OR (now known as New Hope Christian College) and retired from the local power company after thirty-two years. She writes a column in a rural newspaper *Mohawk Messenger*. As chaplain and speaker for The Gideons International, Juanita enjoys opportunities to minister to others. She was a wedding coordinator for fourteen years and now teaches women's Bible studies and writes devotions and fiction stories based on Scripture. Her devotional book *As the Deer* will be available in 2018.

Juanita's email: folks7777@gmail.com